W9-BNU-588

House Privilege

Also by Mike Lawson

The Inside Ring

The Second Perimeter

House Rules

House Secrets

House Justice

House Divided

House Blood

House Odds

House Reckoning

House Rivals

House Revenge

House Witness

House Arrest

Rosarito Beach

Viking Bay

K Street

House Privilege

A Joe DeMarco Thriller

MIKE LAWSON

Atlantic Monthly Press
New York

Copyright © 2020 by Mike Lawson

All rights reserved. No part of this book may be reproduced in any form or by any electronic or mechanical means, including information storage and retrieval systems, without permission in writing from the publisher, except by a reviewer, who may quote brief passages in a review. Scanning, uploading, and electronic distribution of this book or the facilitation of such without the permission of the publisher is prohibited. Please purchase only authorized electronic editions, and do not participate in or encourage electronic piracy of copyrighted materials. Your support of the author's rights is appreciated. Any member of educational institutions wishing to photocopy part or all of the work for classroom use, or anthology, should send inquiries to Grove/Atlantic, Inc., 154 West 14th Street, New York, NY 10011, or permissions@groveatlantic.com.

FIRST EDITION

Published simultaneously in Canada
Printed in the United States of America

First Grove Atlantic hardcover edition: July 2020

This book was set in 12-pt. Garamond Premier Pro
by Alpha Design & Composition of Pittsfield, NH.

Library of Congress Cataloging-in-Publication data is available for this title.

ISBN: 978-0-8021-4847-6
eISBN: 978-0-8021-4849-0

Atlantic Monthly Press
an imprint of Grove Atlantic
154 West 14th Street
New York, NY 10011

Distributed by Publishers Group West

www.groveatlantic.com

20 21 22 23   10 9 8 7 6 5 4 3 2 1

Author's Note

There is a Bear Lake in the Adirondacks, but the Bear Lake in this book, which I located near the town of Tupper Lake, New York, is one I invented. I guess you could call it a man-made lake.

—Mike Lawson

1

Everybody was mad.

Nobody was talking.

Her parents were mad at each other and they were both mad at her because she'd acted like a brat the whole time they were at the cabin. She'd told them that she wanted to stay in Boston, but they'd insisted she come, so she'd ignored them, barely speaking, coming out of her room only for meals. She'd refused to go canoeing or fishing with her dad, wouldn't play Scrabble or make a campfire with him, or anything else he asked her to do. He wanted her to be the way she'd been when she was ten, refusing to accept that she was now fifteen and no longer a little kid.

Most of the time she'd stayed in her room reading because you couldn't do anything *but* read. There was no television or Internet because her dad wanted to "unplug" when he came to the cabin. Nor had she been able to talk to her friends because the only way to get a cell phone signal was to walk to the top of a nearby hill but her calls would fail. So she'd stayed in her room and after a while they left her alone, but then they got into a big fight when her mom said she wanted to remodel the kitchen in the Boston house. *Again*. Her mom considered herself an interior decorator—she watched *way* too much

HGTV—and when she got bored, which was pretty often since she didn't work, she'd remodel one room or another in the house. Well this time her dad put his foot down. He didn't care about the money; he was just sick of the house being a perpetual construction zone and of having to fight with the contractors when something went wrong. Finally her dad, not able to stand her and her mother sulking, decided to cut the trip short and fly back to Boston a day early—which was just *fine* by her.

She looked down at the forest below—nothing but trees as far as she could see—and wished the plane could fly faster. As soon as she got home she'd call Sarah Levy to see what had happened at Jane Whitman's party, which she'd been forced to miss because of the stupid trip. She wondered if Bobby Marcus had gotten back together with Marlee Prentis. She hoped not. Bobby was a—

Her dad muttered, "Shit," and she saw him tap one of the gauges on the console.

One of the reasons they'd gone to the cabin, maybe the main reason, was her dad loved to fly. He'd been flying since he was a teenager and flew every chance he got. He'd take the Cessna on business trips even if it was quicker and cheaper to drive. One thing he'd promised—and it was a promise she meant to make him keep—was that when she got older, like maybe seventeen, he'd let her take flying lessons. She knew he couldn't stay mad at her for the next two years. He couldn't stay mad at her for two days.

"Oh, Jesus," her dad said—and the way he sounded, she could tell something was seriously wrong.

"What is it?" her mom asked, also picking up on his tone.

"The oil—"

There was a metallic screech, followed by a thump, and the propeller stopped turning. She saw her dad frantically pushing buttons—he was probably trying to restart the engine—but he gave up after a few seconds.

He grabbed the radio and yelled into it, "Mayday! Mayday! Mayday! This is Cessna November Seven Four Five Kilo Lima. I have no oil pressure. My engine's failed."

A calm voice came back: "Cessna November Seven Four, is there anywhere you can put down?"

"No. I'm coming up on Dix Mountain in the Adirondacks. There's, there's . . . There's nowhere to land. We're going down. I have a—"

She didn't really hear the rest of what he said; all she could hear was the fear in his voice.

Her mother said, "Jesus, Connor, what's happening?"

At that moment the plane dropped to a steep downward angle, the speed began to increase, and she could see her dad yanking back on the yoke and pushing on pedals to change the downward trajectory and slow the plane. She could tell he was failing.

He turned toward her—he looked terrified—and said, "Cassie, put on your seat belt and put your head down."

"Oh, God, Connor, do something," her mom said.

To her mom, he said, "I'm sorry. I'm so sorry."

The ground—the endless forest—was rushing up at them. Her dad said, "I love you both so much."

Her mom screamed as the plane hit the top of a tree—and maybe she screamed too—but that was the last thing she remembered: her mother screaming.

———————◆◆◆———————

When she came to, she didn't know where she was. All she noticed was the pain. Her head hurt, like the worst headache she'd ever had, and there was a big bump on her forehead and her hand came away sticky with blood when she touched it. Her ribs were sore and it was hard to breathe. Her left arm, her forearm, was throbbing. She looked at it and saw it was swollen and sort of bent in the middle, and she thought, *That's not right.*

She finally realized where she was: in the plane. She had no memory of the crash itself, other than her mother screaming when the plane brushed the top of a tree. Maybe the blow to her head was the reason why.

Her parents weren't moving. They were both sitting upright in their seats, their heads cocked at odd angles, toward each other. It looked as if the whole front of the plane had been shoved into their laps. The plane had no wings—they must have snapped off—and a big tree branch had pushed through the windshield and it appeared to be sticking into her mom's chest. She tried to lean forward to touch them but couldn't, and she realized her seat belt was holding her in place. She unclipped the belt, reached out, and touched her mother's face.

"Mom," she said. "Mom, are you all right?" Her mother didn't move. Her face wasn't injured—but her lower body had been crushed by the console of the plane and the tree branch was embedded in her chest. Her dad, oh God, her dad. His face was barely recognizable. And the yoke had been driven so far into him that—

She threw up, then fell back into her seat and started sobbing. All she could think about was the way she'd acted all weekend, ignoring them, barely talking to them. They'd loved her unconditionally, and she'd repaid their love by acting like a spoiled little shit.

She cried until the sobs turned into hiccups and her throat began to hurt, and when she physically couldn't cry anymore she assessed her situation. She knew, based on what her dad had said about coming up on Dix Mountain, that the plane was in the High Peaks Wilderness Area of the Adirondacks. In other words, in the middle of nowhere, in steep, rocky terrain with no roads and the closest town miles away.

She decided she needed to get out of the plane. She *had* to get out. She couldn't breathe inside the plane. But she couldn't open the doors as the doors were next to the front seats. The door on her father's side was up against a tree. On her mother's side, even if she could crawl over her mother, the tree branch coming through the windshield was blocking the door. She noticed then that the plane was tilted at a sharp angle, canting to the right. The window next to the right passenger seat had shattered, just a little glass left in the frame, and the ground was only a couple of feet below the window. She kicked out the remaining glass with her right foot and slithered headfirst out the window. It was a good thing she was skinny.

She tried to stand and then screamed when the pain hit her, and she immediately dropped to the ground. There was something wrong with her left ankle. It appeared as if the whole left side of her body had absorbed the impact: her forehead, her left arm, the ribs on her left side, and her left ankle.

She started crying again, thinking about her parents, not herself. Her mom was—had been—one of the most beautiful women in Boston. Cassie had actually been jealous of her, knowing she'd never be as beautiful as her mom. Her dad—you couldn't ask for a better dad. He'd absolutely adored her. Called her his princess and treated her like one. He'd spoiled her rotten. Now they were both gone and she couldn't imagine life without them.

She stopped crying after a while and said out loud: "What are you going to do?" Her voice sounded funny, like an old woman who smoked too much.

The first thing she did was check her phone to see if by some miracle she could get a signal. Nope, no bars, which wasn't surprising. The radio, maybe. But she didn't know how to work the radio and, looking at the condition of the front of the plane, she doubted it would work anyway.

She couldn't walk out, not with her injured ankle, and even if she could walk she had no idea in which direction to go. All she'd do was get lost. The best thing would be to just stay where she was. She was positive that someone would come looking for them. Her dad had made the Mayday call and the plane had to have been on someone's radar. And maybe the Cessna had a device that emitted a signal if it crashed. Yeah, they would send out people to look for them, particularly after they learned who'd been flying the plane. Her dad was famous. Then she looked up at the trees above her. Would they be able to see the Cessna from the air? She didn't think so.

What she needed to do was start a fire, a smoky fire. But how could she start a fire? Her parents didn't smoke. They didn't carry matches or cigarette lighters. She had to go back inside the plane and see if there was some sort of survival kit. Maybe there'd be matches in it, or maybe flares. And she'd need water, eventually. Her mom hadn't made a lunch for the short flight back to Boston but she'd packed bottled water and a couple of Diet Cokes. She also had to get all their jackets which were at the back of the plane. It was early November, and although it had been an exceptionally warm fall it was going to get cold at night. She was already starting to feel chilly but wasn't sure if that was totally due to the temperature.

She crawled back into the plane, through the broken window, which turned out to be harder than crawling out because her left arm was useless. Then she cut her arm on some of the glass remaining in the window frame, not badly, but bad enough to bleed. A horrible thought occurred to her. Were there bears in this part of the Adirondacks? Would they smell the blood?

She searched the back of the plane. She didn't find a survival kit—maybe it was behind one of the panels she couldn't open—but found a first-aid kit and put a bandage over the cut on her arm. There were also four little packets of Motrin, two pills in each packet. She dry-swallowed two of the pills for the pain—her whole body was in pain—but doubted it was going to help much.

She thought about just staying in the plane, then she looked forward —at her parents' unmoving heads. No, she couldn't stay in the plane. She *had* to go back outside.

She tossed the bottled water, two cans of Diet Coke, and all the jackets out the window, slithered through the window again—then just sat there. All she could think about was her mom and dad, how they'd always been so good to her, the way her dad had always made her laugh. How was she going to live without them? She may not have been a kid anymore but she knew she was too young to be all on her own.

Three hours later she heard a plane overhead—but she couldn't see it. Even though she knew it was pointless, she got to her feet, trying not to put any weight on her ankle, and began waving her right arm and yelling, "Hey! Hey! I'm down here!"

Moments later the sound of the plane faded and she was alone again in the silence of the woods.

She wondered if she was going to die.

2

Julius Caesar crossing the Rubicon.

MacArthur wading through the surf, returning to the Philippines as promised.

De Gaulle riding into Paris in an open-top limousine at the end of World War II.

Charlie Lindbergh's ticker tape parade through the canyons of New York.

Add now to those historic, triumphant grand arrivals, those glorious moments of victory and validation, John Fitzpatrick Mahoney walking through the doors of the U.S. Capitol the day after the 2018 midterm elections.

Mahoney had been the Speaker of the House for a decade then lost the job when the Republicans took control in 2010. For eight long years he'd suffered mightily as the House Minority Leader, forced to take a backseat to the man who had replaced him. For eight long years, he'd been humiliated by the Republicans, unable to exert his will. For eight long years, he'd been the butt of Republican jokes and forced to suffer their abuse.

All that changed on November 6, 2018, when the Dems took back the House and Mahoney was once again cock of the walk, the man in charge, the king of his tumultuous realm. And Mahoney was a vindictive man; he didn't forgive and he didn't forget. He would give a speech in an hour and make the expected noises about working across the aisle—but the speech would be a lie. His plan was to block the Republican agenda in every way he could and exact his revenge on all those who had debased him. Some in his own party would also suffer, specifically those members who had not strongly supported him during his period of disgrace and exile. A few of those members had even suggested publicly that he should not be elected Speaker again; those blasphemers would be banished to the political equivalent of Mongolia.

Mahoney—blue-eyed, white-haired, a substantial gut, broad across the back and butt—strutted as if on a parade ground as he crossed the rotunda floor toward the marble staircase leading to his office. He was resplendent in a new blue suit, a starched white shirt, a traditional red and blue striped tie. His hair was freshly barbered; his wingtips were shined to a high gloss. A touch of makeup covered the broken veins in his nose. He nodded regally to those who congratulated him but didn't speak to anyone. He smiled broadly at one Republican congressman as he walked up the stairs, the smile making it clear that the man would soon feel the sting of the lash to come.

This morning he would hold meetings, promising committee chairmanships to the faithful while seating the unfaithful down the table where their disloyalty placed them. He would reach out to newly elected members, welcoming them to *his* House, and to warn them of the perils they would face if they chose not to vote for him as Speaker. He would receive numerous calls from those who wished to congratulate him and curry his favor; he would mainly take calls from those who could be of use to him, especially those constituents willing to pay—in one form or another—for his expanded influence. His personal coffers had suffered considerably when he was out of power, and it was time to start reversing his losses.

But at some point during the day he needed to deal with a couple of problems in Boston. Actually, one of those issues was more than a problem. It was a tragedy. He entered his suite on the third floor, marched toward his office, and when his staff stood and applauded, he raised his meaty paws in the air like a boxer who had KO'd an opponent. When he reached his secretary's desk, he said, "Mavis, track down that lazy bastard DeMarco and tell him I want to see him."

3

That lazy bastard DeMarco was where he could often be found on a cool but sunny morning: a golf course. He'd been playing a lot of golf the past four months because he hadn't worked in four months.

Last spring, DeMarco had been arrested for the murder of the House Majority Whip, an ambitious Republican politician named Lyle Canton. The evidence against DeMarco had been overwhelming. The frame had been almost perfect. While he'd been in jail awaiting a trial that would have certainly ended with him being sentenced to life in prison, his enigmatic friend Emma managed to find the people who'd really killed Canton and tried to hang the deed around DeMarco's neck. And that was good. The problem was that even though DeMarco had been proven innocent of murder, simply by being arrested it had appeared as if he might lose his job.

DeMarco had worked for John Mahoney for years—but he'd never been a member of Mahoney's staff. There was no paper trail or organizational chart showing he was connected to Mahoney in any way. The reason for this was because Mahoney wanted *deniability* in case DeMarco was ever caught doing some of the things he did. DeMarco was Mahoney's bagman, the one Mahoney used to collect campaign contributions that some nitpickers might construe as bribes. He was also the one Mahoney called upon when he had some knotty problem that might require crossing that thin line separating criminal acts from legal ones.

To provide the necessary political cover, Mahoney placed DeMarco in an office in the subbasement of the Capitol and gave him the title Counsel Pro Tem for Liaison Affairs. The title was meaningless and intended only to obscure DeMarco's actual duties. DeMarco was also placed in a civil service position, something Mahoney had the clout to make happen as he'd been the Speaker at the time. This meant that the taxpayers paid DeMarco's salary and not John Mahoney, and DeMarco became a GS-13 civil servant, entitled to paid vacations, health benefits, and a pension. His official duties, according to the paperwork on file with the Office of Personnel Management, were *to provide legal services to members of Congress on an ad hoc basis.* This job description was a total fabrication, as DeMarco didn't serve anyone other than Mahoney and he was a lawyer who had never practiced law. But for years everything worked as Mahoney had intended: Joe DeMarco functioned as Mahoney's off-the-books troubleshooter and John Mahoney had the deniability he needed in case DeMarco ever ran afoul of the law.

All that changed with Lyle Canton's murder and DeMarco's subsequent arrest.

DeMarco had always operated in the shadows and hardly anyone in the Capitol knew who he was, much less what he did. More important, no one had ever seriously questioned why the legislative branch of government needed a Counsel Pro Tem for Liaison Affairs. But when DeMarco was arrested for murder, his photo was plastered on the front page of every major newspaper in the country. Worse, the jackals of journalism dug deep and learned that DeMarco was connected in *some* way to Mahoney. There were phone records linking them and DeMarco had been observed going into Mahoney's office many times. The media hacks had concluded accurately, although without any real proof, that DeMarco was Mahoney's fixer—the word *fixer* shorthand for corruption, political shenanigans, and dirty deeds.

Mahoney, of course, vehemently denied that DeMarco worked for him but no one believed Mahoney, a man who'd always had a fickle relationship with the truth. But the worst thing, when it came to DeMarco's future, was that a bright light had been shined on his dubious civil service position and he knew the Republicans would force OPM to abolish the position because doing so would cause John Mahoney pain. In other words, DeMarco would lose his job.

In August, after he was exonerated of the murder charge, DeMarco was banished by Mahoney from the Capitol and was told not to show his face there until November—that is, not until after the 2018 midterm elections. Mahoney didn't want to have to deal with any media flak related to DeMarco while campaigning. So DeMarco was placed on paid administrative leave and the only reason his civil service position wasn't immediately abolished was thanks to his lawyer, the one who'd defended him against the murder charge. She threatened folks with various embarrassing and costly lawsuits if any action was taken against DeMarco until after the midterms. The rationale for this was that, come November, if the Democrats regained the House, DeMarco *might* have a job. But if the Republicans maintained control . . . Well, sayonara, Joe.

No one in the country had been more anxious about the results of the midterms than DeMarco. If he lost his job, it would be almost impossible for him to find another one, at least one that didn't involve picking fruit. Not only had he never practiced law, he couldn't put down on a résumé the things he'd been doing for Mahoney during his so-called career. And if he lost his job, he'd lose that wondrous federal pension—the pot of gold at the end of DeMarco's personal rainbow. So it was with all this in mind that he'd watched the election results come in on November 6, 2018.

In order for the Dems to take back the House they had to wrest twenty-three seats out of Republican hands and DeMarco had little faith that this would happen, not in a country where half the damn people didn't even vote. He'd been glued to CNN until almost all the votes across the country were tallied, and when the Wolfman solemnly declared that the Democrats had retaken the House, DeMarco closed his eyes in relief—but he didn't dance for joy. The fact that the Democrats were now in charge—and even if Mahoney would once again hold the Speaker's mighty gavel—didn't mean that DeMarco's worries about gainful employment were over.

The problem was that for DeMarco to be useful to Mahoney, he had to maintain a low profile, which he could hardly do now since he'd been outed. Now everyone in the Capitol knew that he was Mahoney's guy and Mahoney would have a hard time in the future disassociating himself from anything DeMarco might do on his behalf. Mahoney was not a man who would sacrifice his career for another's; for John Mahoney, loyalty was a narrow one-way street.

Therefore, DeMarco had no idea what was going to happen to him.

Would Mahoney, while feigning reluctance, dismiss him?

Would Mahoney find another job for him, maybe one in the private sector, where he'd actually have to work for a living?

He didn't know.

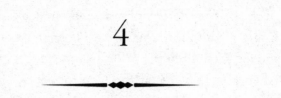

4

DeMarco's phone rang just as he was moving his seven iron forward to hit a shot, and when it rang he shanked the ball and sent it into a water hazard. "Son of a bitch," he shouted. DeMarco took his golf game seriously.

He looked at the caller ID. He was surprised to see the number for Mahoney's office. He'd figured that he wouldn't hear from Mahoney for several days as Mahoney would be too busy appearing on the cable news programs, making promises he wouldn't keep.

He answered the phone, saying, "Hello, this is Joe."

"He wants to see you." The caller was Mavis, Mahoney's secretary. Mavis, for reasons DeMarco would never understand, was completely loyal to the corrupt, self-centered man she served.

"Where?" DeMarco asked. He imagined that Mahoney would want to meet him in some dark watering hole far from the Capitol.

"He said to come to his office."

"Really," Demarco said.

DeMarco told the guys he was playing with that he had to leave immediately, left the golf course, went home, showered and shaved, and put on a dark suit, a white shirt, and a tie. He hadn't worn a tie in four months and it felt confining.

He flashed his ID badge at the Capitol cops as he entered the building, wondering how they'd react toward him. He was certain the cops would recognize him because the person who'd really killed Lyle Canton had been a Capitol policeman and his fellow officers would have followed the case closely. But the cops at the entrance were busy bullshitting about the Redskins' latest loss and they barely looked at DeMarco's badge much less his face. Maybe if he'd set off the metal detector they'd have noticed, but maybe not.

He crossed beneath the glorious rotunda—that hallowed place where dead presidents have lain in state—and headed for the staircase that led to the offices of the party leaders, again apprehensive that someone would point and say: "Hey, aren't you the guy who was framed for killing Lyle Canton?"

DeMarco's form and features weren't particularly distinctive. He wasn't abnormally tall or fat. He didn't have bright red hair or a hunchback. He was a muscular five-foot-eleven, had dark hair he combed straight back, blue eyes, a prominent nose, and a big cleft chin. He was a handsome man but also a hard-looking one. His father, now deceased, had been a hit man for the old Italian mob in Queens and DeMarco, unfortunately, looked like his father—meaning he looked like a guy who could have played the part of a hood in an episode of *The Sopranos*. But other than that, he wasn't all that noticeable and he was hoping that after four months people would have forgotten the photographs of him perp-walking on the front page of the *Washington Post*.

He walked briskly, keeping his head down, and no one noticed him as he moved toward the staircase. Everyone around him appeared to be too busy staring at their cell phone screens. But as he was going up the stairs a girl who looked young enough to be a congressional page said, "Hey, aren't you the guy—"

Aw, shit.

DeMarco entered Mahoney's suite of offices. Aides and interns sat at their desks, jabbering on phones, squinting at computer monitors, studying lengthy, complex documents. DeMarco had no idea what Mahoney's huge staff did all day to serve their master. The one thing he had observed was that Mahoney seemed to have a disproportionate number of female employees who were better than average looking. Only one of the staffers noticed DeMarco as he walked toward Mavis's desk, and her mouth dropped open and her big brown eyes grew large. For a moment he thought she might stand up, point, and say, "Hey! It's him. It's him." Fortunately, she didn't.

Mavis was on the phone. She glanced up at DeMarco but continued talking to whomever she was talking to. Mavis was Boston born and bred, the streets of Bean Town still evident when she spoke. She was now gray-haired and had wrinkles appropriate to her age but DeMarco knew she'd been a stunner when, barely out of her teens, she'd gone to work for John Mahoney. He wouldn't have been at all surprised if Mahoney had slept with her. Mahoney had slept with a lot of women, in spite of having been married to the same woman for over forty years.

Mavis terminated the conversation with: "Well, you just tell the president that Congressman Mahoney will come see him as soon as he can fit him into his schedule."

The president was a Republican and he and Mahoney despised each other. If it were still legal, Mahoney would have challenged the man in the White House to a duel.

Still ignoring DeMarco, Mavis punched a button on her phone, muttered something he couldn't hear, then said, "Go on in. He has ten minutes until his next appointment. And don't dawdle in there. He's already an hour behind schedule."

"Yes, ma'am," DeMarco said. He knew his place in the pecking order.

———◆———

Mahoney was standing behind his desk, gazing out a window at the Washington Monument. His suit jacket was off, his wide red suspenders visible. In his right hand was a tumbler full of bourbon, which was not surprising even though it was only ten a.m. Mahoney, in addition to his many other faults, was an alcoholic.

Mahoney beamed a smile at him and said, "Joe, m'lad, how are we doing on this lovely day."

DeMarco was not at all surprised to find Mahoney in excellent spirits, but *Joe, m'lad*? That was a new one.

Mahoney settled his large rump into the chair behind his desk and said, "I need you to go to Boston. If Mary Pat was here I'd send her but—"

Mary Pat was Mahoney's long-suffering wife. For decades she'd endured her husband's countless affairs, his drinking, his selfish nature. The woman was either a masochist or a saint. Whatever the case, DeMarco adored her.

DeMarco interrupted him. "Hey, wait a minute," he said. "What about my job? Do I still have one or not?"

"Of course you have a job. You've got the same job you've always had."

"But everyone knows—"

"Hey, nothing's changed. You don't work for me. You've never worked for me. You're a freelance lawyer who serves members of the House."

"Yeah, but the papers all said—"

"Fuck the papers. I said you don't work for me, so that's the way it is. And now that I'm the Speaker again, or will be come January, no one's going to screw with your position. But if you fuck up . . . Well, then even I won't be able to save you."

DeMarco had never expected Mahoney to save him. The only one John Mahoney would ever save would be himself. If Mahoney had been on the *Titanic*, DeMarco was certain he would have ended up in one of the lifeboats with women and children floating facedown in the icy sea around him.

Mahoney said, "And I'll have Perry—"

Perry was Mahoney's devious chief of staff.

"—make a few members throw a little work your way just to make it clear that I'm not the only guy you do things for. Anyway, I don't have time to worry about you. I need you to get up to Boston."

"What's going on in Boston?" DeMarco asked.

"You ever heard of Connor Russell?"

"The hedge fund guy?"

"Hedge fund. Real estate. Internet. He was probably worth four or five billion."

"Was?" DeMarco said.

"Don't you read the news?"

Before DeMarco could say not unless the news was on the sports page, Mahoney said, "I was good friends with Phil Russell, Connor's dad. Fifteen years ago, Phil had a grandkid and asked me and Mary Pat to be the godparents. This also made us legal guardians of the kid should something happen to Connor and his wife. I said sure, of course. I wasn't about to refuse a guy as rich as Phil Russell anything, but I never expected, nor did anyone else, that I'd actually outlive Connor."

Mahoney drained his glass and DeMarco had to wait while he pulled a bottle of Wild Turkey from his desk and splashed more bourbon into the tumbler.

Mahoney said, "Connor was a pilot and about a week ago his plane crashed in the Adirondacks. He and his wife were killed but somehow their kid survived. She spent two days alone in the woods before they finally got to her. She had hypothermia, a broken arm, cracked ribs, and God knows what else, but she made it. Tough kid."

"What caused the plane crash?"

"Nobody knows, and the NTSB hasn't really started investigating yet. The crash site is hard to get to and they're all tied up with that United flight that went down a week ago in New Jersey, the one in which two hundred people died. You did hear about that one, right?"

DeMarco ignored the jibe. "So you're telling me that you're now the guardian of a fifteen-year-old girl?"

"Yeah. Phil and his wife are dead too, so I'm the next in line."

DeMarco would have laughed had the situation not been so tragic.

"But what am I supposed to do?" DeMarco asked.

"Like I said, if Mary Pat was here, I'd have her take care of this, but since she's not, I want you to go up to Boston and deal with it."

"Deal with *what*?" DeMarco said, exasperated because he couldn't figure out what Mahoney wanted him to do.

"The girl."

Before DeMarco could ask what *that* meant, Mahoney said, "There's a family trust fund. That's where Connor put most of his money. And tied to the trust is a charitable foundation. The trust and the charity shit are managed by a lawyer who's been doing so for years. Per Connor's will, the lawyer will continue to manage the trust until the kid turns twenty-one. She'll dole out whatever money the girl needs for housing, clothes, education, medical bills, whatever. Connor's businesses will be taken over by a couple of guys he'd named in a succession plan and they'll sit on the boards and handle things until the girl's of age. But as her guardian, I'm the guy who has to figure out where she goes to school, who she's going to live with, and all the rest of it. So I need you to go talk to her, see if she needs anything, and let her know that Mary Pat will be there soon to take control."

DeMarco shook his head. "I don't think I'm the right guy for this."

"I know you're not. So just put things into a holding pattern until Mary Pat gets back from California."

"What's she doing in California?"

"Aw, it's terrible. Her best friend is dying. Some kind of cancer. Anyway, Mary Pat's known her since grade school and she wanted to be there at the end. I talked to her last night, and she said she doubts Becky will last a week."

"Well, I'm sorry to hear that," DeMarco said but was relieved that Mary Pat would be able to step in in a week and deal with the kid. Which reminded him: "What's this kid's name, by the way?"

"Cassie. Mary Pat's always stayed in touch with her, sends her birthday presents, and sees her when she's back in Boston, but I probably haven't seen her since she was five."

"Okay," DeMarco said. "I'll get all the details from Mavis and catch the shuttle up this afternoon." DeMarco rose to leave but Mahoney said, "Hey, sit down. The girl's not the main reason I want you to go up there."

"What's the main reason?"

"There's a guy trying to squeeze me. I want you to pry him off my back. The last thing I need right now is some phony scandal that could keep me from being elected Speaker."

DeMarco knew Mahoney well enough to know that the scandal most likely wouldn't be phony at all.

5

DeMarco caught the shuttle from Reagan National to Boston, and two and a half hours later he was sitting in the office of Erin Kelly, the lawyer who managed the Russell trust fund and the associated charitable foundation. She was the one who would be watching over Cassie Russell's fortune until Cassie was old enough to take charge. DeMarco, mostly to postpone meeting the girl, had decided to drop in on Erin first to get the lay of the land.

From her office on the fiftieth floor of the John Hancock Tower, DeMarco could see Harvard's campus in Cambridge, the Charles River, the Back Bay, and the Boston Cathedral—better known as Fenway Park. The office was large enough to accommodate a family of four. It had an informal seating area with a couple of couches, a wet bar, a conference table that would seat ten, two wide-screen televisions mounted on one wall, and modern artwork mounted on other walls. Behind Erin Kelly's desk was a work station with a Bloomberg Terminal and two computer monitors all displaying financial data. Her chrome and glass desk, and the Persian rug it sat on, probably cost more than most midsize sedans.

As for Erin, she was an attractive, trim lady in her late thirties or early forties. She had a natural redhead's pale freckled skin, hazel eyes, and an upturned nose. She reminded DeMarco of the actress Amy

Adams. (DeMarco had a major crush on Amy Adams.) She was wearing a dark blue suit, a white blouse, and a scarf that functioned as a tie. She offered DeMarco coffee after she learned he was there on behalf of John Mahoney.

DeMarco explained that he was acting as Mahoney's temporary proxy when it came to Cassie Russell, saying that as soon as Mary Pat Mahoney could get to Boston she'd take charge when it came to the girl's future. "Mahoney just sent me to check on her and see if there's anything she needs immediately. How's she doing physically?"

"She's doing fine. She has some sore ribs and a sprained ankle that's almost healed. She also cracked her left ulna in the crash but her arm is mending well."

"Is she still in the hospital?"

"Oh, no. She was released two days after she was found. She's at home."

"By herself?"

"Of course not. I wouldn't leave her on her own. Connor and Elaine had live-in help, an Hispanic couple who worked for them for almost twenty years. The woman is the family housekeeper and cook, and basically Cassie's nanny. She's known Cassie since she was born. Until Mrs. Mahoney arrives and decides otherwise, Cassie will be fine staying with this couple—I trust them both completely—and I'm having a doctor drop in on her every other day. And today she's seeing a therapist to assess how she's coping mentally. But long term, some decisions will have to be made. For example, considering the girl's wealth, I'd suggest Mr. Mahoney think about hiring her some private security, like an armed driver to take her back and forth to school."

"How much is she worth?"

"I'm sure you can appreciate that I can't divulge information about a client, but I can tell you that she's probably the richest fifteen-year-old in America. Anyway, Mr. Mahoney needs to think about her security and where she's going to live in the future. I suppose Cassie could move in with the Mahoneys but as they spend most of their time in

Washington that would mean uprooting her from all her friends here and they'd have to find a suitable school for her in the D.C. area. Or I suppose a good boarding school would be an option."

DeMarco knew there was no way that Mary Pat Mahoney would ship the kid off to a boarding school.

"Where's she going to school now?" he asked.

"The Winsor School."

The Winsor School is a private, all-girls school in Boston, grades five through twelve. The annual tuition is a mere fifty grand.

Before DeMarco could say anything else, Erin said, "I would imagine that becoming the guardian of a fifteen-year-old girl is going to pose a number of challenges for the congressman and his wife, but I have a proposal for you. Or, I should say, for the congressman. My proposal is that he transfer his responsibility as guardian to me. Legally, that isn't hard to do."

"*Really*," DeMarco said. He knew Mahoney would be relieved to hear this. "Would she live with you?" DeMarco asked.

"Yes, and I'd be delighted to have her."

"Connor Russell and his wife didn't have any relatives she could move in with?"

"Connor was an only child and so was Elaine. Cassie's grandparents are all dead and there are no aunts or uncles." She shook her head. "Connor always meant to change his will when it came to Cassie's guardianship but just never got around to it. He was only forty-two and I'm sure he never imagined *both* himself and his wife dying while Cassie was so young."

"And you really wouldn't have a problem with her living with you?"

"None whatsoever. My home has plenty of room, but if Cassie wants to continue to live in her parents' house I'd be happy to move in there. When you see the house, you'll understand why."

"I'm still a bit surprised that you'd want to take on the responsibility of raising a teenager. Are you close to Cassie?" DeMarco asked.

"No. I've met her a number of times, of course, and I genuinely like her. She's very bright. But I'm not offering to become her guardian because we're close. I'm making the offer because it seems like the right thing to do. Mr. Mahoney, considering his job, probably wouldn't be involved with her very much so I imagine the burden would fall to Mrs. Mahoney. At her age, I'd think that would be rather stressful. The other thing, like I said, is that I would hate to see the girl uprooted from Boston so soon after her parents died."

"Well, it's really decent of you," DeMarco said. And he knew Erin was right: Mahoney would have nothing to do with taking care of Cassie; it was Mary Pat who would have to carry the load. Mary Pat had already raised three daughters and DeMarco doubted she wanted to raise another child.

"Are you single?" DeMarco asked Erin. He didn't see a wedding ring. "I'm asking because wouldn't living with Cassie put a strain on your personal life?"

"I'm an old maid," Erin said, then smiled when she saw DeMarco's reaction. "Actually, I've been divorced for a number of years and at the moment I don't have a boyfriend. And if I became Cassie's guardian, I wouldn't allow my personal life to interfere with my responsibilities. And to be completely frank, with Cassie's money, taking care of her wouldn't be the hardship it might otherwise be. It's not like I'd have to scrimp to buy her shoes. Nor would I be taking her to school personally. As I said, I'd hire an armed driver. Any other questions?"

DeMarco decided not to probe deeper into Erin's personal life, such as asking if she had a record for molesting children. He was sure that if Mary Pat was at all interested in her proposal she'd have the woman thoroughly vetted. Hell, she'd probably get the Secret Service to do the job.

"I am curious about something," DeMarco said. "How did you end up managing the Russell trust? Frankly, you're younger than I'd expected." Which was true; he'd been expecting the female version of a grizzled old Boston accountant, some guy who could have played the part of Ebenezer Scrooge.

"I guess you could say that I inherited the job. My dad was Phil Russell's money manager and, when Phil passed away, Connor kept my dad on doing the job, and when my dad died I was already working for him and Connor asked me to carry on. And in case you're wondering about my qualifications, I have a law degree from Harvard, an MBA from the Wharton School, and the Russell family is my only client. I've been their lawyer for the last ten years."

"Well, okay," DeMarco said and rose to leave. "I appreciate your taking the time to talk to me and . . . Oh. Do you have any information on what caused the plane crash?"

"No, but I can almost guarantee you it wasn't pilot error. Connor was a superb pilot and had been flying since he was a teenager. I'm guessing it was something mechanical but that's also hard to imagine. Connor took better care of that plane than they take care of Air Force One. I know that because he'd let me use it when he didn't need it and there was never any sort of mechanical or electrical problem with it."

"You're a pilot, too?"

"Yes. I rent most times when I want to fly as I can't afford to own a Cessna like Connor's, but he'd let me use his plane sometimes. That was one of the perks of this job."

DeMarco left Erin Kelly's office feeling good. The woman was bright, and she seemed to genuinely care for Cassie. He also liked that she was honest enough to admit that taking care of a wealthy kid like Cassie Russell wouldn't be as onerous as it might otherwise be. Whatever the case, he'd pass her offer on to Mahoney.

Erin sat motionless for several minutes after DeMarco left.

DeMarco wasn't going to be a problem; he had no vested interest in Cassie's future. As for John Mahoney, she was positive that he'd snap at her offer. He certainly wouldn't want the responsibility of raising a teenage girl; there was no such thing as a problem-free teenage girl. Mary Pat Mahoney was the one she had to convince. The last thing she needed was Mary Pat's maternal instincts kicking in. As soon as Mrs. Mahoney arrived in Boston, Erin was going to make it job one to charm the pants off her.

As for becoming Cassie's guardian, she wasn't the least bit concerned about that affecting her life negatively in any way. It wasn't like she'd be making the kid's lunch in the morning and taking her to and from soccer practice. The first thing she'd do was pack the brat off to a boarding school, probably one in Switzerland. Then of course she'd be required to drop in on her a few times a year—Cassie's trust picking up the expenses—and would make sure those occasions coincided with the Cannes film festival, fashion shows in Paris, and the ski season in Switzerland. But her plan to assume the role of Cassie's mommy could come completely off the rails if the damn guy didn't finish the job. Men could be such useless creatures.

She pulled the burner phone out of her purse and punched in the number. "Goddamn it," she said when he answered. "When is he going to do it?"

"Aw, calm down. These things take some preparation, especially the way you wanted it done. But I'll talk to him and tell him he needs to get moving."

"You do that, and do it today," she snapped.

He was silent for a moment. "You need to watch your mouth with me," he said.

"I'm sorry," she said. "But I need this to be over and done with."

She tossed the phone back into her purse and closed her eyes.

How could her luck have been so bad?

How in the hell had the damn girl survived the crash?

6

DeMarco glanced at his watch. It was only four thirty. He knew he needed to go see Cassie Russell but figured that could wait until tomorrow. His first priority wasn't really Cassie; it was the guy trying to black-mail Mahoney.

This was not the first time that DeMarco had been forced to deal with people trying to extort money or a favor from his boss and the reason why was that Mahoney had a habit of doing things that made extortion feasible. In this case, the blackmailer was a man named Tommy Hewlett. Hewlett was a former Boston cop who had retired from the force after twenty years then took a job on Mahoney's security detail, serving mainly as Mahoney's driver. Hewlett quit the job about eight years ago and the only reason he gave was that his wife didn't like living in D.C.

Mahoney had said, "Tommy was a good guy. I liked him and I trusted him, which is why I brought him down to D.C. in the first place. So this thing he's doing really shocks me. I guess you can just never tell about people."

Two days ago, right before the midterm elections, Hewlett had sent Mahoney a letter. The letter was brief and to the point: *John, I got something that will cause you and one of your old girlfriends big problems.*

I'm sorry to have to do this to you but I'm in a bind. If you ignore me, I'll take what I have to whatever paper's willing to pay the most. Like I said, sorry about this, but I don't have a choice.

DeMarco called the number that Hewlett had provided. The phone was answered by a man who said, "Yeah?" His voice sounded like a bastard file scraping brass.

"My name's Joe DeMarco. I'm here in Boston on behalf of John Mahoney to talk to you about the letter you sent him."

The phone went silent for a moment.

"Why didn't Mahoney call me himself?"

"Because I'm the guy he sends when he has problems like the one you're trying to cause him."

"Is that right. You some kind of tough guy?"

Before DeMarco could respond, Hewlett said, "Wait a minute. DeMarco. I know you. You were Mahoney's designated hitter back before I left."

"I'm not anyone's designated hitter. I'm just the guy Mahoney sent to find out what you want. So are you going to meet with me or not?"

"Yeah, I'll meet you. But ask Mahoney about me. He'll tell you I'm not a guy who scares easy."

"That's good to know. I want to see you today. We might as well get this over with. Pick a time and place."

7

People could never understand how Mike Kelly ended up becoming the man he became.

Kevin and Maureen Kelly, devout Irish Catholics, had five kids, the kids spaced about twelve months apart. They raised their brood in a ramshackle place in Southie back when Southie still had three-deckers that a Boston fireman could afford. One kid became a priest (the apple of his mother's eye), one a plumber, one a teacher (she was a bit odd), and Francis Kelly, Erin Kelly's father, became a lawyer. A very successful lawyer.

Mike Kelly, the youngest of the brood, became a criminal. A very successful criminal.

After Whitey Bulger went on the lam and the FBI tossed most of Whitey's gang into the slammer, Mike replaced Whitey as the biggest mob boss in Boston. He had his fat fingers into trade unions, garbage removal, construction, and things that fell off the backs of trucks. A good part of his money—allegedly—came from insurance and Medicaid fraud. Another source of income—allegedly—was small businessmen: guys who owned dry cleaners and bodegas and gyms and paid Mike for his "protection." Mike Kelly was just one of the taxes local businessmen had to pay to remain in business.

Mike was currently staying at his beach house on Cape Cod, the place where he usually spent summer and fall. He also had a town house in Boston in the Charlestown neighborhood and a place in Naples, Florida, where he spent his winters. The older he got—he was seventy now—the more he hated winters in Boston. Normally, this time of year, he'd already be in Florida but New England had been experiencing its warmest fall in twenty years and he'd decided to delay going down to Florida until after Thanksgiving. When Erin had called to bug him, he'd been sitting in the living room of his Cape Cod place, watching the news, the commentator's head about to explode over the latest outrageous thing the president had done.

Mike got up from the recliner with a grunt and went to find Paulie. He found him in the kitchen, sitting at the table, on the phone with his mother. When Mike walked into the room, Paulie said, "Ma, I gotta go now. I'll see you this evening. We'll have dinner together."

Mike felt sorry for Paulie, what he was going through with his mom.

Mike had never known a guy as devoted to his mother as Paulie. Except for five years when Paulie had been married to the Bitch from Hell, he'd lived with his mom until she got so bad he had to put her into one of those assisted living places. Now most of what Paulie made went to paying for her care. Everybody loved their mother—Mike had certainly loved his—but he wouldn't have lived with her nor would he have spent almost everything he made to care for her. All he knew, because Paulie didn't talk about it much, was that Paulie's father had been a drunk who beat the shit out of him and his mom until Paulie got big enough and tough enough to put a stop to it.

"How's she doing?" Mike asked.

Paulie shook his head. "She asked why I haven't been to see her this month. I was there just two days ago."

Paulie was sixty, a decade younger than Mike. Unlike Mike, Paulie had stayed in shape, worked out with weights, jogged, and watched what he ate. He'd worked for Mike since he was a teenager and was now

Mike's second in command and also functioned as Mike's bodyguard. He was the guy Mike used to deliver messages when he wanted a message punctuated by a beating.

Mike said, "She just called to bug me. When you going to take care of this thing?"

"Tomorrow. I got everything all worked out. I'm heading back to Boston in an hour, gonna have dinner with Ma, and get it done tomorrow morning."

"Good," Mike said. "The damn woman's a pain in the ass."

Mike still couldn't believe it when his niece called a few days ago and said she wanted to see him.

The last time he'd seen her had been almost ten years ago at his brother Francis's funeral. Before that he'd seen her maybe half a dozen times, and always at family things like baptisms, weddings, and funerals. And when he'd seen her on those occasions, she'd barely said more than hello to him. Francis hadn't wanted anything to do with him, which was understandable, Mike being the black sheep of the family, so Erin calling and saying she needed to see him had been a shock.

When she'd arrived at the beach house, Paulie told her he had to search her purse and wand her. This had not set well with her.

She'd said, "You think I'm carrying a weapon?"

To which Paulie responded, "Guns he's not too concerned about. Recording devices are another matter."

"I'm his niece, for Christ's sake!"

"Still gotta wand you," Paulie said. "And you have to leave your cell phone with me until you leave."

Paulie led her out to the deck where Mike was standing, wearing green sweatpants and a gray, hooded Celtics sweatshirt, looking through binoculars, out at the water. He turned to face her and said, "They've seen sharks out there, right off the beach. Thought I just saw a fin, but I guess not." He took her in. She looked a lot like Francis's wife had looked at that age. "You look good," he said.

"Thanks," she said.

"You wanna beer?"

"No," she said. All business, no time for chitchat, no strolls down memory lane as there was no memory lane.

"Let's sit over here," he said and led her to a patio table. He took a seat where he could see the water and placed the binoculars on the table.

"So what's going on?" he said.

She looked him directly in the eye and said, "I need someone killed."

"Are you shittin' me! I don't see you in ten years, I've probably never said two dozen words to you my whole life, and you come to me with this?"

"I have a serious problem and didn't know who else to go to."

"What in the hell makes you think I'd do something like that, even for you?"

"Because that's the business you're in."

"Hey, girlie, you don't know shit about my business."

"I know enough to know that you can help me. And I'm not asking for a favor. I'm willing to pay you to set this up. I'll pay you a hundred thousand on top of whatever it costs for . . . for the job."

"I don't even know how to react to this."

"You react by saying yes or no."

He shook his head. "What kind of trouble are you in?"

"The kind of trouble that will destroy my life. Now I'm sorry that my dad was never nice to you, but there's nothing I can do about that. Right now, you're the only option I've got and, like I said, I'm willing to pay."

If she hadn't been family, maybe he wouldn't have done anything. He sure as hell didn't need a hundred grand, not at his age and not with all the money he had. But she was family and, well, a hundred grand was a hundred grand. He'd always hated to leave money on the table.

"Who do you want taken care of?" he asked.

"So you'll help me?"

"I haven't decided yet. If it's somebody big, somebody the cops will put a hundred guys on—"

"He's not that big. He's just a businessman. The biggest concern I have is that whoever does the job gets caught and rolls over on me."

Rolls over on me. A line she'd heard in a movie.

Mike said, "The guy won't even know you're the one paying. And he sure as shit won't roll over on me."

"That's good. What does he cost?"

"The last time I used him, fifty g's. But that was a few years ago and with inflation and everything—"

"There is no inflation."

"I'm just sayin'. Anyway, I think he'll do it for fifty. Which means you need to come up with one fifty."

"The money's not a problem. But I can't give you cash. You pay him and I'll pay you through a holding company. The money will go from the holding company to another company that I'll set up so you can get the money from there."

"Sounds complicated."

"It's not. Not for me, anyway. And if we do it my way, there'll be no money trail from me to you."

Mike didn't know exactly what she did, any more than he'd known exactly what his brother Francis had done. He needed to learn more about her because he couldn't help but think that when it came to moving money around she could be useful in the future. And if he did this favor for her, there *would* be a future, whether she wanted one or not.

After she'd left that day, he'd called Paulie out to the deck.

"You seen a shark yet?" Paulie asked.

"Nah, but I know they're out there. What I'd really like to see is what they show on the nature channel, you know, where a shark comes out of the water, jumpin' like a fuckin' trout, and eats a seal."

"More likely to see one eat a guy swimming than a seal."

"Actually, I wouldn't mind seeing that either. Anyway, my niece, she wants someone popped."

"You're shittin' me."

"Yeah, my reaction too. Anyway, she's willing to pay twenty-five grand. I figure, all the money your mom's costing you, you might want to do the job yourself."

8

—◆◆◆—

Tommy Hewlett told DeMarco to meet him at Revere Beach. DeMarco had expected the meeting to take place in a seedy bar—an appropriate venue for extortion—but Hewlett opted for a Dunkin' Donuts on the North Shore Road that had a cross channel view of the Rumney Marshes.

DeMarco hadn't remembered Hewlett when Mahoney said his name but when he saw him, he did. Hewlett was in his fifties, a lanky six-footer, with short dark hair streaked with gray, an aquiline nose, and thin lips. He looked the way DeMarco imagined an old-time Western gunfighter would look, one who'd managed not to end up on Boot Hill in his prime. He was wearing a Red Sox warm-up jacket over a hooded gray sweatshirt, jeans, and work boots. When he'd worked for Mahoney he'd always worn a suit.

DeMarco nodded to him, then walked up to the counter and ordered a cup of coffee. The donut selection caught his eye and he asked for a donut with those little white and blue and pink sprinkles on top. He couldn't help himself.

He took his coffee and donut over to the table where Hewlett was seated and sat down. Seeing no sense in beating around the bush, he said, "So. Tommy. What do you want?"

"I want a hundred and thirty grand. Mahoney's rich. He won't even miss the money."

A hundred and thirty seemed like an odd number. Why not a hundred or one fifty or two hundred? But DeMarco didn't comment on the amount. Keeping his tone casual, he said, "You know, a lot of people make that mistake, thinking Mahoney's rich. I mean, he ought to be rich considering how much he makes both on and off the books, but money goes through his hands like water. He's got a huge house in Boston he should sell, a condo at the Watergate, a sailboat that only his wife uses, and he dresses like a millionaire. So it's easy to understand why people think he's wealthy. But the truth is, he spends a lot more than he makes and is actually carrying a lot of debt."

All this was true, but Hewlett's response was: "Aw, bullshit. All the years he's been in Congress, I know he's got millions. And even if you're not lying, I know he can get the money."

DeMarco took a bite of his donut and some of the little sprinkles dropped into his lap. He brushed them away and said, "And why should he pay you anything?"

Hewlett looked away; he seemed embarrassed. He finally said, "Because I know about an affair he had with a woman. This was fifteen years ago, when I was driving for him."

DeMarco laughed, genuinely amused. "Are you serious? Mahoney's had affairs with a million women. Well, okay, not a million, but a lot. Do you think that you saying he had one more will make any difference?"

What DeMarco meant—and what Tommy Hewlett certainly had to know—was the fact that John Mahoney was a serial adulterer was well known and had been covered extensively by the media. He was like Jack Kennedy or Bill Clinton or Donald Trump in this regard. After having been accused of having affairs with a dozen women, when a new one came to light the reaction now was: *So what else is new?* And all Mahoney would do if Hewlett went to the media was deny that he'd ever had the affair. That was always Mahoney's first line of defense when accused of infidelity: deny, deny, deny until he was forced to do otherwise.

"I got photos," Hewlett said.

"Oh, bullshit," DeMarco said. Mahoney couldn't control his many appetites—his appetites for booze, money, food, and sex—but when it came to sex he wouldn't have put himself in a position where someone could have taken home movies. At least he never had in the past. In the past, it had always been the woman's word against Mahoney's—and people inevitably found the woman more credible.

"Not bullshit," Hewlett responded. "And you don't know who the woman is."

DeMarco took another bite of his donut and again the sprinkles spilled into his lap. "Shit. You'd think they'd make these things so the sprinkles would stick to them better."

"Hey! I'm not fuckin' around here," Hewlett said.

"So who is she, Tommy? And why do you think she'd be any different than all the others?"

"She's Elizabeth Prescott."

Aw, shit. Elizabeth Prescott was now about sixty—a very attractive sixty—and fifteen years ago she would have been even more attractive. She was married, had kids and grandkids. More important, she was now the governor of Massachusetts and a potential—and very viable—2020 presidential candidate.

DeMarco had always liked Elizabeth Prescott. She was intelligent, well spoken, thoughtful, and compassionate. She'd make a good president. Why a woman of her caliber and character would have gotten into a bed with Mahoney was beyond comprehension. But then it had always confounded DeMarco that so many women had succumbed to his roguish charms.

DeMarco didn't say anything for a moment. "I want to see these photos."

Without the photos, who would believe Hewlett? Unfortunately, the answer to that question, and considering Mahoney's reputation, was: a lot of people. And the one who would be hurt personally and professionally wouldn't be John Mahoney; it would be Elizabeth Prescott.

"I didn't bring them with me. For all I know, you got a gun and you'd try to take them from me."

"I don't carry a gun, Tommy. But until I see the photos, I'm not going to believe you, and Mahoney will just call you a liar."

Hewlett rose to his feet. "You tell Mahoney if I don't get the money the day after tomorrow, I'm taking the photos to the *Globe*."

Hewlett left the donut shop but instead of walking to his car and driving away he stood outside the shop, staring across the channel, not moving, apparently thinking over what he'd just done. For a moment, DeMarco thought he might walk back inside and say that he'd changed his mind about blackmailing Mahoney, but then he shook his head and started walking. The head shake seemed to DeMarco the gesture of a man who realized he'd taken the wrong path but knew it was too late to turn back now.

There was something off about Tommy Hewlett. DeMarco had encountered a number of blackmailers and there was usually something ratlike about them. They came across as cowards, onetime school bullies, guys who'd stab an enemy in the back rather than confront him head on. But Tommy Hewlett . . . he didn't come across that way. He didn't strike DeMarco as a back stabber or a coward—but there was no denying he was an extortionist, even if he was a reluctant one.

DeMarco watched Hewlett a bit longer as he walked, head down, the hood of his sweatshirt now obscuring his features. After he was out of sight, DeMarco sat for a couple of minutes, sipping his coffee, mulling things over. Finally, he called Mahoney's cell phone.

As expected, Mahoney didn't answer the call. He may have been at a high-level meeting at the Pentagon being briefed on the invasion of some third world country. Or he might have been at the White House, doing his best to ruin the president's evening. Or he might have just been sitting in his office, drinking bourbon, and he ignored the call when he saw it was only DeMarco calling. DeMarco left a voice mail telling Mahoney to call him as soon as possible.

DeMarco didn't even consider sending Mahoney a text message. Mahoney didn't text; he didn't use email; he didn't Tweet or post comments on Facebook. Mahoney communicated by phone, and if the issue was really sensitive he talked to people face to face. And when people emailed Mahoney, the emails would go to Mavis, Mahoney's secretary, and she would answer them, making it clear she was responding for Mahoney. This of course allowed Mahoney to say that Mavis had incorrectly interpreted whatever Mahoney had told her to say. (Mavis had never incorrectly interpreted anything in her life, but she understood it was her job to take the hits when required.)

Long before Hillary Clinton got in trouble over her emails, Mahoney had recognized that text messages, Twitter, and email could lead to nothing but calamity. He wanted no evidentiary trail whatsoever when it came to his correspondence. Or as he'd told DeMarco on more than one occasion: "The bastards can't subpoena air."

DeMarco left the donut shop, figuring he might as well head back to his hotel and have dinner. He had no idea when Mahoney would return his call. He'd just reached his rental car when his phone rang. It was Mahoney.

DeMarco said, "I talked to Tommy Hewlett. He says he has photos proving that you and Elizabeth Prescott had an affair fifteen years ago."

"Photos?"

"Yeah, so he says. He wants a hundred and thirty thousand."

DeMarco thought Mahoney might make some comment about how it was terrible that Hewlett was going after a fine person like Elizabeth Prescott, but he didn't. He said, "A hundred and thirty?"

"Yeah," DeMarco said. "The simplest thing might be to just pay him, provided he gives me the photos."

DeMarco had paid off a couple of Mahoney's blackmailers in the past, so his suggestion wasn't novel.

Mahoney said, "I'm just baffled by this. Tommy's the last guy in the world I would have ever expected to do this. I'm telling you, he was always a good guy."

"Well, good guys change. Anyway, what do you want me—"

"Shut up. I'm thinking."

A moment later, Mahoney said, "This is the last thing I need right now. Go see Liz and see if she'll cough up the money."

"You want *her* to pay?" DeMarco said. Chivalry was indeed dead, if it had ever been alive in the first place.

"Yeah. She's rich, a lot richer than me, and this will hurt her a lot more than it will hurt me. The fact is, I probably wouldn't do anything if the election for Speaker wasn't coming up."

"Okay, but I'll need you to call her so she'll meet with me."

"I'll call her right now and tell her she needs to see you tonight."

9

The state of Massachusetts was one of four or five states that didn't have a governor's mansion. Why this was the case, DeMarco had no idea. It was hard to imagine any politician not demanding free housing. As for Elizabeth Prescott, she lived in a three-story town house about halfway between the golden dome of the state capitol and the Faneuil Hall Marketplace.

DeMarco arrived at Prescott's place on time, at eight p.m., then couldn't find a parking place within three blocks of her home. He eventually parked in a no parking zone. As he was walking to the governor's town house, he was grateful that the temperature was in the upper forties as he was wearing only a suit. Normally, in November, the temperature at night in Boston would have been close to freezing. Why New England was experiencing such a balmy fall was a mystery, or at least to DeMarco it was. There was probably a flock of scientists out there who would say that the current mild climate was one of the signs of the apocalypse.

He arrived at the town house and started up the front steps when two men—one black, one white—came out of a black SUV parked at the curb in front of the house. Both men were wearing suits, had semi-automatic pistols visible in holsters on their hips, and were big enough to be linebackers for the Patriots.

"Excuse me, sir," one of them said.

DeMarco turned to face them.

The black guy said, "We're the governor's security detail. Do you have an appointment with her?"

"Yeah. My name's Joe DeMarco."

The white guy said, "Can I see some ID?"

As the white guy was studying his driver's license, the black guy took out a phone and spoke quietly into it, then nodded to his partner.

"Are you armed, Mr. DeMarco?" the white man said.

"No," DeMarco said. Why did people think he'd be armed? First Tommy Hewlett and now this guy. Could it be because he looked like his dad? DeMarco held his suit jacket open, lifted the hem, and turned around so they could see he wasn't carrying a gun in the back of his pants.

"Go ahead and ring the bell," the black guy said.

DeMarco rang the doorbell and the door was answered by a slender man with wispy white hair wearing reading glasses perched low on his nose. He was holding a thick book in his hand. He said, "Hi. I'm Dick Prescott. Liz's husband."

"Nice to meet you," DeMarco said and shook Prescott's hand.

Prescott said, "She's on the phone but she told me to take you to the den and she'll be with you as soon as she can."

Prescott led DeMarco to a room that contained an unlit gas fireplace, shelves crammed with books, a threadbare Persian rug, and an old desk with an old Tiffany lamp. On one wall was a small flatscreen TV. It was tuned to CNN but the sound was muted. In addition to the chair behind the desk there were a couple of comfortable-looking green leather club chairs and a worn brown leather couch—a place where a guy could stretch out and read. DeMarco had noticed before that people with old money—and Liz Prescott came from very old money—tended not to waste their fortunes on furniture. They liked things that were practical and comfortable and that lasted a long time.

He also noticed there was no wall of fame in the room: no plaques or photos or certificates documenting Prescott's impressive career. She'd been a Boston assistant district attorney, an assistant U.S. attorney, the Massachusetts state attorney general, a congresswoman, and was now the governor. And in two years she might be the president.

Elizabeth Prescott walked into the room and DeMarco stood. She was barefoot, wearing gray sweatpants and a crimson Harvard t-shirt. Big-framed glasses magnified bright blue eyes, eyes that radiated warmth and intelligence. She was about five-seven, slender, and looked younger than her sixty years. DeMarco had seen videos of her jogging and her security detail appeared to be struggling to keep up with her. How in the hell had a woman like her ever gotten involved with John Mahoney?

She smiled at DeMarco, stuck out her right hand, and said, "Hi. I'm Liz Prescott."

"Joe DeMarco," DeMarco said, shaking her hand.

"John said it was important that I meet with you but he didn't tell me why."

DeMarco looked behind him and noticed that the door to the room was open.

"Governor," he said, "I'd suggest you close the door."

"Why?"

"Because you don't want your husband or anyone else to hear what I'm about to tell you."

She frowned but walked over and shut the door. She took a seat in one of the club chairs and pointed DeMarco to the couch.

"What's going on?" she said.

"There's a man named Tommy Hewlett who used to drive for Mahoney. A few days ago, he sent Mahoney a letter saying he had information that could hurt Mahoney and someone Mahoney knew. I met with Hewlett this evening. He said that fifteen years ago you had an affair with Mahoney and he claims to have photos proving this. He wants a hundred and thirty thousand dollars or he says he'll go to the press."

Prescott closed her eyes and sat for a moment, rubbing her forehead as if she might have a migraine.

"How many people know about this?" she asked.

"Only me, you, and Mahoney."

"What did John say when you told him?"

"He said he was inclined to pay the guy. Actually, he was hoping that you'd pay him."

Prescott made a sound that might have been a laugh. "That figures," she said.

Prescott didn't say anything else for a moment. "I think—no, I'm certain—that the worst mistake I ever made in my life was sleeping with Mahoney. It only happened once—Dick and I were going through a rough patch at the time—but I can't for the life of me explain why I did it."

DeMarco didn't respond.

"Do you believe he has photos?" Prescott asked.

"I don't know. Where did you and Mahoney, uh . . ."

"At a room in the Mayflower, after a fundraiser where I drank too much."

"Which makes it seem less likely that he has photos. I don't see how he could have gotten a camera into the room if this was something that happened only once and on the, uh, spur of the moment."

Prescott again went silent, now looking ill, maybe visualizing photos of herself in bed with Mahoney.

"Why a hundred and thirty thousand?" she said. "That seems like an odd number."

"That's what I thought too," DeMarco said. "The other thing that's odd is that Mahoney said Hewlett was a good guy and they got along fine. Mahoney didn't fire him. He said Hewlett quit because his wife just didn't want to live in D.C. and they parted on good terms."

"And why would he be doing this after so many years have passed?"

"Again, I don't know, Governor. One reason could be because he thinks both you and Mahoney might be particularly vulnerable right now, Mahoney because he wants to be the Speaker again and you because of all the talk about you running for president. If there's some other reason, I don't have any idea what it could be."

"What would you suggest I do?"

"If he really has photos, pay him. I'll get the photos from him but if they're digital there will be no way to guarantee he doesn't have copies. If the photos are on film I'll get the negatives. If he doesn't have any photos, then you and Mahoney just deny anything happened." He waited to hear Prescott's response and when she didn't say anything he said, "Governor, a hundred and thirty thousand is cheap compared to the damage this could do to your reputation. If he comes back for another handout in the future, then we'll have to rethink things."

"Even if he doesn't have photos, he can still make his allegations, and considering John's reputation and the fact that he drove for John, people will believe him."

"They may believe him but—"

She struck a small fist against her thigh. "No! I'm not going to do it. I'm not going to pay him a damn thing. I'm not going to become complicit in a crime, which is what I'd be doing if I pay him. Nor am I going to lie about what I've done. I don't lie. I'll admit that I made a mistake, and let the chips fall where they may. So you tell him that I'm not paying him anything and that I'm going to the police and have him arrested for extortion. Tell him the letter he sent to Mahoney will be used to prove he's guilty and he can look forward to spending the next ten years in jail."

Before DeMarco could say anything, Prescott said, "When I was a prosecutor I used to tell victims and witnesses that they had to have the courage to testify and that if they didn't they were allowing the criminals to win. Well, I'm not going to let this son of a bitch win."

Unlike John Mahoney, Elizabeth Prescott actually had principles.

"Well, don't do anything yet," DeMarco said. "I'm going to meet with him again and I'll try to get him on tape so there's more proof that he's trying to blackmail you. After that I'll tell him what you said, about having him arrested, and see if he'll back down."

DeMarco didn't know how Mahoney would react to this, but he'd cross that bridge after he met with Hewlett again.

Prescott nodded, then shook her head. "One stupid night, and everything I've ever worked for . . ."

"Don't give up yet, Governor. I'm going to make him back down." DeMarco hadn't particularly cared about Tommy Hewlett blackmailing Mahoney, but now that Prescott was involved, he did.

"We'll see," Prescott said.

She just sat there, looking down into her lap. He thought she might start crying, but she didn't. Liz Prescott was a fighter, not a crier.

DeMarco rose and said, "Goodnight, Governor."

10

———◆———

DeMarco could see why Erin Kelly would be willing to move into Cassie Russell's house. It was a four-story, brick Beacon Hill mansion with black hurricane shutters on the windows. According to Zillow, it would sell for about ten million. The amenities included a lap pool, a Swedish sauna, and a rooftop patio with a view of the Boston Common.

A short, stout Hispanic woman, her gray hair tied into a bun, let him into the house. She didn't greet him with a smile; if anything, her expression seemed distrustful. DeMarco assumed she was the female half of the couple who lived with Cassie.

DeMarco said, "I'm Joe DeMarco. I'm here on behalf of Congressman John Mahoney, Cassie's godfather. I called earlier and spoke to a woman and said I'd be coming by this morning to see Cassie."

"That was me you talked to," the woman said. "I'm Mrs. Aguilera. You can talk to her, but if you upset her I'm going to toss you out on your ear."

This coming from a woman who was maybe five-foot-two.

"I'm not going to upset her. I just want to introduce myself and see if there's anything I or the congressman can do for her."

"Oh, the congressman. The one who hasn't seen her since she was baptized. He should have sent his wife, not you."

Sheesh. "You're right, but Mary Pat's in California taking care of a sick friend. As soon as she gets back, I'm sure she'll be seeing Cassie."

"Yeah, I know. Unlike the congressman"—she said "congressman" as if the word were something nasty stuck to her tongue—"Mrs. Mahoney already called and talked to Cassie."

"Hey, I'm not the enemy here, I'm—"

"We'll see about that."

She turned and walked away, leaving DeMarco no choice but to follow. She led him to an elevator, which ascended to the roof of the house. On the roof was a large patio, a barbecue big enough to roast a hog, and a glass-enclosed sunroom filled with plants. Cassie was lying on a couch in the sunroom, fiddling with her phone, wearing a too-big white t-shirt and dark blue shorts. There was a fading bruise on her forehead. Her left forearm was in a soft cast and her left ankle had an ACE bandage on it.

The girl was about as tall as Mrs. Aguilera, maybe five-two, and thin. Not unhealthy thin, just wiry. She had short blond hair, freckles dusting her cheekbones and the bridge of her nose, and DeMarco's first impression was: tomboy.

DeMarco said, "Hi, I'm Joe DeMarco. John Mahoney sent me."

"Oh? He was too busy screwing up the country to come himself?"

Jesus. First the housekeeper and now her.

"He *is* a pretty busy guy," DeMarco said.

"I asked my dad one time how Mahoney ended up being my godfather. He told me Grandpa suggested it, saying that having a family connection to a bigshot politician could be useful. That seems pretty cynical to me."

DeMarco wasn't sure how to respond to that, other than to say she was right.

She said, "I have to admit, though, that Mary Pat is nice. I really like her."

"Yeah, she is nice," DeMarco said. "And she and Mr. Mahoney just want what's best for you. So how are you feeling?"

"How do you think I'm feeling? I just lost my parents."

"I realize that," DeMarco said, "and everyone feels terrible about what happened to them. What I meant was, how are you doing physically? How's the arm?" he asked pointing at her cast.

"It's okay. The bone didn't break completely. I'll be able to take the cast off in a few weeks."

DeMarco said, "Well, that's good. I also wanted to ask—"

"I looked you up online when Rosa said you were coming. You're Mahoney's fixer."

Aw, for Christ's sake. "You know, you can't believe everything you read online. I'm just a lawyer."

"The articles written about you after you were arrested said—"

"I was proven innocent."

"—said nobody could figure out what you did. But most everyone agreed that you were Mahoney's fixer, whatever that means."

"Well, I'm not here to fix anything. I'm just here to see if there's anything I can do for you."

Before she could take another shot at him—the kid really had a quick, smart mouth on her—he said, "Eventually we need to decide where you're going to live, who you're going to live with, where you'll be going to school, all that stuff. I mean, we don't need to make any decisions today but you should think about those things."

"There's nothing to think about," Cassie said. "I'm going to live right here. I'm pretty sure this is now my house. And I've got Rosa and Rafael and I don't need anybody else to live with me. I'm not a child."

DeMarco decided this wasn't the time for an argument.

"Like I said, we don't have to decide anything today. I just wanted to meet you and see if there's anything you need."

"I need to know when I can bury my parents. I was told they can't release their bodies because . . ."

She inhaled sharply, dropped her head into her hands, and started crying.

Mrs. Aguilera, who'd been standing near the door to the sunroom, listening, was on DeMarco instantly. "You need to go now. All this stuff you're talking about can wait and I'm here and I'll take care of her."

Ignoring her, DeMarco said to the top of Cassie's head, "Cassie, I'll find out about the . . . the funeral arrangements." He didn't want to say *autopsies.* "You just get better."

Mrs. Aguilera placed a hard little hand on his arm and pushed. "Go," she said.

"Okay," DeMarco said. "But I need to talk to you before I leave. I'll wait for you by the front door." Seeing the look on Mrs. Aguilera's face, he added, "I'm not leaving until we talk."

<hr />

DeMarco took the elevator back to the first floor, then got lost a bit trying to find the front door. The place was enormous. He couldn't imagine a teenage girl living with just a couple of servants in a place this size. Five minutes later, Mrs. Aguilera arrived and she'd brought her husband with her—for backup, DeMarco assumed.

Her husband was a bit taller than her, maybe five-four, and his complexion was darker. His forearms were corded with muscle and DeMarco suspected he was one of those small guys who'd done manual labor all his life and could bench press three times his weight. He was wearing a navy blue Carhartt t-shirt and worn jeans and wiping what looked like grease off his hands with a red mechanic's rag. He'd probably been doing something useful when Mrs. Aguilera drafted him to help her evict DeMarco. Unlike his ferocious little wife, he was a mild-looking man and seemed embarrassed to be standing there.

DeMarco, speaking to Mrs. Aguilera—clearly the one in charge—said, "Look. I need your help with Cassie. You obviously care for her and—"

"I love her. I've taken care of her since she was born."

"And I can tell she trusts you. But you need to help her adjust to the fact that her living situation is going to change. A fifteen-year-old girl can't be allowed to live on her own and she's going to have to live with someone who can basically act as a parent, meaning someone who will be willing to tell her no if she wants to do something she shouldn't. Someone who will make sure she's not staying out all night, hanging around with the wrong people, doing her homework, and all the rest of it. And I'm sorry to say this but you're her employee and you won't be allowed to assume the role of her guardian."

"I know that," Mrs. Aguilera said. "I'm not stupid."

"I'm sure you're not. Now I don't know yet where she's going to live or who she's going to live with or anything else at this point. Legally, those decisions will be made by John Mahoney. And Mary Pat Mahoney will make sure her husband does the right thing when it comes to Cassie. But I need your help getting Cassie over the idea that she'll be allowed to stay here with just you and your husband."

"She needs time. She needs to bury her parents. She has to adjust to them being gone."

"I realize that," DeMarco said, "but start helping me and quit treating me like I'm the bad guy."

Mrs. Aguilera stared at him a moment, then nodded.

"Okay, I'm leaving now," DeMarco said. "I'll find out when the bodies will be released. I'm also going to ask the family lawyer, Erin Kelly, to help with the funeral arrangements. She seems very competent."

"Huh," Mrs. Aguilera said—just "huh" but it was a disapproving "huh."

"What?" DeMarco said. "You don't think Erin is the right person to do that?"

"No, yeah, she'll do that okay. But—" She stopped.

"But what?"

She looked away, as if she was trying to make up her mind about something, then said, "You live in a house like this for twenty years, you become part of the wallpaper."

"I don't know what you mean," DeMarco said.

"I mean, me and Rafael are always around, especially me, and after a while the family hardly knows you're there and half the time acts as if you aren't there. What I'm saying is, I never snooped on Mr. and Mrs. Russell, but they'd say things when I was in the room and I couldn't help but hear them."

"Okay, but what are you getting at? Did you hear something about Erin Kelly?"

"All I'm going to say is, go talk to an accountant named Jerry Feldman. He's got an office near Copley Plaza."

"Why?"

"Just go talk to him. And that's all I'm going to say."

11

Jerry Feldman was a man who worshipped routine.

He shaved and showered before he went to bed, then laid out the clothes he'd wear the following day so he didn't have to waste time in the morning picking them out. He woke up at precisely five a.m. because he liked to be at the office at six and have two hours to himself before his secretary and his partner arrived. And by starting his day at six, unless something unusual was going on, he'd be able to leave about three and get a jump on the traffic. It was his firm, and he could leave any time he wanted.

He parked each day in the lot where he'd been parking the past ten years. He knew the parking attendants by name and tipped them well at Christmas. From the parking lot, he'd walk to the 7-Eleven on Dartmouth that was a block from his office and buy a large cup of black coffee and a copy of the *Globe*. When he got to his office, the first thing he'd do was make a pot of coffee and, while it was brewing, he'd drink his 7-Eleven coffee and read the *Globe* for half an hour before getting to work.

He had a lot on his mind this particular morning—he still hadn't figured out what he was going to do about the Russell trust—but that didn't alter his routine.

He stepped into the 7-Eleven and waved a greeting to Bolo, the Nigerian guy who had the midnight to eight a.m. shift.

"You hear they're thinking about trading Brady?" Bolo said.

"Aw, they're not going to trade him."

"I don't know. He's getting old."

This was also part of Jerry's routine: chatting with Bolo about the Patriots in the fall, the Celtics in the winter, the Red Sox when summer finally came. Since neither of them cared about hockey the Bruins never came up.

As Jerry was pouring his coffee, another customer walked in, a man dressed in gray pants and a blue short-sleeved shirt that had the name *Stan* stitched over a breast pocket with red thread. Jerry didn't know Stan's last name—Stan wasn't a friendly guy—but Jerry knew he was a maintenance man in a building just down the block. Jerry had seen him going into the building after Stan, too, got his coffee. Like Jerry, Stan was a man who had a morning routine.

Jerry nodded to Stan, Stan nodded back, and as Stan was pouring his coffee, Jerry walked over to pay for his coffee and get a copy of the *Globe* off the rack. At that moment, the bell that rang when the door opened *dinged*, and Jerry looked over at the door.

Oh, shit.

It was a man wearing a black ski mask, holding a gun. He pointed the gun at Bolo and said, "Give me the money."

Bolo said, "Sure, sure, anything you say."

"Hurry up, hurry up," the robber said.

"Sure, sure," Bolo said.

Jerry started to back away from the counter and the guy yelled, "Keep your ass still. Take out your wallet." He pointed the gun at Stan and said, "You, too. Wallet."

Jerry reached for his wallet and put it on the counter and Stan walked over and dropped his on the counter, too. The robber said, "Hurry up, hurry up. Move it, move it, move it."

The robber looked down at the money Bolo had taken from the cash register and placed on the counter and said, "Where's the rest? Where's the rest?"

Jerry thought the guy sounded higher than a kite, talking a mile a minute; he was obviously on something.

"That's all there is," Bolo said. "Everything else is in the safe, and only the boss has the combination."

The robber said, "You lying motherfucker! You motherfucker, you, you" —he shot Bolo in the chest.

Jerry was frozen in place, mouth open, not knowing what to do. Not Stan. Stan spun on his heels and started toward the restrooms—maybe figuring he could lock himself inside the men's room—but the robber shot him as he was running and Stan plowed into a candy rack, knocked over the rack, and fell to the floor.

The robber pointed the gun at Jerry.

Jerry thought, *Oh, dear God. Please.*

12

DeMarco called Tommy Hewlett.

"Did Mahoney agree to pay me?" Hewlett said.

DeMarco recorded that statement on his iPhone.

"Yeah. But only if you give me the photos you claim to have. Meet me where we met last time. Be there at ten," DeMarco said and hung up.

DeMarco was already seated in the Dunkin' Donuts, drinking coffee, when Hewlett arrived, carrying an eight-by-eleven manila envelope in his hand. He walked over to DeMarco's table but before sitting down he looked over at the other customers, as if checking to see whether they might be undercover cops. As the only customers in the place were two women in their eighties sitting together at a table chatting, he must have concluded he was safe.

"You sure you want to go through with this, Tommy?" DeMarco said. "You're about to commit a crime."

DeMarco's phone was recording.

"I told you, I don't have a choice. Where's the money?"

"I'm not giving you the money until you give me the photos. I also need to know that you're not going to come back at some time in the future and try to blackmail Mahoney again."

DeMarco intentionally didn't say Liz Prescott's name. He didn't want her name to be on the recording.

"I won't do that," Hewlett said. "You got my word."

DeMarco laughed. "Your word? You're a blackmailer, Tommy. You're extorting money from a guy who was your friend. I'm supposed to take your word?"

"You're going to have to."

"Let's see the photos," DeMarco said.

Hewlett started to open the envelope, then looked away, out at the Rumney Marshes, which on a gray November day seemed particularly desolate, making DeMarco think of the gloomy fens in England depicted in about every BBC show ever made.

"Tommy, let me see the blackmail photos," DeMarco said again.

As soon as he saw the photos, DeMarco planned to tell Hewlett that he'd recorded the conversation and that, per Liz Prescott's instructions, his next phone call was going to be to the cops. But Hewlett was still staring out at the marsh. DeMarco was shocked to see that tears had welled up in his eyes.

"Aw, what the fuck am I doing?" Hewlett said. "I'm not this kind of guy. Tell Mahoney I'm sorry. And tell him I'm not going to ever say shit about him and Prescott. Mahoney's an asshole but he was always good to me. And Liz Prescott, she's a decent person, and I'd never do anything to hurt her." He got up and stumbled from the coffee shop, bumping into a table before he reached the door, as if partially blinded by his tears. He left the manila envelope on the table.

DeMarco watched through the donut shop window as Tommy walked a few feet down the street, then collapsed onto a bench and sat with his head in his hands.

DeMarco opened the envelope and pulled out the single photo it contained. Attached to the photo with a paper clip was the negative. The photo had been taken at night, and it showed Mahoney and Liz Prescott standing in front of the main entrance to the Mayflower Hotel in D.C. Mahoney had his arm around Liz's shoulders, his head close to hers. Prescott was just staring down at the ground. DeMarco wondered if the photo had been taken after Mahoney and Prescott had had sex and Prescott was already beginning to regret what she'd done. But all the photo showed was Mahoney's arm around her. It was a photo that could be interpreted in a number of ways—like maybe Mahoney was comforting her for some reason—but it didn't prove that anything illicit had transpired between them. What in the hell had Hewlett been thinking? And what had made him so desperate that he'd even consider using the photo to blackmail Mahoney?

DeMarco ripped the photo into twelve pieces and put the negative in his wallet. He'd burn the negative later. When he left the donut shop, he dropped the photo remnants into two different trash cans. He was glad the Hewlett problem appeared to be solved, but he wasn't feeling particularly good about the whole thing. He felt sorry for the guy. He started in the direction of his car and noticed Hewlett was still sitting on the bench, staring once again across the channel at the Rumney Marshes.

DeMarco walked over to him and sat down on the bench next to him. "Tell me what's going on, Tommy. Mahoney said you were a good guy. What made you do this?"

Not looking at DeMarco, Hewlett said, "Four years ago, my wife got cancer. A year later she was dead."

"I'm sorry," DeMarco said.

"We got married when we were both nineteen. We'd been married thirty-six years when she died. Anyway, my health insurance didn't cover some of the drugs and procedures, and by the time she was gone we'd gone through our savings and I had to take out a loan against the house."

"For a hundred and thirty thousand."

"It was for more than a hundred thirty, a lot more. One thirty's what I still owe. But after Colleen died, I became a drunk and drank myself out of a job. I had a good job with a big security company in Boston, did investigations for them, played bodyguard to rich assholes. My boss tolerated the drinking until he couldn't, then he fired me and I couldn't blame him. I found another job as a security guard in a mall that paid minimum wage, and between the mall job and my BPD pension I was barely keeping up with the loan payments. Then I got laid off the mall job. But not because of booze. I've been going to AA for eighteen months and haven't had a drop to drink in all that time. I lost the job because they closed down the whole fuckin' mall."

Facing DeMarco, he said, "I'm fifty-eight years old, and law enforcement and security work are the only things I've ever done, and I haven't been able to find another job. At the end of the month, the bank is going to take my house." He shook his head. "I just needed to make it until I was sixty-two. At sixty-two Social Security will kick in, and with my pension I'd have been all right. Now I'm going to lose my house and have to find some dump to live in and hope I can make ends meet until I'm sixty-two."

A great blue heron with a six-foot wingspan lifted off from the marsh and flew over the bench where DeMarco and Hewlett were seated. The bird was magnificent in flight, yet it made DeMarco think of a pterodactyl, as if the heron had barely evolved over millions of years. By comparison, human beings had managed to evolve—to the point where self-extinction was a distinct possibility.

"The thing about the house," Tommy said, "is that my wife put her heart and soul into it. She loved that place. Painted the rooms herself, stripped down the hardwood floors and restained them all on her own.

She agonized over every picture and piece of furniture, and I haven't changed a thing in it since she died. That house is her."

"I'm sorry," DeMarco said again. "Maybe—"

Tommy said, "What the fuck's wrong with me, sitting here blubbering to some guy I don't even know?" He rose from the bench and said, "Just tell Mahoney I'm sorry for what I did and he'll never hear from me again."

DeMarco watched him walk away and it occurred to him that Tommy Hewlett might go the way a lot of old cops go: he might eat his gun.

* * *

DeMarco was surprised when Liz Prescott answered his call on the first ring. Or maybe he shouldn't have been surprised as her future as a politician might depend on whatever he had to say.

She said, "Hang on." Then he heard her say, "Just keep talking. I'll be back in a moment."

"Okay," she said. "I'm alone."

"The bottom line, Governor, is that Tommy Hewlett isn't going to be a problem and you don't have to do anything or worry about him doing anything in the future."

He heard Prescott exhale in relief.

He told her how Hewlett had gotten in over his head financially because of his late wife's medical expenses and was about to lose his house, which is what had caused him to do what he did.

"I'm very sorry to hear that," Prescott said, "but—"

"The thing is, I didn't have to threaten him with anything. I recorded our conversation but before I could say I was going to have him arrested, he told me that he was sorry and that he'd never bother you and

Mahoney again. And I believe him. Attempting to blackmail you was an act of desperation, completely out of character for the man, and in the end he couldn't go through with it. Mahoney told me that Hewlett was good guy, and I think he still is."

"What about the photos he said he had?"

"He had one photo and it was of you and Mahoney walking out of the Mayflower together. In the photo, Mahoney has his arm around you and is talking into your ear. But it doesn't prove anything. I have no idea why he took it in the first place and I didn't ask him. Anyway, Governor, this thing with Hewlett is over with and you have nothing to worry about. Right now, my biggest concern is that Hewlett might kill himself."

13

———◆———

Having dealt with Tommy Hewlett in record time, DeMarco went to talk to Jerry Feldman, the accountant Rosa Aguilera claimed had information related to Erin Kelly. DeMarco walked into the accountant's office at eleven a.m. where he found an overweight white woman in her sixties sitting behind a desk. He could tell she'd been crying, her eyes red, her mascara running, wads of Kleenex on the desk. She was on the phone, and as soon as DeMarco stepped through the door she put a hand over the phone and said, "We're closed for the day."

"I need to see Mr. Feldman," DeMarco said. "I represent—"

"Jerry's dead," the woman said. "He was killed this morning. Now you have to leave. Nobody can talk to you right now."

"What? How did he die?" DeMarco asked.

She waved a hand at him, shooing him toward the door. "Please. Just go away."

———◆———

Outside the accountant's office, DeMarco pulled out his phone to see if anything had been reported about Feldman's death. Nothing. If the guy had died—the secretary had said "killed"—just that morning, maybe the cops were still notifying the next of kin and that's why there was nothing online. He thought about the word "killed." Killed didn't necessarily mean "murdered." He supposed Feldman could have been killed in an accident, like a car accident. There was no point in speculating but it bothered him that the day after Mrs. Aguilera had said he should talk to Feldman the man dies. But coincidences do happen, and most likely this was one of those occasions.

He thought about going back to Cassie's house and questioning Mrs. Aguilera—she obviously knew more than she'd told him—but he decided to delay doing that until he knew more about Feldman's death.

He hadn't had breakfast so he went to a place he knew only a couple of blocks from Feldman's office. As he was walking there he passed a 7-Eleven with three police cars in the parking lot, their light bars flashing blue and red. There was yellow crime scene tape around the store's entrance. He wondered what had happened.

While waiting for his omelet he Googled Feldman. His firm had a website and it said that Feldman and another man, Clyde Jordan, were partners in the firm. There was a photo of Feldman that showed a round-faced man with short gray hair displaying big Teddy Roosevelt teeth in a wide smile. The bio on Feldman said he was a CPA, had worked for the IRS for twenty-five years, and had graduated from Boston College. His partner was also a former IRS employee. The website listed some of the clients they'd had—mostly big firms in the Boston area—and quotes from clients praising Feldman's and Jordan's work. There was no personal information given about Feldman, such as whether he had a wife or kids. When he Googled "Jerry Feldman, Connor Russell" nothing popped up.

He finished his late breakfast and called Erin Kelly. There was one thing he'd promised Cassie he'd do and he'd nearly forgotten about it.

He said, "The reason I called is to see if you can take care of funeral arrangements for the Russells."

"I'm already doing that," Erin said. "I should have told you when I met you. The autopsies have been completed and the bodies will be released tomorrow. And as I knew would be the case, Connor had no alcohol or drugs in his system, or anything else to indicate he was impaired in any way that would have caused the accident. Cause of death was the trauma sustained in the crash. Connor and Elaine both wished to be cremated and their ashes will be placed in a columbarium at Forest Hills, where Connor's grandparents and parents have their remains."

"Will there be a memorial service?"

"Of course. The service will be held at the Cathedral of the Holy Cross in about a week."

The Cathedral of the Holy Cross was the largest Roman Catholic church in New England. The funeral Mass for John F. Kennedy had been held there.

Erin said, "I'm lining up speakers who will give the eulogies. And I'll be working with Mrs. Aguilera on a reception that will be held at the Russells' home following the service. I'll text you a time and date when everything's finalized, so you can pass on the details to the congressman and his wife."

"It sounds as if you've taken care of everything," DeMarco said. "I'm impressed."

"Somebody had to take charge," Erin said.

"Well, I appreciate it, and I'm sure the congressman will too."

"Have you seen Cassie yet?"

"Yeah, yesterday. She looked okay but, as you can imagine, she's still pretty upset about her parents. She also told me she has no intention of moving and plans to remain in her house with the Aguileras. I decided not to push her on the issue, and until some decisions can be made I'm sure she'll be okay with Mrs. Aguilera. She's, uh, very protective of Cassie."

"Yes, she is. You don't have to worry about her as long as she's with Rosa."

"By the way do you know—"

He stopped.

"Yes?" Erin said.

"Aw, never mind. It's not important. As soon as you have all the arrangements made for the funeral, let me know, and I'll pass them on to the congressman."

"If he comes for the service, maybe I can meet with him and his wife and discuss the proposal I made to you yesterday about becoming Cassie's guardian. If he's not able to attend, I can always fly down to Washington to talk to him."

"I'll let him know," DeMarco said.

He didn't know why, but he'd decided not to ask Erin if she knew Jerry Feldman until he knew more about the guy and how he'd died.

After he finished talking to Erin, and while having a second cup of coffee, DeMarco checked his phone again for information about Feldman's death and found a story that had just been posted. These days you didn't have to wait a day for a newspaper to be printed to get the news.

The article reported that three men—Jerry Feldman, Stanley Kovac, and Bolo Melaye—had been shot during a 7-Eleven robbery. Feldman and Melaye had died; Kovac was in stable condition at Mass General. DeMarco realized then that the 7-Eleven where the robbery had taken place was the one he'd passed on his way to the restaurant.

14

Mrs. Aguilera opened the door to Cassie Russell's mansion. When she saw it was DeMarco, she glowered and said, "Oh, it's you again. You can't bother Cassie now. She's taking a nap. She hardly slept last night."

"I'm not here to see Cassie. It's you I want to talk to."

"What about?"

"You told me to talk to an accountant named Jerry Feldman about Erin Kelly. Well, Feldman was killed this morning."

"*Madre de Dios*," Mrs. Aguilera said, clasping her hands over her mouth.

"Now can I come in?"

"Yeah, sure, sure, come in."

She led DeMarco to a kitchen that would have suited a restaurant with a three star Michelin rating. A gas stove with eight burners, two stainless steel refrigerators, enough pots and pans to prepare a meal for a battalion. They took seats at a small table, most likely the table where Mrs. Aguilera and her husband ate their meals.

"How did he die?" Mrs. Aguilera asked.

"He was killed in a 7-Eleven robbery. Feldman and the guy who ran the store were killed, and another man was wounded. But now I need to know why you told me to go see Feldman in the first place."

She looked down at the tabletop, then looked up and said, "You need to understand, I never eavesdropped intentionally on the Russells. It's like I told you yesterday, I'd just hear things because they'd forget I was in the room and they knew I would never tell people anything I heard. Not ever."

"I believe you."

But Mrs. Aguilera didn't immediately continue. She sat there, her work-worn hands clasped on the table in front of her. It was clearly important to her that DeMarco not think she was the kind of person who would ever be disloyal to her late employers. Or who might be disloyal to Cassie in the future.

DeMarco said, "Mrs. Aguilera . . ."

"A couple of days before the family flew to the cabin in New York, Mr. Feldman came to the house. I met him at the door and he told me his name and said he had an appointment with Mr. Russell. I don't know why Mr. Russell met him at the house instead of his office. Anyway, I take him to Mr. Russell's den. I ask Mr. Russell if he wants anything, like drinks or coffee, and he says no. He was all serious and I could tell this was business not social. Mr. Feldman stayed for maybe twenty minutes.

"Later that evening, Mr. and Mrs. Russell were having cocktails before dinner. Mr. Russell wasn't a big drinker, he'd maybe have a beer or a glass of wine, but Mrs. Russell, she liked a martini, sometimes two, before dinner. I'm bringing Mrs. Russell her second martini, and she says to Mr. Russell, 'Are you sure?' And Mr. Russell says, 'No, I'm not sure and neither is Feldman. But he's one of the best in the business when it comes to this sort of thing.' Then Mrs. Russell says, and this is word for word, 'I just can't believe that Erin would steal from us.' And Mr. Russell says, 'I can't either and I don't want to jump to any conclusions. I'm not going to do anything until Feldman finishes the audit.'"

Mrs. Aguilera stopped. "And that's it. That's what I heard. Word for word. But . . ."

"But what?"

"I've just never trusted Erin Kelly."

"Why not?"

"I don't know. You know how you get a feeling about people? Well, I can't tell you why, but I've never trusted her."

Mrs. Aguilera was the family watchdog. And like all good watchdogs, she could sense when someone posed a threat to her masters, and for whatever reason Erin Kelly had caused her hackles to rise. No matter how attuned her protective instincts might be, however, it was apparent she had no proof that Erin had done anything illegal.

But DeMarco couldn't ignore what he'd just heard.

———◆———

DeMarco got back into his rental car, sat for a moment thinking about what he should do next, then called Mahoney's office. Mavis answered and he said, "I need to talk to him."

"He won't be free until after two. He's over at the White House having lunch."

DeMarco wondered if he'd soon be reading about a food fight at the White House and Mahoney slinging mashed potatoes at the president's head.

"Yeah, well, when he's done with that he needs to call me. It's about Cassie Russell. It's important."

Knowing it could be hours before Mahoney called him back, DeMarco went to a sporting goods store that had a setup where your golf swing was videoed. So he pretended he was interested in buying a new driver and spent an hour trying out drivers and looking at the videos of himself hitting the ball. His swing didn't look like Jordan Spieth's.

He'd just walked out of the sporting goods store and was trying to decide what else he could do to kill some time when his phone rang. He was surprised to see it was Mahoney calling.

Mahoney said, "What's going on that's so important? I only got five minutes. I'm meeting with a reporter to leak something the president said during lunch."

Jesus. Whenever DeMarco thought the state of politics in this country couldn't get any lower, a conversation with Mahoney always served to remind him that the pit was bottomless.

DeMarco said, "I called to talk to you about Cassie but I also wanted to let you know the Tommy Hewlett problem is gone. He's not going to do anything."

"Liz paid him?"

"No. She was going to have him arrested. But when I met with Hewlett to tell him that no one was giving in to extortion—"

"Well, I would have," Mahoney said.

"—he started crying and said that he wasn't going to do anything. He said to tell you he was sorry."

"Then why the hell did he send me the letter in the first place?"

"Because he's broke and a bank is going to take his house. He blew all his money on his late wife's medical expenses."

"Geez, sorry to hear that," Mahoney said. "What was the other reason you called? You said it had to do with Cassie."

That was apparently Mahoney's idea of empathy: *Geez, sorry to hear that.*

DeMarco continued, telling him how Erin Kelly—the very bright, very competent lawyer who managed Cassie Russell's trust—had selflessly volunteered to become Cassie's legal guardian.

Mahoney instantly responded with: "Sounds good to me."

"Well, maybe not. Since you don't have time for me to go into all the details, I need you to call the superintendent of the BPD and tell him that I need to talk to whoever's in charge of the murder of a man named Jerry Feldman. Feldman was killed this morning. Can you remember that? Jerry Feldman, killed this morning?"

Mahoney's memory, when sober, wasn't all that sharp. When he was drunk . . .

"What? What in the hell are you talking about?"

"Do you have time for me to tell you?"

"No."

"Then call the superintendent and tell him to call me."

DeMarco knew that if the soon-to-be Speaker of the House and Boston's preeminent politician told the superintendent to set his own ass on fire, the superintendent would reach for a box of matches.

Half an hour later, while DeMarco was wandering through a bookstore, the superintendent called.

15

The detective assigned to the Jerry Feldman case agreed to meet DeMarco at the Starbucks on Boylston. At ten after the appointed hour, a heavyset guy in a rumpled suit walked into the coffee shop, looked around, and decided DeMarco wasn't the girl with the blue hair or the young man with the dreadlocks. He raised a hand in a just-a-minute gesture and walked over to the counter. After getting coffee and a Danish he clearly didn't need, he sat down at DeMarco's table and introduced himself as Andy Lannigan.

"You must have some serious juice," Lannigan said, his tone light, not at all confrontational. "The superintendent calls the chief of d's, the chief of d's calls my boss, and my boss tells me I'm to meet with you and tell you everything we got on the 7-Eleven thing. When I ask why, I'm told to shut the fuck up and do what I'm told. So here I am. What do you want to know?"

"Whatever you know about the robbery and the murders."

Lannigan shrugged. "There's not much to tell. A guy walks into the store and tells the guy behind the counter to give him all the cash. There's two customers in the place at the time, Jerry Feldman and Stan Kovac. The shooter tells them to give him their wallets, which they do.

But when the cashier—his name was Bolo Melaye—puts the money on the counter, the guy wigs out because it wasn't very much. So then he shoots everyone, after which he grabs the money, the wallets, and boogies on out of there."

"In what order did the shootings happen?"

"He shot Melaye first. One shot in the heart. When he does that, Kovac, the guy who survived, starts running and the shooter pops him. Hits him in the back, the upper shoulder. Then he shoots Feldman, who was just standing there like he was too scared to move. He shot Feldman twice, also in the heart."

"How do you know all this?"

"From the surveillance camera behind the counter, and what Kovac told us matches what the camera shows."

"When you say the guy wigged out, what do you mean?"

"The camera in the store didn't have sound, but you could tell just looking at the video that the guy was hyper, waving his arms, acting all agitated. Then we have Kovac's testimony. He said the shooter sounded high and he flipped out and started screaming when Melaye didn't have much money."

"Why would he shoot Feldman twice and the others only once?"

"Hell, I don't know. He was using a semiauto and just squeezed the trigger more than once. What difference does that make?"

DeMarco didn't answer the question. "Do you have any idea who the shooter could be?"

"Nope. He was wearing a ski mask and gloves, didn't leave anything behind but four shell casings on the floor, and the casings didn't have any prints on them."

DeMarco sat for a moment thinking, turning his coffee cup in his hand. "Was there anything at all about the killer that makes you think he might not have been a junkie?" DeMarco asked.

"I don't understand what you're getting at."

"What I'm getting at is, could this guy have been *pretending* to be a junkie. Could he have been a pro who'd been sent to kill the people in the store?"

"A pro? Why would a pro kill them?"

"I don't know. It's just a possibility worth thinking about. So let me ask again. Was there anything about the killer that might make you think he wasn't some hyped-up addict?"

"Well, when you put it that way, there were a couple of things. We were surprised the casings didn't have prints on them and that he was smart enough to wear gloves. Usually junkies aren't thinking all that clearly when they decide to do something stupid. And the gun he used wasn't some cheap ass Saturday night special. It was a Glock that retails for about five hundred bucks new. Then there's the ski mask. Most junkies don't have ski masks. They might have a stocking cap but not a mask. And his clothes looked good. I mean, no big stains on his jacket, no rips in his jeans, but that doesn't mean much. There are a lot of opioid addicts out there and they're not all street people. He could be a guy who has a decent job, or maybe had one at one time, gets hooked on heroin, loses his job, blows through all his money, and gets desperate enough to rob a store. But he still had an expensive gun and good clothes because he hadn't yet gotten to the point of hocking everything he owned."

"Did it strike you as odd that he put one bullet directly into the clerk's heart, two into Feldman's heart, then only wings Kovac?"

"Not really. Melaye and Feldman were just standing there. Kovac was moving, hustling to get away, and the guy just didn't hit him in a place that killed him. It's not easy to hit a moving target, even one a few feet away."

"How did the robber get away? Did he have a car?"

"Don't know. We looked at cameras in nearby stores, but none of them were pointed at the 7-Eleven. All we got was the guy running out of the store, but where he went from there I can't tell you."

Then Lannigan said, "How come you're so interested in this? And if you've got information that makes you think this wasn't an ordinary holdup, you need to tell me."

"Not yet. I just needed to hear what happened."

"But why?"

DeMarco said, "Remember, Andy, that I'm the guy with the juice. But I promise if I learn anything that will help you solve the case I'll call you."

"Yeah, all right," Lannigan said. He wanted to know what DeMarco knew and why he was asking questions, but he didn't care all that much. He was a man treading water until he could collect a pension.

16

DeMarco drove to Jerry Feldman's office, hoping his partner would be there, but the office was closed. He spent the next half hour tracking down Clyde Jordan's address, then another forty-five minutes fighting his way through rush hour traffic to Jordan's home in Brookline.

A plump, gray-haired woman, holding a dish towel in her hands, answered the door. DeMarco said, "Hello, my name's Joe DeMarco. I need to speak to Mr. Jordan. It's a matter of some urgency."

"Oh, you need to come back some other time. Clyde's business partner was killed this morning and he's too upset to talk with anyone."

"The reason I need to see him is about Mr. Feldman's murder. Like I said, it's important."

The woman—DeMarco assumed she was Jordan's wife—hesitated then said, "Wait here. I'll see if he'll talk to you."

"Tell him I represent Congressman John Mahoney."

Clyde Jordan was a tall, stoop-shouldered, balding man in his sixties wearing wire-rimmed bifocals. One of those skinny guys with a small potbelly. He was dressed in a white dress shirt and pants from a suit but had his shoes off. He was wearing blue and red argyle socks.

He met DeMarco in a room that appeared to be his man cave. There was a brown leather recliner aimed at a television set, a worn couch with a hassock in front of it, bookshelves filled with novels, and a number of framed certificates on the walls. There were also a lot of photographs in the room. A few showed Jordan and his wife together—on a cruise ship, celebrating a birthday or an anniversary at a restaurant—but lot of the photos were of men: men tailgating at Fenway Park; a foursome on a golf course holding beers; men proudly displaying strings of fish. Jerry Feldman was in almost all of those photos.

Jordan shook DeMarco's hand. "My wife said you're here about Jerry's death and representing John Mahoney. Why's Mahoney involved?"

"Mr. Mahoney is Cassie Russell's guardian."

"I didn't know that. But I still don't—"

"I've been told that Mr. Feldman was doing an audit of the Russell trust and may have found some irregularities."

"Who told you that?" Jordan said.

"I can't tell you."

Jordan mulled over DeMarco's response, then asked, "You got some ID?"

DeMarco showed him his driver's license and the badge that gave him access to the Capitol.

"This just shows you work for Congress. How do I know you really represent Mahoney?"

"Call him. I'll give you his cell phone number. Or if you want, you can look up his office number online and his secretary, a woman named Mavis, will answer the phone."

Jordan hesitated, then said, "No, that's all right. You want a beer?"

"Sure," DeMarco said.

Jordan removed two cans of Coors from a small refrigerator behind the couch and handed one to DeMarco. "So what do you want to know?"

"Like I said, I know that Mr. Feldman was doing an audit of the Russell trust. I also know he met with Connor Russell and, after that meeting, Connor told his wife that he was concerned that Erin Kelly might be embezzling from the trust."

That wasn't exactly what Mrs. Aguilera had said, but close enough.

Jordan hesitated. "I don't know what Jerry told Connor Russell. What he told me was that he found something that bothered him."

"Like what?"

"I don't know. I caught him in his office as I was leaving one night and asked him how the audit was going, and that's when he told me he'd found something that didn't make sense to him, something about a stock transaction, but he never told me exactly what it was. I asked him flat out, 'Are you saying that Kelly is stealing from the trust?' and he said he wasn't sure but something smelled. And that was the only time we talked about the audit before he was killed. But I don't know what he found after I talked to him, and I don't know what he told Connor Russell."

"Wouldn't he have kept notes or records related to the audit?"

"Yeah, in his laptop. But Jerry was paranoid about security. He wouldn't even connect his work laptop to the net. He had the wireless function permanently disabled. And his computer is password and fingerprint protected. I'll probably have to get a kid from MIT to break into it."

"Why was he asked to do the audit in the first place?"

"Do you know who John William Henry is?"

"Are you talking about the owner of the Boston Red Sox?"

"Yeah. Jerry told me Russell and Henry had dinner one night, and Henry tells Russell about one of his players getting completely screwed by the guy who was managing his money. This happens to athletes and entertainers all the time. They make millions, don't know diddly about how to handle their money, and they hire some guy who rips them off. Anyway, Henry told Russell this story, then a couple more about supposedly intelligent people getting shafted by people they trusted to handle their finances."

"And this led to Russell asking Feldman to do an audit?"

"I guess."

"Why did he pick your partner?"

Jordan seemed to puff up. "Jerry and I spent twenty years in the Criminal Investigation Division of the IRS. You've never heard of us, but we've been involved in some of the biggest cases in this country involving tax evasion and money laundering. When we retired, we decided to set up our own shop and hire ourselves out to anyone— individuals, corporate boards, nonprofits—who wanted an independent audit conducted to make sure they weren't getting screwed. Connor Russell wasn't our first big name client."

"I see. So why did Jerry say he *thought* something smelled funny when it came to the Russell trust? With his experience, wouldn't he have known if Erin Kelly was embezzling?"

Jordan laughed. "The Russell trust and associated charitable foundation have assets worth about five billion dollars. It's invested in real estate, stocks, bonds, start-up companies, cutting-edge research labs. Hundreds of thousands of dollars are going in and out of the trust every day. Profits and losses from stocks and other investments. Money going to charities. Money coming back in the form of royalties or rent on real estate. Expenses for security, office space, maintenance, lawyers, investment advisers, and so on."

"So it's complicated," DeMarco said, "but—"

"Then you have Erin Kelly. She's a very bright lady—I met her once at a tax seminar—and if she decided to embezzle there wouldn't be some obvious discrepancy in the accounts."

Jordan paused to take a sip of beer. "Look, Erin has been managing the trust since 2007 when her dad got sick. Let's say, just for the hell of it, that she embezzled a million bucks. A million is not even a quarter of one percent of the trust's value. And she probably wouldn't have embezzled it all at once. Let's say she did it over a ten-year period, between 2008 and 2018. That's only a hundred grand a year disappearing from a five-billion-dollar pot, and the losses would most likely be spread over multiple accounts within the portfolio and be barely noticeable.

"On top of that, almost the whole time Erin has been managing the trust, it's gotten *bigger*, not smaller. The way the stock market has been performing the last few years, the size of the trust is probably fifteen percent larger than it was when Erin started managing it. You see what I'm getting at here? It's not like Connor Russell would wake up one day and say, 'Oh, my God. My trust is down a million bucks. Where did the money go?' No, Russell would look at the reports Erin gives him and they would show that the trust is a moneymaking machine and that Erin is doing an incredible job."

"But how would she do it? How would she steal the money?"

"A zillion different ways. She claims an expense for something was a couple percentage points more than it actually was. She sends money to a company for some service they supposedly performed when in reality the company is a shell corporation that Erin set up. She says a stock lost two percent, when the stock lost only one percent. There are all sorts of ways a woman as smart as she is could have nibbled little pieces off the trust, particularly if she did it over a long period of time."

DeMarco said, "But wouldn't Connor Russell have been involved in money the trust was spending?"

"Sure, for big things. Like when he decided to give five million to MIT a couple of years ago for Alzheimer's research. Or if he decided to spend twenty million on real estate or pour a boatload of money into some start-up, he would have been involved in those decisions. But he wouldn't have been involved in minor transactions involving property maintenance or legal fees or legitimate operating expenses. And he wouldn't question every stock loss, not when total gains exceeded losses."

"You said Jerry thought something was off about one stock transaction, and that was what made him suspicious in the first place. What could that have been?"

"I have no idea. Maybe he saw a loss on the books for a particular stock and he was personally invested in that stock and knew it hadn't taken that big of a hit. But I have no idea. What I do know is that if Jerry smelled something fishy that probably means there's a great big dead carp rotting away in Erin Kelly's books but he just hadn't found it yet."

Then it was as if a lightbulb went on inside Jordan's head. He said, "Do you think Erin could have had Jerry killed? Do you think this 7-Eleven robbery was really used to hide a murder to silence him?"

"I don't know," DeMarco said, "but it's hard to imagine her going to that extreme. She just seems too, I don't know, too uptown for that. I have to go think about everything you've told me and figure out what I'm going to do next."

"Well, I know what you should do."

"What's that?"

"You should hire me to finish the audit Jerry started. If Jerry found something, I'll find it too."

"I don't know if that can be done. Connor Russell obviously had the authority to demand an audit, but I don't know if Mahoney, as Cassie's guardian, has the same authority. I have to talk to Mahoney and probably a couple of lawyers. In the meantime, you need to keep this discussion to yourself. We don't want to do anything to let her know that she might be investigated or that someone else might come in to audit her books. Do you understand?"

"Yeah, I understand, but you have to do something. Jerry Feldman wasn't just my business partner. He was my best friend."

———◆———

DeMarco called Erin Kelly. He needed to know something, but he didn't want to alarm her.

When she answered, he said, "Mahoney asked me something, I don't know why, but I figured the easiest way to get the answer was to call you."

"Sure," Erin said. "What does he want to know?"

"He wants to know how the Russell trust is managed."

"I don't know what you mean. I manage the trust."

"No, he knows that but he was wondering if, as Cassie's guardian, he was responsible for overseeing the trust in any way. Knowing Mahoney, he's probably afraid he might actually have to do something."

"Oh, I see. Well, when Connor was alive, he oversaw the trust personally and I reported directly to him. We'd get together periodically and I'd go over the financial statements in some detail and I'd recommend changes to portfolios or suggest investments that I thought he should consider. Mostly what we discussed were charitable contributions Connor wanted to make. But now that Connor is dead, and per his will, the trust will be overseen by a board consisting of Cassie's guardian and two of Connor's old friends who are Boston businessmen."

"So Mahoney's on this board?" DeMarco said.

"That's correct. And I'll be reporting to him and the other two board members and they'll be concurring in any major decisions I make."

"How often does the board meet?"

"That hasn't been established. I would imagine quarterly, but I need to discuss it with the board."

"Oh, boy," DeMarco said. "Mahoney's not going to be happy having to attend a quarterly meeting."

"Well, I imagine he could appoint a proxy, like yourself for example."

"I'm the last guy he'd appoint. The only person who knows less about managing money than John Mahoney is me. Anyway, I'll pass on what you've said and let him decide. Thanks for taking the time to talk to me . . . Oh, I'm just curious about something. If Cassie hadn't survived the crash, what would have happened to all her money?"

"Well, I would have continued to manage the trust and would be overseen by the two men I just mentioned. Cassie's guardian obviously wouldn't be involved if Cassie were gone. As for the trust, it would become an institution like the Gates Foundation and my job would have been to ensure that it remained solvent and did as much good for others as possible."

"I see," DeMarco said. "Anyway, I was just curious."

Erin Kelly hung up the phone and thought: *Goddamn it. Why the hell is he asking these questions?*

17

DeMarco went back to his hotel to mull things over.

He took a seat at the bar, figuring a martini would be the perfect lubricant for his thinking machine. The bartender walked up to him, smiled, and asked what he wanted—and DeMarco's heart did a backflip.

She was wearing a white dress shirt with thin black suspenders, a black bow tie, and tight black tuxedo-like pants that clung to what DeMarco thought might be the best backside in New England. She had gray eyes and long, thick dark hair that she'd tied into a ponytail, and for an instant DeMarco imagined what her hair would look like fanned out over a pillow. She appeared to be a few years younger than him, maybe five years or so, and had smile crinkles next to those amazing eyes. Her name tag said her name was Shannon.

He ordered his martini and Shannon moved down the bar to make it. When she returned with it, she said, "Here you go. Enjoy," and smiled at him again.

There'd been moments in DeMarco's life—albeit not that many—where he'd felt an instant connection with a woman and could tell the woman felt the same. This was one of those moments. He followed her with his eyes as she went over to a table and took an order from a couple seated there.

Okay, enough, he told himself. Get to work.

<hr />

The simple story—the most likely story—was that Connor Russell and his wife died in a tragic accident and that Jerry Feldman was just the unlucky victim of a convenience store robbery.

The other story was not so simple. Connor Russell hires superaccountant Jerry Feldman to audit the trust. Erin Kelly, who's been embezzling from the trust, becomes worried that Feldman is going to figure out that she's a crook. Maybe Feldman even said something to her during the audit that showed he was suspicious. So Erin, realizing that life as she knows it is about to end and that she might spend years in prison, decides to kill Feldman *and* the Russells. If she killed only Feldman, Connor Russell would just hire another auditor. But if the Russells were all dead, per Connor's will she would have almost complete control over the trust. There was this board she'd mentioned, consisting of a couple of Connor's old buddies, and they could order another audit, but why would they? They wouldn't know anything about the audit that Connor had ordered Feldman to conduct or what Feldman had told Connor. Most likely, and unless they got suspicious about something, and as long as the trust was making money, they'd probably give Erin a free hand in running things the way she always had.

What Erin hadn't counted on was Cassie Russell surviving the plane crash. She probably concluded that Cassie surviving wasn't really a problem; a teenager was not going to question her management of the trust and it was unlikely that Cassie's guardian, a busy politician like John Mahoney, would question it either. But to ensure that Mahoney doesn't become a problem, she selflessly volunteers to become Cassie's guardian, eliminating Mahoney's involvement completely.

Yeah, maybe.

But still unlikely.

———◆———

Shannon was standing near him cutting limes and lemons, but her eyes kept flicking over to the television on one side of the room. A hockey game was in progress: Boston Bruins versus the Pittsburgh Penguins. Pittsburgh sports teams had great names: the Steelers, the Pirates. The city once had an ABA team called the Condors, which was also cool. But Penguins? Why would you name a hockey team after a bird that waddled on the ice?

DeMarco had never been big on hockey, but he had been to a few games and enjoyed the sport during the Olympics. But he could tell Shannon was clearly a fan when she stopped cutting the limes and shouted at the television: "Come on LeBlanc, you putz. Pass the puck!"

Then she noticed DeMarco watching her, looked embarrassed, and said, "Sorry. The guy just drives me nuts. They paid fifteen million for him and I swear, I can play better than him. I know I can outskate him."

"You play hockey?" DeMarco asked.

"I used to, in college. At BU."

"And you still have all your teeth?"

"The girls aren't as dumb as the guys," she said. "We wear helmets with face shields and we don't take off our helmets when we fight."

When we fight? Before DeMarco could react to that statement, a phone behind the bar rang and Shannon answered it, and after that she was occupied making four margaritas for a room service order.

Back to Erin Kelly—and the possibility she was a murderer and a thief.

First, what motive would she have for embezzling? Judging by her office and the way she dressed, she most likely made an outstanding salary. Yeah, people always wanted more than they had, but becoming a thief? That seemed doubtful.

Second there was no proof that Erin had embezzled. Feldman had smelled something fishy but there was no evidence that he'd found a dead fish. Based on the conversation that Mrs. Aguilera had overheard, he certainly hadn't told Connor Russell anything definitive, as Russell had wanted him to complete the audit before he decided anything.

Third, there was nothing so far to show that the plane crash had been anything other than an accident, and an accident was more likely than foul play. And as he'd told Feldman's partner, he had a hard time imagining the stylish lady lawyer as a saboteur.

Fourth, Jerry Feldman's death. Again, it was more likely that Feldman had been killed by a junkie in a robbery than it was that Erin Kelly had hired a professional killer to bump him off. Not to mention, where would Kelly find a professional killer? It wasn't like they advertised on Facebook.

Okay. He needed to do a couple of things.

He needed to learn more about Erin Kelly. For all he knew, she was a degenerate gambler up to her eyeballs in hock to a loan shark. Or maybe she was just a woman in debt, living above her means. In any case, he needed to find out more about her financial situation.

Second, he needed to call the NTSB to see where the agency stood on investigating the accident. Per Mahoney, it'd been too busy lately to give the case its full attention, which meant that he needed to give some bureaucrat a sharp kick in the ass.

Okay, so that was the plan for tomorrow. Now there was just one more thing he had to do this evening.

DeMarco pulled out his phone and checked the Bruins schedule. They had two home games this week, one against the Montreal Canadiens and the other against the Anaheim Ducks —another goofy name for a hockey team.

Shannon came back and asked if he wanted a second martini. He did but he didn't want to come across as a lush, yet he wanted to spend more time talking to her. "Just one more," he said. He noticed she wasn't wearing a wedding ring. "You usually work nights?" he asked.

"Yeah, the four to ten shift. It's perfect for me. Gives me all day to focus on my real job."

"Your real job?"

"I'm a writer, or at least I think I am. Two years ago, I got divorced and got this job so I could concentrate on my novel. Also, since I haven't been published yet, so I could make enough to pay the rent."

The part about her being divorced was very good news. DeMarco said, "But they must give you a night off." Before she could answer, he said, "The Bruins have two home games this week and I can get really good seats, like right behind the Bruins' bench. I was thinking that would give you a chance to yell at LeBlanc in person."

"You can get those kind of seats?"

"I know a guy who knows a guy," DeMarco said.

"What's your name?" Shannon asked.

18

The first call DeMarco made the following morning was to the NTSB. He identified himself as John Mahoney's lawyer—which was sort of true—explained that Mahoney was Cassie Russell's guardian, and that he wanted some answers regarding the plane crash. DeMarco, flexing the political muscle he didn't really have, said he expected a call back within the hour. He didn't know who he'd talked to at the NTSB, but he was certain that his demand would rocket to the top of the agency.

While waiting to hear back from the NTSB, he called a lady named Maggie Dolan. Maggie was an overweight, overworked, harried woman who ran Mahoney's office in Boston, the office where he met on occasion with his constituents. One of the positive things DeMarco could say about Mahoney was that he actually liked meeting with his working-class constituents and cared about most of them. The Boston office was typically staffed by bright kids from Harvard who worked for free, Maggie convincing them that being an intern for John Mahoney would look good on their résumés. More important, as it related to DeMarco's current assignment, Maggie Dolan knew everybody who was anybody in the city of Boston.

Maggie came to the phone saying, "What do you want, DeMarco? I'm busy."

So much for small talk. "I need the name of someone wired into the legal network here in Boston. Someone who can give me the dirt on Erin Kelly."

"Which Erin Kelly? There are probably a million Erin Kellys in Boston."

"The Erin Kelly who's the attorney managing the Russell family trust."

"Why would Mahoney care about her?" Maggie asked.

"You don't know?" DeMarco said.

"Know what?"

"Mahoney is now Cassie Russell's guardian."

Maggie was silent for a second then said, "That poor girl." DeMarco didn't know if *that poor girl* referred to Cassie's status as an orphan or if the phrase expressed Maggie's opinion of Mahoney's suitability as a guardian. He suspected the latter.

"So do you know someone?"

"Give me a minute, will ya?"

DeMarco waited patiently as the gears within Maggie's smart brain spun around.

"Peter Blackwell," she said. "He's a high society lawyer. Been here forever, comes from old Boston money, and would have known the Russell family socially. And he likes to gossip. Keep that in mind because he's likely to tell people whatever you tell him."

"Can you call him and get me an appointment with him? Or better yet, see if he'll just have a drink with me." What DeMarco meant, and what Maggie surely understood, was that she was to use Mahoney's name to make this happen.

———◆◆◆———

DeMarco's phone rang.

"Hello?"

"Mr. DeMarco?"

"Yes. Who's this?"

"Steve Schommer. I'm the NTSB's Eastern Regional Office director. I was told that Congressman Mahoney wanted an update on the Russell accident investigation and that I was to call you."

"That's right, and thanks for calling."

"So what do you want to know?"

"I'm going to cut right to the chase here, Mr. Schommer. I want to know if the accident could have been deliberately caused."

"You're kidding."

"I'm not."

"Well, right now, I can't tell you what caused the accident. We know from Russell's Mayday call that he lost oil pressure. But that's all we know at this point." Schommer paused. "Look, the plane went down in the middle of the Adirondack mountains. To get to the crash location, it's a four-hour hike. You can't drive to it, not even with ATVs. The bodies had to be airlifted out with a chopper. We had to cut the top off the cockpit to free the bodies, then we had to put them in baskets, like the ones used to transport injured people, then airlift them out of there one at a time. It took us two days to get the bodies out. And the investigator who's seen the crash wasn't able to determine the cause, not from an in situ visual inspection. We're going to have to send a team in there, find as much of the plane as we can, like the wings, which snapped off and aren't near the fuselage, then we're going to have to send in a rigging team to get the plane out with a heavy lift chopper. You understand what I'm saying? We can't just put the plane on a flatbed truck and drive it out of there."

"Yeah, I get it," DeMarco said.

Schommer wasn't through. "After we've choppered the plane out, we'll have to take it to a shop where we can do a detailed analysis for things like metal fatigue or a mechanical failure of some kind, such as an oil fitting or a brazed joint coming apart, to see what could have resulted in a loss of oil pressure. If there's evidence of sabotage, maybe we'll see it and maybe we won't. It's not like we're going to find a hole in the fuselage from a rocket hitting the plane. So if the plane was sabotaged, it will depend on how it was done and if we can tell from what's left of the plane in its current condition."

"How long will all that take?"

"At least a month, and that's if we really push it and say money and overtime be damned."

"Well, you need to push it."

"Why do you think the plane could have been sabotaged?"

"I can't tell you that. All I can tell you is that it's a possibility and Congressman Mahoney has a legitimate reason to be concerned."

"Yeah, okay," Schommer said, yielding to the political weight coming down on his head.

"Let me ask you something," DeMarco said. "If you were going to cause a plane to lose oil pressure, how would you do it?"

The only thing DeMarco knew about engines and oil was that if an engine didn't get oil bad things happened.

"The simplest way would be to drill a small hole in one of the oil lines and slap a piece of tape over the hole."

"Tape? Like duct tape?"

"Yeah, but maybe not duct tape. The oil pressure in a Cessna engine, like the one in Russell's plane, varies between fifty and a hundred psi. And the oil heats up as the engine runs. So you drill a hole, slap a piece of tape over the hole, the heat from the oil loosens the tape a bit, and eventually the oil pressure blows off the tape, all the oil is lost, and the engine freezes."

"Huh," DeMarco said. "So it's not that complicated. I mean, it's not like you'd have to build an explosive charge with a timer or something."

"No, a person with a drill, a roll of tape, and the knowledge of where to drill could do it."

"Well, if somebody drilled a hole, won't you be able to see it when you, uh, autopsy the plane?"

"Maybe. It depends on the condition of the oil lines after the crash."

Everything was *maybe* with this guy.

The call ended with Schommer assuring him that he'd expedite the investigation and the only thing DeMarco concluded was that an experienced pilot like Erin Kelly could have caused the crash. Maybe. But because the plane didn't crash on the way to Russell's cabin, she would have to have had access to the plane while the Russells were at the cabin.

He was having a hard time imagining that: Erin Kelly sneaking into some airport, camo paint on her face, wearing black ninja clothes, and drilling a hole in an oil line.

19

Peter Blackwell wore what DeMarco suspected was a very expensive hairpiece and a red bow tie. Bow ties may have been popular at some point in the history of men's fashion but these days the guys who wore them were usually pretentious putzes who wanted to stand out from the crowd. Okay, maybe that was too harsh, but DeMarco tended to automatically dislike bow tie wearers.

He met Blackwell at his club—the Somerset Club at 42 Beacon Street. Established in 1826, the Somerset Club was the most exclusive and, reportedly, the most expensive social club in Boston. No one knew for sure how much it cost to join as that information was not made available to the unwashed public. It was said to be a case of *If you're concerned about the price you probably can't afford it*. DeMarco was surprised he was even allowed to enter through the front door.

He and Blackwell sat across from each other in high-backed red leather chairs. Blackwell was drinking a gin martini. As it was only noon, DeMarco suspected the man might be a lush. His red tie not only matched the color of the chair but also the veins bursting in his cheeks. Blackwell, who appeared to be in his seventies, had explained to DeMarco that he ate lunch at the club almost every day, but so far the only thing he'd ordered was a drink.

Blackwell intimated that the only reason he was speaking to a lesser mortal like DeMarco was because of DeMarco's connection to John Mahoney. (Mahoney, by the way, would never be permitted to join the Somerset Club. He didn't have either the bankroll or the proper lineage. His political influence, however, could not be ignored.)

DeMarco said, "I'd like to ask what you know about a lawyer named Erin Kelly. As you may know, Ms. Kelly manages the Russell family trust fund."

"May I ask why you're asking about Erin?" Blackwell said.

"I'm not," DeMarco said. "John Mahoney is. And he's asking because he's Cassie Russell's godfather and her legal guardian now that her parents are dead."

"Really," Blackwell said. "Do you have some concern about Erin?" His beady eyes were twinkling; he was just dying to hear something scandalous.

Yeah, I think she might be a murderer and an embezzler.

"No," DeMarco said. "No concern at all. I'm just doing my due diligence as Mahoney's attorney and I was told you might be helpful in that regard. Can you think of any reason why Erin shouldn't continue to manage the trust?"

Blackwell shook his head. "I knew Erin's father, Francis, quite well. He came from an impoverished background and pulled himself up by his bootstraps, as they say, but was as honest as the day is long."

The way Blackwell said this DeMarco got the distinct impression that bootstrap pullers would be automatically excluded from membership in the Somerset Club.

Blackwell continued. "Francis was a good lawyer and outstanding financial manager. And judging from what I've heard about the size of the Russell trust, which Erin managed through the recession, she's as competent as he was."

"Do you know anything about her personal life?"

"Not really. I've met her at a few social occasions, usually charity events put on by the Russell Foundation, and she was very charming. I know she went to the right schools."

Meaning Harvard, of course. For a man like Blackwell that was the only right school.

"I know she was married once to some banking person and got divorced. The rumor I'd heard was that he'd cheated on her with a secretary but I don't know if that's true or in any way relevant to your inquiry."

"It's not. Let me put it this way," DeMarco said. "Would you have any qualms at all about Erin Kelly managing your money?"

Blackwell laughed. "Don't you know who Erin Kelly's uncle is?"

"Her uncle?"

"Her uncle is Mike Kelly."

DeMarco figured if he looked in the Boston phone book he'd probably find five thousand Kellys listed and maybe a third of the males would be named Mike. Seeing DeMarco's confusion, Blackwell said, "I'm talking about the gangster Mike Kelly."

"You gotta be shittin' me," DeMarco said, causing Blackwell to grimace. Such a crude expression was apparently frowned upon in the hallowed halls of the Somerset Club.

Blackwell said, "As far as I know, neither Erin nor her father before her had any association with Mike. But still—"

"Do you think Connor Russell knew about Erin's uncle Mike?"

"I'm sure he did. And Phil Russell, Connor's father, certainly would have known. He wouldn't have hired Francis Kelly without having thoroughly vetted the man. But when you ask if I'd hire Erin Kelly, I must admit that her most famous relative would give me pause. Most apples do fall near the tree."

Blackwell was an unrepentant snob. On the other hand, DeMarco figured if you wanted to outsource a murder, Mike Kelly would certainly be a viable source.

Blackwell ordered his third martini as DeMarco was leaving. He wondered if the club's amenities included a chauffeured limousine to take its drunken members home.

———◆———

Blackwell sat sipping his martini, pondering.

It had been his experience that life, at a certain level, was mostly about connections and favors. Knowing the right people opened doors for you. His connections had gotten him into Harvard Law. His grades certainly hadn't. The first law firm that hired him had done so because his name was Blackwell, knowing that the name alone would tend to draw clients with money to the firm. His name combined with his connections ensured invitations to distinguished gatherings, inside information on financial matters, a degree of deference from pesky regulators. He'd also learned that in the circles in which he traveled, money didn't have all that much purchasing power because everyone in those circles had money. What purchased a tactical advantage in certain circumstances were *favors*. You do a favor for a man, he owes you and might do one for you when the time was right. And he'd just done a favor for John Mahoney and someday Mahoney might reciprocate. Now the proper thing was to do a favor for Erin Kelly. A woman who managed a five-billion-dollar trust could at some point be helpful. He didn't know how, but the possibility was always there, and it would cost him nothing but a phone call to get into Erin Kelly's future good graces.

He called her office and when she came on the line he spoke slowly and carefully as the last martini appeared to be affecting his speech if not his mental acuity. He said, "I just thought I'd let you know that I had a meeting with a man named Joseph DeMarco, a lawyer representing John Mahoney."

"Really," Erin said. He could tell she was trying to sound casual but he could hear the tension in her voice in that short, simple word.

"Mr. DeMarco just wanted to know what I thought about you. He said he was doing due diligence for his employer who, as I understand it, is now Cassie Russell's guardian."

"And what did you tell him, Peter?"

"I told him that if I had a young ward I could think of no one better than you to handle her financial affairs. The only reason I called was to let you know that he's making inquiries about you."

"Well, I appreciate that but I'm not really surprised. If I were John Mahoney, I would certainly vet the person managing Cassie's trust."

"There is one other thing he asked that I thought you should also know. He asked me if Mr. Mahoney should be concerned because of your family ties to Mike Kelly."

He thought he heard Erin inhale sharply when he told this small white lie.

"And what did you say, Peter?"

"I said he shouldn't be concerned at all. That, as far as I know, there's never been any connection between you and your infamous uncle."

"Again, I appreciate that, Peter. And, of course, you're right. The last time I saw Mike was at my father's funeral, nine years ago. I could hardly ban him from his own brother's funeral. Is there anything else Mr. DeMarco asked about?"

"No, that was it. And as I said, the only reason I called is because you're a friend—"

Now she was.

"—and I wanted you to know that Mahoney's man was making inquiries."

Blackwell disconnected the call, thinking, *Another favor in the bank.*

20

How had it come to this?

In 2008 she'd been riding high, flying above the clouds, practically touching the sun. She had a job that paid two hundred thousand a year. She had a one-point-five-million-dollar condo in the Back Bay and a million-dollar town house she rented out to a gay couple for an exorbitant amount. Her stock portfolio was producing a steady stream of extra income. She knew she was walking a financial tightrope—any prolonged cash flow interruption and it would all come crashing down—but she was confident of her moneymaking skills, a strong stock market, and a seemingly ever expanding real estate market.

The problem was that her job demanded a certain lifestyle. As the manager of the Russell trust, she was required to mingle with Boston's upper crust, the people who socialized with Connor Russell and attended his charity events. These were people whose net worth was anywhere from a few hundred million to several billion—and she didn't want to be thought of as the hired help, even though she was. She needed a suitable home for entertaining on Connor's behalf, stylish clothes, a luxury car. You didn't hobnob with the Russells' set in dresses from Macy's, driving a Prius.

Then those greedy bastards on Wall Street, those sonsabitches, destroyed the economy and it all came crashing down. The couple who rented her town house lost their jobs, couldn't pay the rent, and she was forced to sell the place and lost three hundred thousand when she did. As for the condo in the Back Bay, it had gone underwater. The city of Atlantis occupied higher ground. If she'd sold the condo in 2008 or 9, she would have taken a half-million-dollar bath and be swimming in debt. Bankruptcy hadn't been a possibility; it had been a certainty. She figured the economy would bounce back eventually—it always did—but the only way to survive until things improved was to skim money from the trust, money she'd eventually pay back when her financial apple cart righted itself. She wasn't a thief, for Christ's sake; she just had a temporary cash flow problem, and as soon as it was resolved she'd make things right. She'd sworn to herself that she would.

She took small amounts at first, just enough to help pay her mortgage and utility bills. Then the damn Mercedes broke—fuck German engineering—and she had to buy another car. An eighty-thousand-dollar Tesla seemed appropriate, not to mention environmentally correct. Then there was just *life*: hair salons, pedicures, massages, Christmas in Aspen, shopping in New York, the occasional brief getaway to St. Barts. It was the life she was *expected* to live—she had a reputation to preserve—and there'd been no way to stem the outgoing financial tide, the one that washed her salary away in the blink of an eye.

In 2009 she'd been worried that Connor Russell might audit the trust because, although the trust still had several billion in it, it had taken a hit along with everyone and everything else. Then the economy turned around, the market bounced back, and the trust began to grow again. The past eight years Connor had always seemed delighted with her management skills, constantly praising her for the fine job she was doing. But no matter how hard she tried and how much she scrimped, she just couldn't live within her income.

She was extraordinarily careful and never got outlandishly greedy. The trust was like a giant scoop of ice cream and the amount she stole was the little bit that melted and ran down the side of the cone. As for the trust's accounts, she made sure they showed exactly what she wanted them to show: tiny losses here and there from multiple portfolios, expenditures that had never occurred but were easily explained and perfectly reasonable. As for the spreadsheets, they were an absolute *mess*—a bean counter's nightmare—and intentionally so. She wanted the spreadsheets to be as hard to audit as possible and she was about a hundred percent certain that no one would be able to navigate them without her help.

And then along comes fucking Jerry Feldman.

She'd been speechless when Connor told her that he was having the trust audited. He explained that it had nothing to do with his faith in her, it was just that a friend had suggested an audit was a "prudent" thing to do and might identify ways to make the trust more "efficient." Bullshit! He was checking up on her and she'd been furious that he would even *think* she might be untrustworthy—but she hadn't been able to come up with a way to stop the audit.

She started worrying the third day of the audit. The first two days, Feldman had been professional but friendly, taking a few minutes to chat before he got to work. But by the third day he seemed guarded. He had to use a computer in a room adjacent to her office to examine the spreadsheets; she'd refused—for security reasons, she'd said—to allow him to copy the files to his computer. (Her accounting program in fact made copying the files impossible without a password.) The first two days, the office door remained open, and when he went for lunch he left the computer on and open to whatever spreadsheet he was reviewing. (She'd peek at the screen whenever he left the room.) But on the third day he started shutting off the computer every time he left the room, even to go to the bathroom or get coffee, and he always took his briefcase, which she assumed contained his notes, with him. His attitude became if not exactly frosty, certainly more formal.

She knew something was wrong and that's when she decided to learn a bit more about Jerry Feldman. Who was this pudgy, fussy little accountant? She knew from his website he'd worked at the IRS so she called a lady at Treasury who she'd gone to school with—and that's when she learned that Feldman was a legend within the gray halls of the Treasury Department. He was a man who'd caught some of the most famous tax dodgers in recent American history.

She knew the audit would take at least two weeks, maybe three, so she was certain that Feldman hadn't issued a formal report. But if he was suspicious—and he was certainly beginning to act that way—she wondered if he'd spoken to Connor. She decided to call Connor and ask for a meeting. Not a meeting about the audit but about a gala being planned during the Christmas holidays. All she wanted to do was see how he acted, to read his body language. But when she asked for the meeting, he said he didn't have time as the family was flying to their cabin in the Adirondacks for a long weekend.

He'd just sounded *off* to her. Cool. Reserved. Not as chatty and friendly as he normally was. Was she reading too much into Feldman's guardedness and Connor's brusqueness? Was she being paranoid? Maybe. But she couldn't afford *not* to be paranoid. If she was caught for what she'd done, she was facing prison, disgrace, and abject poverty. She could imagine being forced to live in some halfway house for paroled felons, surrounded by addicts and old whores. She'd rather commit suicide.

So when Connor mentioned that he was flying to the cabin in New York, her first thought was, *Dear Lord, let them all die in a plane crash.* Although she doubted God would answer such a prayer, the entire family dying might be her only salvation. If they were all dead, she could terminate the audit and no one in the future would question her management of the trust. And then the trust would become her very own piggy bank, a piggy bank that would sustain her for life.

Then it occurred to her that she didn't have to rely on prayer. She had the skills to turn prayer into reality. But did she have the courage? Did she have the will?

She did.

After Connor and his wife died—she still couldn't believe the brat had survived—Jerry Feldman sealed his own fate. She hadn't planned to kill Feldman. She'd been thinking that as long as he couldn't complete the audit there'd be no reason to do so. He might suspect something, but suspicions weren't proof. Then the guy had the gall to show up at her office the day after Connor's death was reported, saying he felt he had an obligation to complete the audit, saying that he'd been paid in advance—which she knew was bullshit. She told him that she was in no condition emotionally to deal with him and that she was postponing the audit, at least until after the funeral. But she knew, sure as God made little green apples, that Jerry Feldman wasn't going to go away. She could tell, just looking at the little bastard, that he was like a dog with a slipper and he wouldn't quit chewing on it until the slipper was in shreds. And that's when she drove to Cape Cod to see Uncle Mike.

But now DeMarco was sniffing around and asking questions about her. Then there was the question he'd asked about how the trust was managed. He'd said that the question came from John Mahoney but she sincerely doubted Mahoney was even thinking about Cassie Russell's trust; he was too busy trying to come up with ways to impeach the president. No, the question was DeMarco's and she couldn't understand why he'd asked it. Had he learned something in the short time he'd been in Boston?

It was then that she realized she could spend the rest of her life in a state of perpetual anxiety, wondering if another audit would be performed by someone as competent as Jerry Feldman. Per Connor's woefully outdated will, and as she'd told DeMarco, a board now controlled the trust and would continue to control it until Cassie Russell was twenty-one. The board consisted of Connor's two buddies and Cassie's guardian, John Mahoney. Connor's pals—two rich guys he trusted and played golf with—were a pair of nitwits. The only reason they were rich was because they'd inherited their money. They both trusted her and would buy any story she gave them regarding the financial health of the trust and they were each too busy to spend any time looking over her shoulder. Not to mention, the money in the trust wasn't their money and they really didn't have anything personally at stake. But if Cassie's guardian became suspicious of her *he* could ask for an audit. And when Cassie turned twenty-one *she* could ask for an audit.

But if Cassie was gone . . .

21

Mike Kelly couldn't believe his niece wanted to see him again. He figured now that the accountant was gone, she'd avoid him like the plague the way she always had.

The thing with the accountant had turned out okay. He'd made a hundred and twenty-five grand, Paulie had made twenty-five, and the police didn't have a clue. He knew this because he had a couple guys in the BPD he paid for information. The only oddity was that there was some guy named DeMarco who worked for John Mahoney—talk about a fuckin' crook!—who was asking about Feldman's death. He didn't know why Mahoney's guy was asking but didn't see that it mattered as the cops were still looking for a junkie as the killer.

Mike had never spent a lot of time thinking about what his brother Francis did before he died and what Erin was now doing. He knew she worked for Connor Russell, and knew that Russell and his wife had been killed in a plane crash, but that's about all he knew. He'd figured that his brother, being a lawyer, had probably done things to help Russell avoid paying taxes and that his niece was now doing the same thing.

After Erin came to him the first time, he talked to a couple of lawyers he knew in Boston. These were criminal lawyers—meaning their clients were criminals, although they were too—and they didn't know what his niece did either, so he told them to ask around. They did, and they told him his niece was sitting on a fucking gold mine, managing several billion dollars for a dead guy, investing it, buying and selling real estate, giving money to charities, and doing whatever else rich people did with their money. The next thing that occurred to him—because *he* was a criminal—was that his high society niece must be skimming from this trust she managed. Why else would she want an accountant killed? Or maybe the accountant had figured out what she'd been doing and had been blackmailing her. Whatever the case, she had control over a pile of money, more money than he could even imagine, and there just had to be some way he could get a little taste of it.

One time a cop had asked him why he continued to be a gangster. The cop said, "You're seventy years old. You're a rich man. How much fuckin' money do you need?" The answer to that question was complicated. The truth was that he didn't really need any more money. He was going to die long before he spent all he had. But the thing was, this is what he did. It's what he'd been doing his whole life: he stole. He started stealing in grade school and had never stopped. It didn't matter how much he had; if there was an opportunity to steal he took it.

So when his niece said she wanted to see him again, the first thought that occurred to him was to wonder how he could steal from her.

She showed up at the beach house wearing a baseball cap and sunglasses, her red hair under the cap. A disguise? Paulie wanded her again, which again pissed her off, and then led her out onto the deck where Mike was sitting, keeping an eye out for sharks. He still hadn't spotted one but had heard on the news yesterday that another one had been seen about a mile down the beach, scaring the shit out of some guy in a kayak.

He was dressed in jeans and a blue sweater his sister had given him. (His sister, a total nutcase, was the only one of his siblings he'd stayed in touch with.) It was brisk on the deck with the wind coming off the water, but not real cold, and he still couldn't believe what a warm fall it had been. On the news they were saying that sharks didn't normally hang around the cape this time of year but global warming and warmer oceans and fish migrating to places they didn't normally go was the reason. Whatever the case—he wasn't sure about all that global warming shit, the winters were still cold enough to freeze your ass off—he wanted to see a shark.

He offered her a beer, which she again declined, then said, "So. What's up?"

She didn't hesitate. "I want someone else taken care of."

"You're shittin' me. What kind of trouble are you in?"

"What makes you think I'm in trouble?"

"Why else would you be killing people? Because you're a psycho? Because you hate them?"

"What difference does it make? I'm willing to pay you. A hundred thousand, just like the last time."

"Who do you want taken care of?"

Now she hesitated. "Cassie Russell," she finally said.

"Who's—"

"The daughter of Connor Russell, the one who survived the plane crash."

"A kid? You want to kill a kid?"

"Yeah. You have some kind of rule against that?"

She said this all snooty, like she couldn't imagine him having any kind of scruples, which pissed him off.

"As a matter of fact, I do," he said. "I've never killed a kid in my life."

"What difference does it make? A kid's nothing but a short person."

Jesus, she was a cold bitch. "It makes a difference," he said. "At least to normal people it does."

"All right. I'm willing to pay you *twice* as much as I paid you last time. That's two hundred thousand just to be the middle man."

Now *that* was a lot of money. And now he had no doubt she was skimming.

"You actually have two hundred grand, plus what the guy will want?" he asked. "I know him and he's going to want more than fifty to whack a kid."

"I got the money. You got paid the last time, didn't you?"

"I don't know," he said.

"You don't know what?"

"A kid. I don't know."

"Will you quit saying that! Will you do it or not?"

Mike stuck a cigar in his mouth, patted his pockets as if hunting for a lighter, then reached into a pocket. He shut off the tape recorder and pulled out a lighter.

After she left, he walked back into the house. Paulie was sitting there watching a talk show, these two fat chicks yelling at a scrawny, tattooed, long-haired guy sitting between them. Something about how the guy was balling both of them. Paulie watched some weird shit on TV.

"Get us a couple of beers," Mike said, "and come on outside. I need to talk to you about something."

Paulie got the beers and took the chair where Erin had been sitting. "You seen a shark yet?" he asked.

"No. But I know they're out there. Guy in a kayak spotted one just a mile from here. I was thinking, maybe we could buy a pig, tape a life jacket to it, then row out there and toss it in and see what happens."

"Where would you get the pig?"

"Hell, I don't know. Anyway, that's not what I wanted to talk to you about." Mike took a sip of his beer, burped, and said, "My niece. She wants someone else taken care of."

"You shittin' me. What is she, some kind of psycho?"

"I think she's what they call a sociopath, but what do I know? Anyway, she wants someone else offed."

"Okay. Who?"

"Well, here's where it gets kind of tricky. She wants a kid killed."

"A kid?"

"Yeah, I know. Well, not a little kid, a teenager, but still. Anyway, I know this isn't the kind of thing that would, uh, appeal to you, but she's willing to pay a lot."

"What's a lot?"

"Let me ask you something. How old is your mother?"

"My mother? She's eighty-four. Why are you—"

"And how much does that assisted living place cost?"

"Thirty-six hundred a month. But the cost keeps going up, the more they have to do for her. If she needs total care—you know, somebody feeding her, dressing her, giving her baths, and all that shit—it'll eventually be six grand a month. Talk about a fuckin' racket."

"So say six grand a month. That's seventy-two grand a year."

"And she's eighty-four now. Her mom lived to ninety-two."

"So say she needs total care and lives ten more years, that's more than seven hundred grand you'll need."

"I hadn't thought about it that way but you're right."

"What if I can get my niece to pay for the assisted living place for as long as your mom lives? Then your mom's set for life and you can quit using everything I pay you to take care of her."

"Your niece will do that?"

"Not up front. Up front she's willing to pay you fifty to take care of the kid. But after you do the job, she'll do it because I got a recording of her asking me to set up the hit."

Mike figured that was the least he could do for Paulie. The guy deserved a life and it wasn't like it was his money. And he'd make two hundred and fifty grand, his two hundred to set it up and half the hundred thousand he'd told Erin the hit would cost. Then Erin, after he had a little talk with her, and with this trust she managed that gave buckets of money to charities every year, could easily make the monthly payments for Paulie's mom's nursing home. It was a good deal for everyone.

Paulie looked away, out at the surf. "I don't know. I mean . . . Jesus, a kid."

"Well, think it over."

Paulie turned back to face Mike. His eyes were flat and dead, the way a shark's eyes looked in photos Mike had seen. "There's nothing to think about. A kid I don't know versus my mom."

22

The air rushing past the windows screamed like a factory whistle blowing. The ground—the forest—was coming toward her at an unbelievable speed and there was nothing she could do to stop it. The nose of the plane brushed the top of a two-hundred-foot evergreen, and continued downward, toward a virtual wall of trees. The plane hit another tree and the left wing broke off, sounding like a twig being snapped, and she saw it propeller away from the body of the plane. The plane pitched wildly to the right, headed toward another evergreen, and one of the evergreen's largest branches was now pointed directly at the plane—then the branch morphed into a spear with a sharp iron point. The branch, the spear, penetrated the front windshield but before it could stab her as she sat terrified in her seat she screamed—and woke up. She always woke up just as the branch—the one that had killed her mother—went through the windshield. The t-shirt she'd worn to bed was soaked with sweat and her heart was beating like a hamster's.

She'd been having the dream almost every night, and after she had it she couldn't get back to sleep for hours. She should talk to the therapist about it but he'd probably give her a pill to help her sleep and she didn't want to start popping pills.

She supposed she was lucky that she couldn't remember the crash, which would have meant remembering watching her parents die. But the two days she spent in the woods—the two longest days of her life—she remembered vividly and would never forget.

After the crash, after she'd crawled outside the plane the second time, she remembered hearing about the rule of threes: three minutes without oxygen, three days without water, three weeks without food—and you died. She had two bottles of water and two cans of Coke, so if someone found the plane in less than a week she'd be okay if she rationed the liquids.

Food was the bigger problem. She didn't have the weapons or the skills to hunt squirrels or birds for dinner, and even if she had she couldn't imagine eating raw meat. Her problems were compounded by her inability to make a fire for cooking or warmth or light, and her sprained ankle and broken arm made it difficult to forage. She found a fallen tree branch to use for a cane and limped around the crash site, always keeping the plane within view because she was afraid she'd get lost if she didn't. She hunted for a stream in case she needed more water and for things to eat. There was no stream but she found a plant with some small red berries on it and some sort of mushroom attached to the trunk of a tree, but she didn't know if they were edible. She decided to wait as long as she could before eating the berries or the mushrooms; she didn't want to poison herself.

She again thought about the option of walking out. By the position of the setting sun she knew which direction was west. If she traveled west long enough she'd reach her parents cabin and long before then would encounter civilization. But she had no idea if the nearest town was east, west, north, or south. And with her injured ankle how far would she be able to travel? She concluded the best thing would be to wait and hope that someone found her. She should have paid more attention when her dad talked about the plane; if she had she would have known if it had some sort of device that emitted a distress signal.

The first night, she decided to stay outside the plane. With her mom's and dad's coats as well as her own, she figured she'd be warm enough. She'd rather be cold than sit in the Cessna with her dead parents. When night fell she couldn't believe how dark it was. It occurred to her that she'd never been in a place before where there wasn't *some* light—lights from nearby houses, street lights, lights from passing cars. But where she was in the woods it was pitch black; there wasn't even a moon to provide any illumination.

She'd sat huddled in the coats all night, trying to sleep, but couldn't. She couldn't stop thinking about her mom and dad being dead, and how if she'd behaved better her dad wouldn't have left when he did. Then the noises started—the sounds of things moving about in the woods. She was sure she was hearing small animals—not something big like a bear or a deer—but the noises were disturbing as she didn't know what was making them. Then at one point something *screamed*. She didn't know what had screamed—prey or predator—but when she heard the scream, she screamed too, then immediately clamped her hand over her mouth terrified that whatever had caused the scream might come after her.

The second day, as much as she hated to do it, she went back into the plane again. She looked over at her mom; her face was becoming waxy and had a blue tinge. It occurred to her that her parents were literally decaying before her eyes—and the thought of that made her gag. She searched the plane a second time for matches and food but again couldn't find anything, and again wasn't able to open some of the small compartments as their doors had been jammed shut by the crash.

On the afternoon of the second day, as she sat there with her back against the plane, a large black bear came out of the woods, stopping on the perimeter of the crash site, about thirty yards from her. It probably weighed four hundred pounds. *Oh, God.* She wondered if the smell of her dead parents had attracted the bear. She was afraid to move and at the same time she wanted to crawl back inside the plane. If the bear attacked she'd be better protected in the plane and able to use her walking stick to fight it off. While she was trying to decide what to do, the bear stared at her, and then, as if it was bored and had seen enough, turned and disappeared into the woods. But now she knew the bear was out there and she didn't know if it would return.

At this point her head ached and her broken arm began to throb. She'd used up all the Motrin tablets she'd found in the plane. She wasn't hungry but she was incredibly thirsty, and it took all her willpower not to drink the remaining water she had. She strained to hear the sound of an approaching plane or helicopter but the only thing she heard was something moving through the brush a few yards from where she was. She didn't call out, however, because she was afraid it might be the bear.

The worst thing was she couldn't stop thinking about her parents, her mind spinning with guilt and remorse and unfathomable loss. They'd both been extremely busy people but she realized now that they'd always been there for her when she needed them. She'd been the selfish one, not her mom and dad.

Nightfall of the second day, feeling fearful of things in the woods, she crawled inside the plane to sleep, then couldn't. She didn't believe in ghosts but she had the eerie sensation that any moment her parents would turn their heads and speak to her. She could imagine them saying: *Cassie, if it wasn't for you, we wouldn't be here.* Finally, she decided that she'd rather take her chances with bears and whatever else was in the woods. She crawled out of the plane, then sat shivering, huddled in all the coats, until daylight finally came. She'd never been so happy to see a sunrise in her life.

On the morning of the third day, she told herself that she had to make a decision. Tomorrow half her water would be gone and she was beginning to feel lightheaded from lack of food. If she wasn't rescued today, and while she still had the strength, tomorrow she'd begin walking. Maybe she'd find something edible, like blueberries or wild strawberries, and maybe she'd cross a stream and be able to fill her water bottles. Her ankle would make walking difficult but what choice did she have? To just sit there and die of starvation or thirst? Before she left she'd leave a note on the plane saying she'd headed west, west being as good a direction as any to go, and perhaps someone would find the note and come looking for her.

She'd just had this thought when a man wearing a large backpack, hunter green clothes that looked like a uniform, and a goofy-looking tennis hat walked out of the woods. He appeared in the same spot where she'd seen the bear and she wondered if she was hallucinating.

———◆———

She picked up her phone on the nightstand next to her bed and saw it was eleven thirty. She'd slept for only an hour before she'd had the dream. She thought, *Eleven thirty. Sarah will still be up.* Sarah was always up until at least midnight.

She called her and Sarah softly said, "Hey."

"I'm sorry but I can't sleep. Had the stupid dream again."

"That's okay, I'm glad you called. I'm watching YouTube and there's this cat—"

"Sarah, I can't stop thinking about that weekend. If I hadn't acted like a brat, we wouldn't have left that day, then maybe everything would have been different."

Sarah, who was not only her best friend but also the smartest girl she knew, didn't say anything for a moment. "My mom says you should come and stay with us for a few days. We'll sleep together in my room and binge watch shows on Netflix. You shouldn't be alone in that big house."

"I'm not alone."

"Yeah, I know, but you sorta are. So tomorrow, you should—"

"What's the name of the cat video on YouTube?" Cassie asked, hitting the YouTube icon on her phone.

23

DeMarco decided it was time to go see Cassie again. He needed to tell her the date for her parents' funeral had been set.

He'd already told Mahoney about the funeral. Mahoney said he wasn't sure he'd be able to make it, all the stuff he had going on right now in Congress, but Mary Pat's friend in California was reaching the end so Mary Pat would be attending. The good news, for DeMarco, was that Mary Pat would be in Boston soon and she could get into it with Cassie regarding her future.

He still hadn't told Mahoney his suspicions about Erin Kelly; he'd do that right after he'd talked to Cassie.

He rang the bell and Mrs. Aguilera answered the door, frowning when she saw it was him.

He said, "I'm just here to tell Cassie the date for the funeral has been set."

"I'll tell her."

"No, I want to tell her myself. I want to see how she's doing."

He followed Mrs. Aguilera up a staircase wide enough for a Volkswagen to the second floor. While walking down a long hallway, he saw a fitness room containing free weights, an elliptical machine, a stationary bicycle, a treadmill, and a rowing machine. On one wall was a television with a seventy-inch screen. He imagined that Connor and Elaine Russell had had his and hers personal trainers.

They eventually reached Cassie's bedroom, a room bigger than the living room in DeMarco's Georgetown town house. She was lying on a king-size bed, surrounded by about a dozen pillows, wearing a ratty-looking old sweater and jeans with holes in the knees. There was a television mounted on one wall, shelves filled with novels and school books, posters of bands he'd never heard of, and sports equipment—soccer balls, a field hockey stick, an aluminum baseball bat, and a ball glove—piled in a corner. Cassie was on the phone talking to somebody, but when she saw it was DeMarco she said, "Sarah, I'll call you back."

DeMarco said, "How are you doing?"

"I'm all right," she said.

He thought she looked tired but otherwise she seemed okay. She still had the cast on her left arm but the bruise on her forehead was fading. How she was doing mentally, he had no idea, but he was about to find out.

DeMarco said, "Erin Kelly called and said the funeral is scheduled for Saturday. Ten a.m. at Holy Cross."

Cassie nodded.

"Ms. Kelly's taking care of everything. Flowers, speakers, all the other arrangements. And Mary Pat will be attending the funeral."

"I know, she told me," Cassie said. "She called again yesterday."

"Anyway, I just wanted to see if there's anything I can do for you. When Mary Pat gets here, you and she can talk about the future."

"I can't think about the future right now."

"Well, right now you don't have to. Like I said, when Mary Pat gets here—"

"I want to go back to the cabin."

"The cabin?"

"The place where we were before my mom and dad died. The last time we were there, I acted like a little bitch and I just can't stop thinking about it. I want to go back there for a couple of days. I want to feel close to them. I want to . . . I can't explain it, but I have to go back and I want you to take me. Rosa doesn't drive."

"Oh, well, I don't know if that's—"

"All you have to do is drive me, for Christ's sake. It's a big cabin, you'll have your own room, and you can just lay around for a couple of days. I'd go by myself if I could drive."

How the hell could he get out of this? He knew if he called Mahoney, Mahoney would tell him to take her. Then something occurred to him.

He said, "Cassie, I'd be happy to take you. When do you want to go?"

"Tomorrow. I want to leave first thing tomorrow morning."

"Honey, you can't go tomorrow," Mrs. Aguilera said. "You have a doctor's appointment."

"And I can't do it tomorrow either," DeMarco said. "There's something I have to do for Mr. Mahoney."

"Then the day after tomorrow," Cassie said, her expression making it clear she wasn't going to take no for an answer. This was a girl used to getting her way.

DeMarco looked over at Mrs. Aguilera. She nodded.

"Okay, day after tomorrow," DeMarco said.

"Mavis, I need to talk to him. And for more than five minutes. It's about his goddaughter."

"How she's doing?"

"Okay, I think. Anyway, get me on his schedule for fifteen minutes or so. And get me on it before he's completely stewed."

"I don't appreciate those kinds of comments, DeMarco," loyal Mavis said.

"Yeah, well, you know what I mean."

And what he meant was that by seven or eight at night, Mahoney was likely to be completely in the bag and DeMarco wanted to talk to him while he was still semi-sober. He was never completely sober.

Surprisingly, Mahoney called him back a few minutes later. "What's going on?" he said.

"I think Erin Kelly might be embezzling from Cassie's trust. And I think there's also a possibility that she might have killed the Russells."

When dealing with Mahoney, and knowing Mahoney's attention span, DeMarco knew it was always best to start with a headline.

"What the fuck are you talking about?" Mahoney shrieked. "Are you drunk?"

Talk about pots and kettles.

DeMarco told him everything: what Mrs. Aguilera had overheard Connor Russell say to his wife and what Jerry Feldman's partner had said.

"And you seriously think Erin could have had Connor and Feldman killed?"

"I think it's a possibility, but obviously I'm not sure. And even if she's not a murderer, you can't keep her in charge of the trust if she's skimming from it."

"But how would she have killed these people? She's a damn lawyer, not a mob hit man."

"Well, speaking of mob hit men, there's something else you need to know. Her uncle is Mike Kelly."

"Which Mike Kelly. I probably know—"

"The Mike Kelly who's the biggest mobster in Boston."

"Are you shitting me!"

"No, sir."

"So what are you going to do?" Mahoney asked.

"I want to hire someone to dig into Erin Kelly's financial life. I also want to know where she was the weekend the Russells were killed."

"You think she killed them herself, sabotaged the plane or something?"

"Erin's a pilot and Connor used to let her fly his plane. And I talked to an NTSB guy and he said it wouldn't take a CIA agent to cause a plane to lose oil pressure. Anyway, I want to know where she was that weekend. And there's something else. Cassie wants me to take her back to the cabin where she spent the last couple of days with her parents. Some sort of pilgrimage, I guess, but don't ask me to figure out what's going on inside her head. I'm going to take her because I want to see the airport where Connor kept his plane. I want to see if there are security cameras and how hard it would be to get access to a plane."

"Geez, I just can't believe people," Mahoney said. "First, Hewlett and now this woman."

DeMarco decided not to tell his boss what he had in mind for Tommy Hewlett.

<hr />

DeMarco called Maggie Dolan. She came on the line saying, "Now what is it, DeMarco? I don't have time for you today."

"You're gonna have to make time. It's for Cassie Russell." Before Maggie could interrupt, he said, "First, there's a guy named Tommy Hewlett. He used to drive for Mahoney."

"I remember Tommy. He was a sweetheart."

"After he quit working for Mahoney, he went to work for a big security firm here in Boston. I want a meeting, right away, with the guy who runs the firm."

"Why?"

"It's complicated. Just get me a meeting. Today. Then there's one other thing. At the end of the month a bank is going to foreclose on Tommy. They're going to take his house."

"Oh, that's terrible."

It was time for a wee lie. "Yeah, that's what Mahoney thought, too. Mahoney really likes the guy. Anyway, Mahoney said to see if you can find a banker to buy Tommy's loan and give him some breathing room. He only owes a hundred and thirty grand, so we're not talking major money. I figure there must be a dozen bankers in this town who want to stay on Mahoney's good side and will be willing to do him a favor."

"I can think of three weasels off the top of my head," Maggie said.

"Great. So make this happen. First get me a meeting with the security company honcho and, while I'm meeting with him, you get a banker to take over Tommy's loan and give him some time to pay it back."

"DeMarco, did I miss the memo that said I was now working for you?"

"Thanks, Maggie."

24

Thurston Security was one of the largest security firms in Boston, employing about seven hundred people. It provided guards to businesses, bodyguards for individuals, installed security systems, did cyber security work. The firm also did "discreet" investigations. The company's main office was in Exchange Place, a forty-story glass skyscraper in Boston's financial district.

The head of the company was a stocky woman in her forties with short dark hair, wearing a navy blue Hillary Clinton pantsuit. Her name was Nora Thurston. On the wall behind Thurston's desk were plaques and certificates showing her membership in business organizations, recognition for various charitable activities, and a degree from a university. What caught DeMarco's eye was a photo of a young Nora Thurston in military fatigues, standing with three other women in front of a camouflaged personnel carrier. There was a desert landscape in the background of the photo and he wondered if it had been taken in Afghanistan or Iraq.

Thurston said, "I was told you wanted to retain my firm on behalf of John Mahoney."

"Maybe," DeMarco said. "It sort of depends on if we can come to an agreement about something."

"What's that?" Thurston said.

"I want your firm to investigate the whereabouts of a woman on a certain weekend. Second, I want you to look at this woman's finances and see if there's any evidence that she might be living above her means or otherwise in need of money."

Thurston shrugged. "Not a problem. We do that sort of thing all the time. And we never mention the name of the client."

"The other thing Mr. Mahoney wants is a specific person assigned to the case."

"Who would that be?"

"A man named Tommy Hewlett. He used to work for your company but you fired him a couple of years ago."

"I don't remember the name. A lot of people work for me. Why did we fire him?"

"Because he was a drunk."

Thurston shook her head. "You're asking me to rehire a drunk I fired?"

"He doesn't drink anymore. He's been sober for eighteen months."

Thurston studied DeMarco for a moment, then picked up her phone and said, "Look up a guy named Hewlett, Thomas. We apparently fired him a couple of years ago." There was a brief pause before Thurston said, "Okay. Tell Clark to come see me."

To DeMarco, Thurston said, "I looked you up when Maggie Dolan made the appointment for you. Saw the spot of trouble you got into last spring."

"If you can call being framed for murder a spot of trouble."

"The papers said you were Mahoney's fixer. But Mahoney always denied it."

"So who you gonna believe? The papers or the next Speaker of the House?"

Thurston smiled.

There was a knock on the door and Thurston said, "Come in."

A bulky guy with short, gray hair and a dark mustache entered the room. DeMarco wondered why his hair was gray and the mustache wasn't.

Thurston said, "Clark, this is Joe DeMarco. He wants to hire us for something but there're some strings attached."

DeMarco liked the fact that Thurston didn't mention Mahoney's name.

Thurston said, "Do you remember a man named Tommy Hewlett who worked for us? You apparently fired him."

"Sure, I remember him. He was a good guy. I hated to let him go but didn't have a choice."

"Good guy" was the way everyone seemed to remember Tommy Hewlett.

Clark said, "He retired out of BPD. Did a lot of robbery, fraud investigations for them. Then he took a job in D.C. doing security for some politician and, when he quit that, we hired him. He was a good investigator. You remember the Cavendish thing?"

"Sure," Thurston said.

"Well, Tommy's the one who solved it. But then his wife died, he fell apart, and tried to drown himself in scotch. So I fired him."

Thurston said, "DeMarco says he's sober now. Has been for eighteen months. DeMarco wants us to hire him back, temporarily, and use him on a case. Would you have a problem with that?"

"If he's sober, I guess not."

Speaking to Thurston, DeMarco said, "I'm not coercing you into doing anything. You don't want to hire Hewlett, I'll take my business somewhere else. And if you take him back I'm not going to squeal if you decide to fire him again if he doesn't work out. All I want you to do is give him a second chance. I also figured you'd be the best firm to use based on your reputation and the fact that Tommy knows what the firm can do. And you can never tell when doing a favor for my, uh, employer might be good for you."

"Who's your employer?" Clark asked.

Thurston said, "That's irrelevant."

———— ⬩ ————

DeMarco called Maggie Dolan. "Did you have any luck with Tommy's loan?"

"Piece of cake. Took one phone call. First Fidelity agreed to buy it and Tommy won't have to start paying them back for six months. Since it will cost the bank a few thousand to do this, the CEO wants a one-on-one meeting with Mahoney."

"Maggie, if you were here, I'd kiss you on the lips."

"I don't want you kissing me anywhere, DeMarco."

DeMarco said, "Tell the CEO that the meeting with Mahoney will have to wait until Mahoney's the Speaker again in January."

That would give DeMarco time to break the news to Mahoney that DeMarco had used his name to cut a deal for Hewlett. But Mahoney could wait. Right now the important thing was to find out if Erin Kelly was a murderer and/or a thief.

———— ⬩ ————

DeMarco called Tommy Hewlett next.

"What do you want, DeMarco? I told you I wasn't going to do anything."

"I want you to meet me at my hotel this evening. I've got a job for you. Some other good news too when it comes to keeping your house."

"What?"

"I'm staying at the Boston Park Plaza. Can you get there by five?"

"Yeah, sure. Hell, yes."

⬥

Tommy hung up the phone and placed it next to the .45 on the side table. The gun lay on a cloth to make sure it didn't scratch or leave an oil stain on the table. His wife, had she been alive, would have strangled him if she'd seen it on the bare wood. Tommy had owned the gun since he was a Boston cop. He'd never fired it in the line of duty and could recall only two instances when he'd removed it from his holster during arrests. He couldn't help but think that it would be kind of funny if the only time he used it for real was to kill himself.

In his lap was a photo of his wife in a silver frame. He'd been looking at it when DeMarco called. Colleen had been twenty when he'd taken the picture; they'd been married just a year. She was standing on the boardwalk in Atlantic City, barefoot, wearing red shorts and a white tank top, the waves rolling onto the beach behind her. Her hair was blowing to one side thanks to a breeze and he'd caught her in mid-laugh, her eyes sparkling, her mouth open, her teeth white as pearls. He couldn't believe how beautiful she'd been—and this was the way he wanted to remember her, at twenty, and not the way she'd looked at the end, withered by disease, her face contorted with pain.

The photo was the last thing he wanted to see before he joined her.

He stood up and placed the photo next to the .45.

He'd see what DeMarco had to say.

⬥

Tommy entered the bar, clean shaven, wearing a suit that had seen better days. DeMarco was seated at a table away from the bar, drinking a Coke. He didn't want to tempt Tommy with alcohol in any way.

The bartender came over to ask what Tommy wanted. The bartender wasn't Shannon; it was her night off. Tommy said, "Give me a tonic water, with lime."

"So what's going on?" he asked DeMarco as soon as the bartender departed.

"There's a woman named Erin Kelly that I want investigated."

DeMarco told Tommy about Connor Russell's plane crash, Jerry Feldman's suspicions that Erin could be embezzling from Cassie Russell's trust, and Feldman's death.

"You think she might have killed the Russells?" Tommy said.

"I think it's a possibility that needs to be looked into. I want to know if she could have been in the vicinity of Tupper Lake, New York, the weekend Russell's plane went down. So I'm guessing what I need is any location information you can get from cell phone data, toll booth charges, credit card charges, that sort of thing. What I also need is Erin Kelly's financial profile. I'm looking for anything that would indicate she might have a motive for embezzling."

"You want to hire *me* to do this?"

"I'm not hiring you. I'm hiring Thurston Security. I cut a deal today with Nora Thurston to take you back on a temporary basis. But if you screw up or start drinking again—"

"I'm finished with booze. Forever."

"Good. Anyway, Thurston's willing to give you a shot. Whether she agrees to keep you on afterward is up to her."

"Jesus, DeMarco, I don't know what to say."

"And there's one other thing. A bank called First Fidelity here in Boston bought the loan you took out on your house. It did this because the CEO wants some political suck with Mahoney. But what this means is that you're being given a six-month reprieve on making your loan payments, so you might be able to keep your house."

Tommy didn't say anything. He was looking at DeMarco as if he were some sort of apparition that had descended from heaven.

DeMarco took a yellow Post-it out of a pocket. "Call this guy. He's the banker now handling your loan. You can get all the details from him."

"Why are you doing this for me, DeMarco. I tried to blackmail—"

"Karma, Tommy. I believe in karma. You got some bad breaks and I figured if I helped you out, maybe my short game would improve."

"Your short game?"

"That was a joke. But investigating Erin Kelly isn't. Tomorrow I'm taking Cassie Russell to her folks' cabin in New York. While I'm there I'm going to check out the airport where Connor Russell kept his plane. And when I get back I want some answers on Erin Kelly."

DeMarco rose, leaving Tommy stunned motionless sitting at the table. DeMarco turned to go, then turned back and said, "Oh, I'm curious about something. Where'd that photo of Mahoney and Liz Prescott come from?"

Tommy shook his head. "I've always been into photography, you know, back before everybody's phone became a camera. That night, I'd just gotten a new lens for taking low-light shots and while I was waiting for Mahoney I was fiddling around with the camera. When Mahoney and Prescott came out of the hotel I took their picture, but it was just to see how the shot would turn out. I wasn't thinking about . . . Hell, I'd forgotten I'd even taken it, until, well, you know."

DeMarco nodded. "I'll talk to you soon," he said. "Now I gotta go. I got a date tonight."

25

———✦———

DeMarco met Shannon at the TD Garden ticket booth. She'd told him that her apartment was just a couple of blocks away and that he didn't need to pick her up. He wondered if this was true or if meeting him at the stadium was a first date strategy so if she decided he was a creep he wouldn't know where she lived. Whatever the case, she looked terrific in a tight pair of jeans but he made sure he didn't ogle her in a creeplike fashion.

They entered the stadium and Shannon was appropriately impressed by their seats. She should have been impressed as they'd cost DeMarco five hundred bucks. One nice thing about a hockey game was that DeMarco didn't have to strain to make conversation, Shannon being completely absorbed in the game, pointing out to DeMarco every error the Bruins made—particularly LeBlanc's, the guy the Bruins had paid fifteen million for.

At one point, however, she did say: "I looked you up, by the way."

That was the thing about dating these days, people checking out their dates on Google and Facebook and, for all DeMarco knew, some women's-only NSA database. All DeMarco had told her about his job was that he was a lawyer employed by the House of Representatives and he did mundane legal chores to keep the politicians from being indicted. He'd said this as if he was joking although when it came to Mahoney he was being serious.

"You didn't tell me that the politician you worked for was John Mahoney," Shannon said. This statement was accompanied by an eye roll.

DeMarco decided not to go into the spiel where he claimed he was an independent counsel who served many members of the House and that Mahoney wasn't really his boss. He just didn't feel like lying to this woman.

"Well, I didn't want to scare you off," he said. "And Mahoney does have some good qualities, it's just hard to name them."

Shannon laughed. "I also read about that thing with Lyle Canton last spring."

That *thing* being almost spending his life in prison for a crime he didn't commit.

"Well, I'd be happy to tell you all about it. I—"

Shannon came out of her seat, screaming, "Are you blind, LeBlanc? Ouellet was wide open!"

After the game—which the Bruins won thanks mainly to LeBlanc—they went to a coffee shop and had apple pie for dessert. (The meal preceding the pie had been hot dogs and beer purchased at the game.) While they were eating, DeMarco told her all about being framed for murder. She said that would make for an interesting book, though it wasn't the sort of thing she wrote.

He learned that she had gotten a degree in literature and creative writing at Boston University. While at BU, in addition to playing hockey, she met her future husband, a guy studying to become a dentist. After she graduated she got a mind-numbing job working for an insurance company to support him until he got his degree, then went to work for him so he wouldn't have to pay for a receptionist.

"The first few years, we were swimming in debt but those were the best years of our marriage. Jeff started out as this fun-loving, adventurous guy with a sense of humor, and he would spend a weekend every month treating poor people at a clinic in Dorchester. By the time we got divorced, he'd morphed into this dour creature who was obsessed with money, constantly bitching about his taxes and worrying about how to increase the size of his practice. Then, like a bad movie, he had an affair with a dental hygienist, this mousy little creature who acted as if he walked on water. By then I'd had enough anyway, divorced him, got a job as a bartender, and started working full time on my novel. And, by the way, I got screwed when it came to splitting up all the money I'd helped him make when we were married."

To change the subject, DeMarco asked, "What's the novel you're working on about?"

She grew even more animated, although in general she was a pretty animated person, as he'd seen during the game. Her gray eyes flashing, she told him her novel was about a single mother, battered by divorce and abuse, who lived with her obnoxious sixteen-year-old daughter in a lighthouse off the coast of Nova Scotia. The daughter, by the way, was pregnant and refused to get an abortion. DeMarco said it sounded interesting, even though it didn't, at least not to him. He preferred crime fiction and not the literary equivalent of a chick flick.

She said, "A really big deal literary agent in New York agreed to represent me. I found out just today." She clutched his hand and said, "Joe, I might not be tending bar much longer."

26

DeMarco arrived at Cassie Russell's mansion on time, exactly eight a.m. He was in an excellent mood. He'd told Shannon that he had to take Cassie up to her parents' cabin and would be gone a couple of days, but maybe after he got back he could take her out to dinner to celebrate her landing a big shot agent.

Cassie and Mrs. Aguilera were waiting in the foyer with a pink backpack and a large cooler. Mrs. Aguilera said, "I've packed enough food for two days. Sandwiches, fruit, things you can heat up in the microwave. Also, water and soft drinks. No alcohol," she said, looking pointedly at DeMarco.

To Cassie she said, "You sure you have everything, honey? A heavy jacket in case it gets cold? You know, it could snow there. You got extra shoes? Your medicine, your toothbrush, your—"

"I have everything, Rosa," Cassie said. Cassie hugged her. "Don't worry, I'll be fine."

"And you, you drive careful," Mrs. Aguilera said to DeMarco. "No speeding."

DeMarco tossed Cassie's backpack in the trunk of his rental car and placed the cooler on the backseat. Judging by the cooler's weight, Mrs. Aguilera had packed enough food for a week.

Cassie settled into the passenger seat and immediately put in the ear pieces attached to her iPhone. She said, "I really appreciate you taking me to the cabin, but I don't feel like talking."

"That's fine," DeMarco said. He didn't know what to say to her anyway and had been concerned about how well he'd be able to communicate with a teenager. But it was going to take five hours to drive from Boston to the cabin in the Adirondacks, and he doubted she'd be silent the whole way.

They headed west out of Boston on I-90. Two and half hours later, at the halfway point in the trip, they reached Albany, where DeMarco made a pit stop to use the restroom and get coffee. For the first part of the trip, Cassie hadn't said a word. She sat there listening to music, her eyes closed, falling asleep periodically. From Albany, they took I-87 north, cruising through Saratoga Springs, and when they approached Lake George the scenery improved dramatically as they entered the High Peaks Wilderness Area. The fading fall colors were spectacular. When they passed Lake George, Cassie took out the earbuds and reached into the backseat and opened the cooler. "You want a Coke?" she asked DeMarco.

"Sure."

She opened his Coke for him, then settled back into her seat. "You ever lost anyone you were close to?"

"Yeah, my dad," DeMarco said. "He died young, when I was in my twenties."

He wasn't about to tell her that his dad had been a hit man for the old Italian mob in Queens and he was shot three times by a crooked cop. But it was true that he'd been close to his father. He'd loved the man deeply, and he'd been loved deeply in return.

"How long did it take you to get over him dying?"

He wasn't sure what to say. He didn't want to make her feel worse than she already did but figured it would be better to tell her the truth than to make up something. He wasn't a psychiatrist.

He said, "I've never gotten over it. But as time passes, the grief becomes less intense. When he died, at first I was constantly thinking about him, about things we'd done together, about things I wished we'd done. I still think about him frequently, but not every day. Or I'll think about him when I see something that reminds me of him. It's a cliché but life goes on."

"But I'll bet you didn't feel guilty when your dad died, wishing you could take back the last thing you ever said to him." Her voice broke when she said this but she didn't start crying.

"Actually, that's not true. I did feel guilty, but not because of anything I said to him. I felt guilty that I didn't make the effort to get to know him better. I hardly ever asked him questions about how he became who he was. I felt guilty because I never, ever really told him how much I loved him. My dad and I . . . We weren't big talkers when it came things like feelings. Now I regret that."

"Do you still feel guilty?"

"Yeah, but it doesn't nag at me. I realized—and you will too—that your parents loved you and knew that you loved them and anything you might have said or done on any single day would never change that."

"I don't know," she said. "I can't imagine either one of them having had nice thoughts about me that last weekend."

"Trust me. They loved you," DeMarco said. Then he added, even though he didn't know if he believed it: "This thing you're doing, going to the cabin to get the feeling of being near them, is a good thing. But don't dwell on the negative stuff. While you're there, think about the good times you spent together, the fun times, the family times. Think about things that make you laugh."

She didn't answer him. She turned her head and stared out the window, and they drove on in silence, both of them thinking about their fathers.

———◆———

The Russells' cabin was five miles north of the town of Tupper Lake. The boundary for the High Peaks Wilderness Area—the region Connor Russell had flown over on his last flight—was about ten miles to the east. The cabin sat on the west side of a small hundred-acre lake called Bear Lake. It was a classic—and most likely very expensive—log cabin with a stone chimney. DeMarco was surprised by how isolated the cabin was. He could see a couple of other cabins across the lake but there were no nearby neighbors. He wouldn't have been surprised if a guy with Connor Russell's money had bought a lot of the surrounding property so he would have the lake and the woods mostly to himself.

Cassie got the key hidden in the well house and unlocked the front door and DeMarco lugged his suitcase, her backpack, and the cooler packed by Mrs. Aguilera inside. The interior of the cabin was comfortably and expensively furnished. Four bedrooms, two bathrooms, wide-plank hardwood floors, a fireplace, Oriental rugs, a kitchen with a large farm table and copper-bottomed pots and pans hanging from hooks above an island counter. They wouldn't be roughing it. Almost every room had a window facing the lake and DeMarco could see a small flotilla of ducks swimming near the dock; a rowboat and a canoe were on the dock, secured with a chain. In the mudroom off the back door—the door facing the lake—were fishing poles, life jackets, snowshoes, three different sizes of hiking boots, and backpacks.

Cassie showed DeMarco his room then went to her room and unpacked. While DeMarco was putting the food from the cooler into the refrigerator, she said, "I'm going for a canoe ride."

It hadn't occurred to DeMarco, until then, that he should be concerned about her safety. If he was right about Erin Kelly, she'd tried to kill Cassie by bringing down Connor Russell's plane. She also might have hired someone to kill Jerry Feldman. But would Erin try to kill Cassie again? Probably not. Her primary target had been Connor Russell, not his daughter. And with Connor and Feldman both gone, why take the risk of attempting to kill Cassie a second time? Then there was the fact that the only ones who knew where Cassie was besides himself were Mr. and Mrs. Aguilera. Yeah, Cassie would be okay while they were at the cabin, plus he doubted she was going to tolerate him hovering over her like a bodyguard.

"You sure you should be paddling a canoe with your arm?" he asked, pointing at the cast.

"My arm'll be fine," she said. This was delivered in a tone that said, *Quit trying to mother me.* Nonetheless, DeMarco felt compelled to say something parental, like dress warm, wear your life jacket, stay close to shore—words along those lines—then decided to keep his mouth shut.

27

Paulie stood in the woods, watching as the girl paddled a canoe out to the middle of the lake.

Mike had told him there was no rush on this job. The important thing, Mike had said, was that the kid's death had to look like an accident and not an outright murder. So just as he'd done with Jerry Feldman, Paulie planned to spend several days following her to get some sense of her routine and then come up with a way to make an accident happen. So far he'd had only a couple of ideas. A small kid like her, a broken neck in a fall was a possibility. Then there was drugs; teenagers experimented with drugs and accidental overdoses occurred all the time. But so far those were the only ideas he'd had and he needed to follow her and see what else occurred to him.

He'd shown up at Cassie Russell's house—actually, a fuckin' *mansion*—after he had breakfast with his mom. God, that had been depressing; she kept calling him Jack, his dead father's name. She was really going downhill fast. It was a shame about the kid—he really didn't want to kill a kid—but that was the only way he could guarantee his mom didn't end up in some shitty state facility. He'd seen some of those places: peeling paint, smelling of piss and death and decay, old ladies wandering around in a daze, nobody paying any attention to them. He couldn't let that happen to his mom.

He'd just parked his car when a midsize Nissan with a Hertz sticker stopped in front of the house. The driver went into the house and a few minutes later he came out with the girl, lugging a big cooler. The girl was clutching a pink backpack. The driver was a strong-looking guy with dark hair and a hard face. He looked like some of the guinea hoods Paulie knew in Providence, and he wondered if he could be the girl's bodyguard. She was rich enough to have bodyguards, which would really complicate things. Whoever he was, he didn't have a gun on his hip, so unless he had a piece in an ankle holster he wasn't armed.

When the Nissan took off he followed it. Following the guy was easy in Boston with all the traffic, but then they just kept going and going. Where the hell were they going? He wondered if the girl was planning to spend the night somewhere—that would explain the backpack—but where? It was a good thing he'd filled up the gas tank the night before.

Paulie was still behind him when the guy pulled into a gas station in Albany. Thank God, because Paulie had to pee like a racehorse. Paulie pulled into the same station, and while the guy was filling up his tank Paulie did the same thing, and the guy never even looked over at him. While the guy was getting coffee and the kid was using the restroom, Paulie used the men's room, then got a cup of coffee, too.

By the time they got to Saratoga Springs, Paulie was beginning to think, *Fuck this*. He hadn't counted on the guy driving so damn far. He was probably going to have to find someplace to spend the night and he hadn't brought along a change of clothes or his toilet kit.

When they reached Lake George, Paulie finally figured out where they were going. He'd read that Connor Russell had a place in the Adirondacks—that's where he'd been before his plane crashed—and he figured that's probably where they were headed. But now following them was becoming a problem because there wasn't that much traffic.

When they reached Tupper Lake, all Paulie could do was hang back, sometimes intentionally losing sight of the Nissan, then speeding up to make sure it was still ahead of him. When the guy turned onto a narrow gravel road, Paulie's was the only car behind him and he had to drop back again. He was sure he was going to lose him—which meant he'd just wasted five fuckin' hours. He hit the gas to see if he could get a glimpse of the Nissan but didn't see it. Where had the damn guy gone? There was some lake off to his right and he'd passed a couple of cabins and wondered if that's where they'd gone: to one of the cabins on the lake.

He almost missed him. He just happened to look over at the right time and spotted the Nissan parked in front of a big log cabin. This had to be the place where the kid was going to spend the night, but what the hell was he going to do now?

He drove past the cabin and noticed that there weren't any nearby neighbors. He drove half a mile and still didn't see another house. He made a U-turn and drove past the cabin again, then drove half a mile farther. There wasn't a neighbor within a mile of the place. He pulled over and parked in a wide spot in the road a quarter mile from the cabin and walked into the woods. He wanted to find a spot where he could see the cabin. He wasn't dressed for hiking in the woods, wearing a light jacket, slacks, a polo shirt, and loafers, but nothing to be done about that. It was a damn good thing it wasn't colder or snowing.

Fortunately, he didn't need a machete to get through the woods and finally made it to the shore of the lake where he could see the cabin off to his right. He leaned against a tree, thinking it was not going to be good if he had to spend a couple of days standing in the woods. It occurred to him that a fire was a possibility. Come back at night while they were sleeping, bar the doors in some way so they couldn't escape, and just burn the whole fucking house down. The problem with that bright idea was the order to make the kid's death look like an accident and he didn't have the skills to make arson look like anything other than arson. He hoped something else would occur to him.

Ten minutes later, to his surprise, he saw the girl come out a door facing the lake, wearing a life jacket over a hooded sweatshirt. She unlocked a chain securing a canoe to the dock, got into it, and paddled toward the center of the lake.

One thing he knew about canoes: they were notoriously unstable.

Paulie decided to stick around for a day or two to see if an opportunity would present itself. He figured the guy and the girl would spend at least a couple of days at the cabin; you didn't drive three hundred miles to stay a single night. The most it would cost him would be a couple hundred bucks, and if he couldn't figure something out, then he'd follow the girl when she returned to Boston.

He drove back to Tupper Lake and found a sporting goods store, a place called Raquette River Outfitters. He asked the clerk if there was a public boat launch on Bear Lake. The guy said, "Yeah, a small one on the north side, but gas motors aren't allowed on the lake, just electric trolling motors." The clerk added, "Some rich guy named Russell owns most of Bear Lake and he was able to convince the other folks who live there to ban gas outboards."

After talking to the clerk, Paulie bought a fishing pole—just the pole, no reel, no line, no bait—a baseball hat with a long bill, and a hooded sweatshirt in case it got chilly. He also bought a cheap inflatable raft and some rope to secure the raft to the roof of his car.

He drove to a gas station, pumped up the raft, then had a bitch of a time getting it tied to the roof of his car. Next stop, a grocery where he bought a small cooler, a bag of ice, a six-pack of beer, three bottles of water, four sandwiches, and a couple of candy bars. Also a toothbrush and some toothpaste. His last stop was a place where he could buy a change of underwear and some inexpensive, canvas tennis shoes. He didn't want to fuck up his loafers; they weren't cheap.

All set for tomorrow, he found a motel, paid in cash for two nights, then had dinner, accompanied by a couple of stiff drinks. But only a couple. He didn't want to wake up with a hangover. Before going to bed, he called Mike on the burner phone. He told Mike he was going to be out of town for a few days "to take care of, you know." Lastly he called his mom. When he said goodnight, she said, "Don't hit me tonight, Jack." *Aw, geez.*

Paulie's dad, Jack McGuire, had been the biggest prick to ever walk the earth. Couldn't hold down a job, drank like a fish, and blamed everyone for his problems but himself. And when he got really drunk he'd beat the shit out of Paulie and his mom.

When Paulie had been little his mom had protected him as best she could. Her left shoulder hadn't felt right since she was thirty thanks to her husband almost tearing it out of the socket. There'd been half a dozen times when Paulie and his mom had sported matching black eyes—their left eyes, because his ham-handed dad had been right handed.

One night his old man came home drunk after being fired from his latest job and started drinking Jack Daniel's to comfort himself. Paulie, twelve at the time, made the mistake of coming into the kitchen and saying something that set him off. To this day, he couldn't remember what he'd said, but whatever it was his dad whipped off his belt and started whaling on him. When his mom grabbed his father's arm to stop him, he turned on her, smashed her as hard as he could in the nose, then started kicking her in the stomach with steel-toed work boots as she lay there on the floor.

Paulie, without even thinking about it, ran into his room, got his Little League bat, and swung it at the back of his old man's head. He swung hard enough to drive a ball over the Green Monster at Fenway. He killed the son of a bitch with a single swing.

He and his mom had sat there for a while, breathing hard, looking at the body, the head caved in, blood all over the floor, some on the refrigerator door and the stove. Paulie said, "Should we call the police?"

"No," his mom had said. "I'm not going to let them take you away from me."

At two in the morning, they drove down to where the Tobin Bridge passed over the Mystic River and dumped the asshole in the river. His mom didn't have a plan. Her broken nose hurt so badly she could hardly think. She figured the body would be found eventually, and when it was she'd tell the cops that her husband was a drunk and maybe he fell into the river. Or maybe he pissed somebody off and they killed him and threw him into the river. Her final option, if it came to that, was to tell the cops that she'd killed him because he'd been hitting her and Paulie, but no way was she going to say that Paulie was the one who'd killed him. She told Paulie she'd go to jail for life before she'd ever let him be arrested.

Incredibly, the body was never found. They hadn't weighed it down or done anything else to keep it submerged but, thanks to some fluke of nature, Jack McGuire was never seen again. When the neighbors asked Paulie and his mom where his dad was, they'd say they didn't know, that one night he left and just never came back. Good riddance, all the neighbors said. Jack McGuire turned out to be like Earl in that Dixie Chicks song: a missing person who nobody missed at all.

His father's body not floating to the surface of the Mystic was maybe the only break Paulie's mom ever caught in her entire miserable life and now she didn't even know who her son was.

28

There was something DeMarco needed to do but he didn't want to leave while Cassie was on the lake in the canoe. He grabbed a paperback he'd brought with him and took a seat on the back porch in one of the two rocking chairs facing the lake. He wished he had a beer to drink.

It was a miraculous November day. This time of the year, snow wasn't abnormal in the Adirondacks; it was typical. DeMarco had been concerned when Cassie said she wanted to go to the cabin that they might be snowed in until spring. But today, for reasons defying the history of New England weather, it was almost sixty.

He looked out at the lake. Cassie had paddled to the center then laid back in the canoe and just let the boat drift along, the sun shining down on her, as she thought about her parents.

An hour later, she returned to the cabin and said to DeMarco, "I'm going to go take a nap."

"Sounds good," he said. It seemed to him that she was sleeping a lot for a girl her age, but then figured that carrying around so much grief and guilt was making her unusually tired. "While you're doing that, I'm going to drive back to Tupper Lake and get a couple of things I forgot to pack. But I want you to promise me you'll stay here in the cabin until I get back."

"I'm not going to promise you that. I'm not a little kid you need to babysit."

Sheesh. "I realize that, but I'm responsible for you. And it's going to be dark pretty soon and I don't want you wandering around in the dark. They probably call this place Bear Lake for a reason."

"We've never seen a bear here."

That was a relief to hear. "I don't care," he said. "I don't want you leaving the cabin. If you won't promise me you'll stay inside with the door locked, you're going to have to go with me into town."

"Fine," she said, dragging out the word *fine*. "I promise I'll stay here until you get back."

⸻ ❖ ⸻

DeMarco hadn't forgotten to pack anything. He wanted to see the airport where Connor Russell had kept his plane.

He drove into Tupper Lake and stopped at a general store. Behind the counter was an old codger wearing blue suspenders to hold up sagging blue jeans. His right cheek bulged with what DeMarco assumed was tobacco. DeMarco bought a six-pack of beer then said, "I've been told there's an airport near here. Can you tell me where it is?"

The guy laughed. "There's no airport here. There's a landing strip outside of town. I wouldn't be surprised if the place was used by Canadian drug dealers."

Yeah, those Canadians are a wild bunch.

"Can you tell me where it is?" DeMarco asked.

The place was a couple of miles west of Tupper Lake and, as the guy at the store had said, it wasn't an airport. It was an asphalt landing strip in the middle of a weedy field, the runway maybe half a mile long. There were ground lights on both sides of the runway that could be turned on after dark but no control tower or terminal. There was also no fence around the place. There were three small single-engine planes parked near the runway, a gas pump, and a metal Quonset hut that probably functioned as a hangar. Near the Quonset hut was a small building that might be some sort of office. What he didn't see were any security cameras.

DeMarco drove over to the small building, stepped out of his car, and peered inside. The door was locked and there was no one home. There was a desk and a couple of old chairs, shelves filled with books and three-ring binders that might have been technical manuals or parts manuals, and a table on which there was some sort of radio setup. On the door was a phone number to call. He tapped the number into his phone and was about to hit dial when a man came out of the hangar.

The man was in his fifties or sixties and wore gray mechanic's coveralls and a grease-stained red baseball cap. He hadn't shaved in three or four days.

"Can I help you?" he said. DeMarco figured he must have heard his car pull up to the office.

"Yeah, maybe you can. Do you operate this place?"

"My family owns it. I'm Jim Hodges."

DeMarco didn't want to tell Hodges that he was looking into Connor Russell's death if he didn't have to. So he lied.

"My brother and I bought a cabin near here. My brother's got a plane and he asked me to come over and check out the landing strip."

"What kind of plane does he have?"

"An old Piper Cub, but that's all I know about it. My brother's the flier, not me. Anyway, he talked to some other pilot who's landed here before, so he knows the runway's long enough, but he was wondering about security if he has to leave the plane here for a few days."

Hodges said, "There isn't any security. I don't have guards patrolling the place at night. And if your brother decides to fly in here, I'm not responsible for anything that happens to his plane."

"You don't have any security cameras?"

"Nope. But I can tell you that I've never had a problem with theft or vandalism. A couple of years ago some of the local kids were drag racing on the runway, but the cops figured out who they were and put a stop to it. Since then, there hasn't been any kind of problem. I mean, I guess leaving your plane here is no different than leaving your car on the street in town."

"Well, that's good to hear. I put your number in my phone. Will it be okay if my brother gives you a call if he has any questions about fees, landing here at night, or whatever."

"Sure, tell him to call me."

DeMarco thanked Hodges and left, thinking you wouldn't have to be a navy SEAL to sneak onto the airstrip and sabotage a plane.

———◆———

DeMarco returned to the cabin and found Cassie on the back porch looking out at the lake. So much for her promise to stay inside.

For dinner, DeMarco heated up Mrs. Aguilera's casserole in the microwave. It was delicious. The woman could cook. While they ate, DeMarco made an attempt to have a conversation with Cassie.

He said, "I saw you had a baseball bat and a glove in your bedroom. You play baseball?"

"Softball."

"What position do you play?"

"Shortstop. This spring I'm going to be starting for the varsity team."

"You must be pretty good," DeMarco said. He could imagine her, the way she was built, being quick and having the range to play the position.

"I am," she said, for the first time showing a little spark.

"You ever go see the Red Sox play?"

"Of course. My dad has—had—season tickets. We used to go together all the time when I was little, but after I turned twelve I didn't go with him all that often. I like playing softball but watching baseball's actually kind of boring."

She looked away and DeMarco could see she was now regretting not having gone to more games with her dad. He wished he hadn't brought the subject up. DeMarco could remember going to a few Yankees games in the Bronx with his dad when he was a kid. Those were some of the best memories he had of his father, although his dad, not a big talker, had barely said a thing while they'd sat there in the bleacher seats. But just being together had been enough.

Cassie rose from her chair and said, "I'm going to go make a campfire. Dad and I always used to do that when we came up here."

"Great," DeMarco said. "I'll give you a hand splitting the wood."

"I don't need any help. There're two cords of wood on the side of the house and the kindling is in a box in the mudroom. Anyway, I want to do it myself."

Half an hour later, Cassie was sitting in a lawn chair in front of a crackling fire, a blanket wrapped around her shoulders. She looked so small and alone, staring into the flames. It broke DeMarco's heart.

29

DeMarco got up at eight the next morning, took a shower, found the coffee, and made a pot. He went out onto the back porch to drink the first cup, again sitting in one of the rocking chairs. It was a cool morning, the temperature in the upper thirties, but there wasn't a cloud in the sky. The same flock of ducks he'd seen yesterday was swimming along in a V formation near the dock. When he hit the lotto he'd buy the Russells' cabin if Cassie would be willing to part with it.

Cassie got up at ten. She came into the kitchen wearing red boxer shorts and a too big t-shirt, her short blond hair rumpled from sleep. DeMarco thought she looked about five years old.

"You want some breakfast?" DeMarco asked.

"Sure," she said.

So DeMarco made breakfast—meaning he used the microwave again to heat up an egg dish that Mrs. Aguilera had made.

"You got plans for the day?" DeMarco asked as she was eating.

"Yeah. There's a little cove down at that end of the lake." She pointed. "You can't see it from here, but there's a grassy spot over there. In the spring, wildflowers grow all around it and a stream runs through it, into the lake. We used to go there for picnics and my dad would try to catch fish with a fly rod, but he never caught any. All he ever did was get the line tangled in the bushes." She smiled slightly, which DeMarco was glad to see. "Anyway, I'm going over there in the canoe and have a picnic like we used to. I'd invite you but, and I'm sorry, I'd really just as soon be alone."

"Hey, that's fine," DeMarco said, wondering what the hell he was going to do all day.

As if reading his mind, Cassie said, "There are fishing poles in the mudroom, lures and hooks and stuff in the cabinet over the washing machine. You could take the rowboat and go fishing if you want. They stock the lake and there's some kind of trout, rainbow I think, or maybe browns."

"Yeah, maybe I'll do that," DeMarco said. No, he wouldn't. If he caught a fish, then he'd have to clean it and cook it, which seemed like way too much work. He wondered if there was a golf course nearby, someplace where he could rent clubs, then rejected that idea as he knew he couldn't leave the girl alone for the time it would take to play a round.

Cassie took a shower and came back dressed in jeans and the same hooded sweatshirt she'd worn yesterday. She said, "I'm going to walk up the hill and call my friend Sarah. I'll be right back."

"Walk up the hill?"

"Yeah. In case you haven't noticed, you don't get a cell phone signal here. You have to go across the road and walk up this little hill. There's a trail that leads to it. Sometimes you get a signal, sometimes you don't."

"Good to know," DeMarco said. He'd been thinking about calling Tommy to see what he'd learned about Erin Kelly. Also, he wanted to see what Shannon was up to. After Cassie went on her picnic, he'd trudge up this hill and make some calls.

Cassie left the cabin, with DeMarco watching her through a window. She crossed the road and disappeared into the woods. Again, DeMarco momentarily wondered if he should be concerned about her safety and again he decided she'd be okay. He poured another cup of coffee and went back to sit on the porch. He noticed a guy in a black, inflatable raft fishing on the other side of the lake. He wondered if he was catching anything.

Cassie came back into the cabin only fifteen minutes later. DeMarco asked, "Were you able to talk to your friend?"

"Yeah, for like a minute. The call kept dropping. That's the one thing I really hate about this place."

Again DeMarco felt like saying something parental, like it's good not to be plugged into a cell phone twenty-four seven, but he kept his mouth shut.

She went into the kitchen and put one of the sandwiches Mrs. Aguilera had made, potato chips, and two Cokes into a plastic bag. She grabbed a blanket, a paperback—DeMarco wondered what she was reading but didn't ask—her life jacket, and her picnic lunch and headed toward the door. "See you later," she said.

"Maybe you ought to take a heavier jacket in case it rains or gets chilly."

She said, "It's supposed to be about sixty today and there's not a cloud in the sky. Quit worrying about me."

He watched as she got into the canoe. She was an athletic kid and had no problem balancing herself as she got into it. She took off paddling, a blond Sacagawea with a flotilla of ducks leading her way.

30

Thank God, Paulie thought, although he wasn't sure that was not blasphemous. He started rowing the raft in the direction the girl was going. He was hoping she'd head for the point he could see; if she rounded the point she wouldn't be visible to the guy who'd come with her. He didn't know if there were people in the other cabins around the lake—there were only five other cabins—and so far he hadn't seen anyone. He imagined the cabins were vacation places and not occupied most of the time, especially in November. Whatever the case, as near as he could tell, the only ones on the lake were the girl and the guy she'd come with, and again he wondered who the guy was. If he was a bodyguard, he wasn't much of one.

She rounded the point as Paulie had been hoping and he watched as she beached the canoe at a grassy spot where a small stream ran into the lake. She took off her life jacket, tossed it into the canoe, then took a blanket and a plastic bag from the canoe. She spread the blanket on the grass, then just sat there with her legs crossed looking out at the lake.

Paulie stopped rowing and sat for a couple of minutes trying to decide if he should do it now or not. He didn't like to do things on the spur of the moment; he liked a solid plan, a plan where he could make sure there were no surprises. Like the way he'd dealt with Feldman, where he followed the guy for three days to make sure he knew exactly where Feldman was going to be that morning and how many people were likely to be around. What he was thinking of doing when it came to the kid was simple—simple is always best—but things could get dicey if anyone saw him. Again, his eyes scanned the shoreline. He didn't see a soul, not even another vehicle parked near the other cabins. "Let's get this over with," he said out loud.

He didn't feel good about what he was planning to do but it had to be done. For his mom, it had to be done.

Okay, this is the way it would work. He'd row up to her but he didn't want to scare her off or make her think he was coming ashore because of her. A girl her age, all alone, would be leery of an older man. He'd say, "Hey, sorry to disturb you but my raft's got a slow leak. I just need to pump it up a bit before I head back to the boat landing."

Then he'd beach the raft and, without thinking about it, run up to her and drag her into the water and drown her. After she was gone, he'd toss the blanket, her life jacket, and whatever else she had back into her canoe, then push the canoe out into the lake, tip it over, and put the body near it. It would look as if she'd decided to take off the life jacket for some reason, like maybe she got hot while she was paddling, and then had tipped the canoe over. He'd have to be careful not to bruise her as he was holding her under the water. He'd grab her by the hair and the sweatshirt she was wearing so he didn't leave marks. As small as she was—she couldn't weigh ninety pounds—that should be easy enough to do.

Yeah, he was going straight to hell when he died.

31

Jimmy Montgomery was sure he was going to get laid today, for the first time in his life. At seventeen he had to be the only virgin in his class. Well, no, that probably wasn't true. There were a few dweebs in his class who couldn't get laid in a whorehouse if they owned the place.

He'd been dating Kathy Lee for three months now and they'd gone from French kissing to heavy petting and the last couple of times they'd gone out he'd managed to get her bra unhooked. He thought he'd died and gone to heaven the first time he touched her breasts. He also knew she wasn't a virgin, which was maybe one of the reasons he'd started dating her. Before she began dating him, she was going out with that asshole Jenkins, and Jenkins, being Jenkins, had to let everyone know they'd slept together. But it wasn't as if he didn't like her and was dating her just to get laid. She was actually a lot of fun to be with. He just didn't want to marry her.

The problem was finding a place to do it. They couldn't do it in the backseat of his car because his car didn't have a backseat. He drove an old Ford 150 pickup that had a hundred eighty thousand miles on it. Then he noticed the weather was amazingly good for November, checked the forecast and saw no rain or extreme cold predicted, and came up with the idea of a picnic, one where he was hoping Kathy would be dessert.

He could tell when he'd asked her if she wanted to go to Bear Lake for a picnic that she knew what was going to happen. There was something about the way she had looked at him that made him certain. Bear Lake in November was about as isolated a place as you could find.

So today was the day—and he was ready, he was *prepared*. He'd watched a lot of porn to make sure he knew what to do. He stole six condoms from the box under his big brother's bed, hoping six would be enough. He also stole a six-pack of Bud from the fridge. He was going to catch holy hell for that—but hey, it was a price he was willing to pay. He had not one but three blankets: two to put on the ground and one to put over them if it got chilly when they were naked. *Naked*. He loved that word. As for the picnic lunch, Kathy said she'd take care of that. When she'd asked him what kind of sandwiches she should make, he told her he didn't care because he really didn't. Food was the last thing on his mind.

He parked the pickup and Kathy followed him down the trail to the grassy point on Bear Lake. He carried the beer and all the blankets. The condoms were in the back pocket of his jeans. She carried the bag with the food and he thought she looked really good today in this tight white sweater she had on. The girl could *really* fill out a sweater. He prayed there wouldn't be some dumbass fisherman out near the point. Not today of all days.

He picked up his pace. God, he could hardly wait to get to the lake.

He walked off the trail and onto the grassy area where he planned to put the blankets—and there was this guy, a dark-haired older guy who hadn't shaved in a couple of days. He was pushing a kid *under* the water. The kid's arms and legs were thrashing. He was trying to drown the kid. What the fuck was going on?

"Hey!" Jimmy yelled. "What the hell are you doing?"

Jimmy dropped everything he was carrying and charged. The guy was only about five feet from the shore, in water up to his knees. Jimmy wasn't afraid of him, whoever the hell he was. Jimmy Montgomery played right guard on the high school football team, weighed two hundred and thirty pounds, and lifted weights almost every day. This guy, this asshole, had to be sixty and wasn't anywhere near as big as him.

Jimmy reached the edge of the water—and stopped.

Oh, shit!

———————◆◆◆———————

Paulie didn't even think about it. He didn't have *time* to think about it.

He pulled the Glock out of the back of his pants and shot the big kid rushing at him. Who was he? Where the fuck had he come from?

He'd had to let Cassie go to deal with the kid, and as soon as he did she sprinted farther out into the lake and started swimming. But she'd put only a few yards between them. He turned and aimed the gun at her head then hesitated, thinking again how he'd been told to kill her in a way that looked like an accident. Then he thought, *Too late for that now,* with a dead boy lying on the shore. He started to squeeze the trigger before Cassie could get any farther—but then he heard a scream, a scream that would peel the paint off a wall. He spun his head to look back at the shore to see who was screaming and there was a girl in a white sweater standing there.

His first thought was: witness. He aimed at her, pulled the trigger, but she was fifty yards away and he missed. She screamed again then turned and ran into the woods, still screaming. He figured he'd have a bitch of a time finding her in the woods and, as soon as the girl could, sure as shit, she'd call the cops. He turned back again to look at Cassie. The little squirt was swimming like she was in the Olympics. Every couple of strokes, she'd turn her head to take a breath and look back at him. He aimed at her head again, but she dove under the water just as he fired.

Okay, it was time to get the hell out of here. He didn't know how long it would take the cops to respond in a rural area like this—probably not that fast—but he had a major problem. His car was half a mile away, at the boat landing. He could row the raft back to the boat landing, catch up with Cassie as he did, and finish her off but it would probably take him twenty minutes to reach the landing in the raft. He'd be better off running. He could make it back to his car in ten minutes if he ran.

He ran in the direction the girl in the white sweater had gone, barely looking at the big kid lying on the shore, on his back, the front of his sweatshirt soaked red. He didn't see any sign of the girl; she was probably crouched down in the bushes, whispering on her phone. When he reached the trailhead he saw a beat-to-shit old pickup that most likely belonged to the boy he'd shot. He checked to see if by some miracle the kid had left his keys in the ignition; he hadn't.

He took off running on the road that ran around the lake. He ran as fast as he could and was sweating like a mule and panting by the time he reached his car. He would have had a heart attack if he hadn't kept himself in shape. He jumped in his car and took off. He had to get the hell away from this area before the cops arrived.

Jesus, he'd fucked up big time. He needed to call Mike and tell him what had happened. Mike was going to be royally pissed.

32

DeMarco, tired of sitting around on the back porch reading, decided to walk up the hill and call Tommy. Cassie had been gone a couple of hours but he wasn't concerned. It was a nice day and he could imagine her lying on her blanket, thinking about her folks, maybe crying a bit now and then. He hoped she was also doing like he'd told her and thinking about the good times they'd all had.

He left the cabin, crossed the road in front of it, and saw the trail, the one that should lead to the hill. The hill turned out to be just that—a hill, not a mountain, only about a hundred feet higher in elevation than the cabin. He looked at his phone and saw one signal bar—then the bar disappeared, then came back again, like the lights flickering off and on in a thunderstorm. He called Shannon to see how she was doing but got her voice mail. He called Tommy Hewlett next.

DeMarco said, "It's DeMarco. I just called to ask if—"

"What?"

"I said, I just called to ask if—"

"What?"

DeMarco could hear him but he couldn't hear DeMarco. After screaming futilely in the phone for a minute or two, he gave up and headed back down the trail to the cabin. He'd just reached the front door when a Tupper Lake police cruiser pulled into the driveway and parked near DeMarco's rental car. The driver's-side door opened and a uniformed cop stepped out but, before DeMarco could ask what he wanted, the passenger door opened and Cassie ran to him, wrapped her arms around his waist, and started sobbing. Her hair was matted down and her clothes were damp. Then he noticed there was blood on her sweatshirt, a lot of blood.

"What the hell's going on?" DeMarco asked the deputy. Had the son of a bitch arrested Cassie for some reason? And whose blood was it?

The deputy, a heavyset man in his fifties with a sizable beer gut, said, "This girl says you're her guardian. Is that true?"

Technically, it wasn't true, but DeMarco said, "Yeah. What's going on? Why's she crying? And why's she wet?"

"Somebody tried to kill her," the cop said.

DeMarco told Cassie to go take a shower and change clothes, and while she was doing that he asked the cop what had happened.

The cop, whose name was Blake, said, "According to Cassie, she was sitting on a blanket near the stream that goes into Bear Lake when a fisherman in a raft rows up. He said he needed to pump up his raft but when he gets ashore he grabs Cassie and tries to drown her."

"Son of a bitch," DeMarco muttered.

"Fortunately for Cassie, Jimmy Montgomery and Kathy Lee showed up."

"Who are Jimmy and Kathy?" DeMarco asked.

"A couple of high school kids from Tupper Lake. They were planning to have a picnic in the same place where Cassie was. And Jimmy—he's a big kid—saw the guy holding Cassie's head underwater and he charged the guy. And the guy shot him."

"Aw, shit. Is he going to be all right?"

"He lost a lot of blood before the ambulance arrived to take him to the hospital. They don't know if he's going to make it or not. Anyway, according to Kathy, after the guy shot Jimmy, Cassie started swimming to get away and Kathy screamed, and this bastard, whoever he is, took a shot at her. Luckily, he missed. Kathy ran into the woods and hid and called 911 but she doesn't know what happened after she ran away. Cassie said the guy took a shot at her, then he split, ran into the woods, and she thought he might have been going after Kathy.

"By the time I got there, the guy was gone and Kathy and Cassie were trying to stop Jimmy from bleeding to death by pressing a blanket on his wound. After the ambulance took Jimmy away—he's a good kid, I hope he makes it—I took Kathy and Cassie to the station in Tupper Lake to get statements from them. After that I called the state police and the Franklin County sheriff. Bear Lake isn't in our jurisdiction. I just answered the 911 call because I was the closest cop to the area, but either the state police or the sheriff will be taking over the case and they'll send someone out to interview Cassie again, probably later today."

As the cop was talking, DeMarco was fuming. And not only because someone had tried to kill Cassie but because he'd failed to protect her.

Blake continued. "Right now, a Tupper Lake cop is waiting at the scene for the state forensic techs to show up. The guy left the raft he was using on the shore and maybe they'll be able to get prints off it or the oars or the fishing pole he was using. By the way, the fishing pole didn't have any line in it so he obviously wasn't trying to catch fish. So you got any idea who would want to drown Cassie, Mr. DeMarco? We didn't get much of a description from either girl. It all happened too fast. All they noticed was that he was an older guy and had dark hair."

DeMarco asked, "How long ago did this happen?"

"About two hours ago."

Which meant, if DeMarco was right about who the killer was, he would be back in Boston in three hours. He needed to move quickly.

He told the cop, "Officer, I think I know who this guy might be. Or I should say, I think I know who he works for."

"You do?"

"Yeah, but I need to make a phone call right away and I can't get a signal here."

"Why do you need to make a call?"

"Officer, you gotta trust me on this and there isn't much time."

The deputy hesitated, then said, "Head down the road that goes around the lake, toward the point where Cassie was. You'll get a signal there."

"Okay. But I need you to stay here with her until I get back."

DeMarco sped down the road, constantly checking his cell phone until he had two bars. He stopped the car and called Lannigan, the detective assigned to Jerry Feldman's murder.

He said, "This is Joe DeMarco. I need you to—"

"If you're calling to ask about Feldman, I don't have anything new to—"

"Shut up and listen to me. Someone just tried to kill Cassie Russell, Connor Russell's daughter."

"Sorry to hear that but why are you calling me?" Lannigan said.

"I'm calling you because you're the only Boston cop whose phone number I have. Now I can call John Mahoney and he can call the superintendent to get what I need, but there's no time for that. And if the guy who tried to kill Cassie gets away, I'm going to blame you and encourage Mahoney to get you fired."

"What the hell do you want?"

"I want you to get as many photos as you can get of guys currently working for Mike Kelly. Then I want you to—"

"Mike Kelly?"

"The mobster, Lannigan. Your organized crime people will have mug shots and surveillance photos of Kelly's men in their files. So I want you to get photos of people currently working for him, meaning guys not dead or in prison. Then I want you to email the photos to the cops in Tupper Lake, New York. You need to move fast, because I think the guy who tried to kill Cassie is headed to Boston right now and he'll be there in less than three hours. If Cassie can ID the guy, you might be able to arrest him before he gets there and disappears into the city. Do you understand?"

Lannigan didn't understand. So DeMarco had to repeat everything two more times before Lannigan got it.

DeMarco drove back to the cabin. Cassie was out of the shower, dressed in clean, dry clothes, sitting on the couch. She had a blanket wrapped around her shoulders even though it wasn't cold in the cabin. She looked almost catatonic, staring straight ahead without blinking. Blake, the Tupper Lake cop, was sitting at the kitchen table, looking uncomfortable, not knowing what to say to her.

DeMarco asked Blake to step outside. He didn't want to talk in front of Cassie. On the porch he said, "I'm having a bunch of photos emailed to your office. I'm going to bring Cassie in to look at the photos and see if she can ID the guy who tried to kill her. You need to get that other girl, what's her name, Kathy, to the station so she can look at the photos too."

"I told you this isn't our case. The state police or the sheriff will be handling it."

"I don't give a shit who's handling it. There's no time for some kind of jurisdiction squabble. The photos are being sent to your office."

After Blake was gone, DeMarco said to Cassie, "Honey, I need you to pack and you need to do it quickly. We're heading back to Boston and when we get there I'm going to hire some security guys to watch over you."

"Why did that man try to drown me?"

DeMarco hesitated, not sure he should tell her what he knew. He didn't want to scare her more than she already was. He said, "I don't know. After you're packed, we're going to the police station in Tupper Lake and you're going to look at some photos and see if you can ID the guy."

"You didn't answer me. Why would someone try to kill me?"

"I told you, I don't know for sure."

"I think you're lying to me."

"Cassie, we need to get moving. Go pack."

As they were driving toward Tupper Lake he looked over at her. She was staring straight ahead, biting her lower lip. Her right knee was bouncing, probably uncontrollably. He couldn't even imagine how she must be feeling: the plane crash, losing her parents, surviving on her own in the mountains for two days before she was rescued, and then some asshole tries to kill her. He hoped she was strong enough mentally to handle everything that had been thrown at her. He could see her having a breakdown, afraid to leave her house or be left on her own. But he didn't think that would happen. Even though he didn't know her all that well, he could tell that she was a resilient kid. She'd be okay, or at least he hoped so.

DeMarco was also pissed at himself. He'd been a fool for not protecting her better. But he'd honestly never thought that Erin would try to kill the girl a second time. When Erin sabotaged Connor Russell's plane—and DeMarco knew she had even though he couldn't prove it—Cassie would have been collateral damage and not the primary target. It was Connor Russell that Erin wanted dead so the audit would be stopped. Then she'd decided, maybe at the same time she decided to kill Connor, that the accountant, Feldman, also had to go because of what he knew and might eventually reveal. But DeMarco just hadn't thought that Erin would take a second shot at Cassie. She must have been concerned that John Mahoney, acting as Cassie's guardian, would ask for another audit, but if Cassie were dead Mahoney would be out of the picture and most likely the other two guys on the board wouldn't question her management of the trust. And who did Erin Kelly turn to to help her kill people? Her uncle Mike; DeMarco was sure of that. He had thought that as long as no one knew Cassie was at the cabin she'd be safe, but he'd underestimated Mike's capabilities—and he felt like a fool for having done so.

If the cops could catch the guy who'd tried to kill Cassie, he'd give up whoever had hired him to avoid going to prison for the rest of his life— meaning he'd give up Mike. Then Mike, to reduce *his* time in prison, would likely admit that he'd conspired with Erin to kill the girl—and it was Erin that DeMarco really wanted to see in a cage.

But first they had to catch the prick who'd tried to drown a fifteen-year-old girl.

———◆◆◆———

DeMarco parked in front of the Tupper Lake police station. He and Cassie went inside, where they found Blake and a deputy from the Franklin County Sheriff's Office.

Blake said, "The state police are on their way. We're still not exactly sure who will end up with jurisdiction for this, the sheriff or the state police."

"And I told you, I don't care who has jurisdiction," DeMarco said. "You can sort that out later. Right now what you need to do is—"

"Who the hell does this guy think he is?" the Franklin County deputy said to Blake.

"My name's DeMarco," DeMarco said to the deputy. "I represent John Mahoney, the guy who's about to become Speaker of the House. He's also Cassie Russell's guardian."

"So what? Mahoney is Massachusetts. This is New York," the deputy said.

"The governor of New York is a Democrat and he cares about what John Mahoney thinks. Which means you're going to be looking for a new job if you fuck this up." Turning to Blake, DeMarco said, "Did Boston email you the photos I asked for?"

"Yeah, they're on the computer in the office over there."

"And is Kathy here?"

"She's in one of the interview rooms with her mother."

"Then let's go take a look at the photos," DeMarco said. "We'll have Cassie look first then the other girl so they don't influence each other."

Blake, the Franklin County deputy, Cassie, and DeMarco went into a small office. Blake got the photos emailed from Boston up on the screen of a computer and placed Cassie in a chair—then all the men stood in a semicircle behind her, looming over her, as she looked at the screen.

"Just scroll down and see if you recognize the guy," DeMarco said.

There were about forty photos. Some of the men looked like criminals—hard faces, scars, beady eyes, bent noses—but most of them just looked like ordinary middle-aged guys. Cassie scrolled down, looking at about a dozen photos before she pointed at the screen and said, "That's him. He's the one. He's a little younger in this picture but it's him."

"You're sure?" Blake asked.

"Yeah, I'm sure. He tried to kill me."

DeMarco looked at the name beneath the photo. Paul S. McGuire.

Five minutes later, Kathy Lee also identified McGuire, although she was less certain than Cassie, which was understandable as she'd been fifty yards away and McGuire's face hadn't been six inches from hers, shoving her head underwater.

DeMarco called Detective Lannigan in Boston. "The guy's name is Paul S. McGuire," DeMarco said.

"Paulie McGuire. Now there's one nasty piece of work."

"You know him?"

"Everyone in the department knows him. He started working for Mike Kelly when he was maybe seventeen and eventually ends up as Mike's second in command. He's spent some time inside for extortion, assault, nothing big, but he's the main suspect in at least half a dozen homicides. If he's the one who tried to kill Cassie Russell—"

"He is."

"Then she's lucky to be alive. The reason Mike uses Paulie is he doesn't screw up. At least not usually."

DeMarco said, "I think McGuire is headed back to Boston right now. He's probably on I-90 and he's going to be in the city in about an hour. You need to—"

"I'm working for you now?"

"Shut up. You need to get his license plate number out to the highway patrol and every cop in Boston. Like I said, he's probably on I-90, about an hour from Boston. Pull him over and arrest him and Cassie will ID him as the guy who tried to kill her."

33

At first, Paulie thought he might be able to get away with it. It had all happened so fast, the two girls had been scared, and they couldn't have gotten a very good look at him. As for the boy, he had to be dead; he'd hit him right in the chest. Once he got to Boston, Mike would set up an alibi for him if the cops came sniffin' around.

But that's when he remembered the raft. He'd been in such a hurry to get out of there he hadn't thought about it at the time. The truth was, he'd panicked. He'd worn gloves but he couldn't be sure he hadn't left prints someplace on the raft or the oars or the fishing pole. He'd been planning to wipe everything down thoroughly after he'd finished the job. Then there were the beer bottles in the bottom of the raft. He'd worn gloves when he drank from the bottles, but he supposed there might be DNA on the bottles. His plan had been to chuck the bottles into the lake but . . .

He could be fucked.

When he got to Boston he'd head straight for the docks. Mike had a couple warehouses down there and he could hide in one of them until Mike could get him out on one of the ships they used for smuggling shit into the country. After that, and after Mike got some idea of any evidence the cops might have, they'd figure out a plan. The plan could be to return to Boston if it looked like he was in the clear. If not, he'd get a fake passport and head for some country where they'd have a hard time extraditing him.

But what was going to happen to his mom? He sure as shit wasn't going to get paid for a job he'd bungled, and he doubted Mike would be able to force his niece to pay for his mom's nursing care since he'd failed to kill the kid. And if he had to leave the country, Mike probably wouldn't continue to give him a slice of the action. Mike didn't pay people who didn't earn for him. And if he was arrested or had to go on the run, there was no doubt they'd kick his mom out of the nice assisted living place and dump her into some human warehouse.

How in the hell could his luck have been so bad, those two kids showing up just as he was trying to drown the girl?

As for his mom, her luck had always been bad.

He'd just had this thought when he looked into the rearview mirror and saw the blue and red lights of a highway patrol cruiser behind him. The cruiser was coming up on him fast. Why the hell were they pulling him over? He hadn't been speeding. The good news was that he'd tossed the gun into the woods not long after leaving Tupper Lake.

That turned out to be the only good news.

34

"Why did that guy try to kill me?"

Cassie hadn't said anything for almost an hour after they left the Tupper Lake police station, apparently just thinking everything over. She had the blanket from the cabin still wrapped around her shoulders and partly covering her head, as if trying to hide inside it. At least she wasn't shaking as she'd been earlier. But now she wanted some answers and DeMarco wasn't sure what he should tell her.

When she saw him hesitating, she said, "You obviously know something. You're the one who arranged for those photos to be sent to the police station. So tell me what's going on."

"It has to do with your trust fund. I think somebody has been stealing from it and they're trying to cover it up."

"How would killing me cover anything up? I don't have anything to do with the money in the trust."

"Look, it's complicated and—"

"Don't tell me it's complicated. I'm not stupid and I want to know what's going on."

"I know you're not stupid but I can't tell you anything yet because I'm not sure of anything yet. We need to wait and see what the cops find out."

"I think you're BSing me."

He was. "The important thing is you're alive and the cops are going to get the guy who tried to kill you and make him talk. And I'm going to make sure nothing happens to you until I've got this whole thing sorted out."

"Yeah, we'll see about that."

Talk about a vote of confidence. But he was glad to see she was angry. Anger was better than her being paralyzed with fear.

They drove on in silence for a while.

Cassie, looking out the window and not at DeMarco, said, "My dad had my whole life figured out. He used to tell me that he and his dad had made a lot of money so I wouldn't ever have to worry about making money. He said that my life should be devoted to making things better for other people. He said we were kind of like the Kennedys, you know, where old Joe Kennedy made all the money and his kids went into politics to try to make the world a better place."

"Your dad wanted you to go into politics?"

"Not necessarily, but he wanted me to do something more than just be a rich kid who'd inherited a pile of money. He said he'd talked to Melinda Gates one time, and when I got out of high school that maybe I'd spend a summer working for the Gates Foundation to see how they operated and how they decided to do the things they did. He said he might get me a job in Washington, maybe with Mahoney if Mahoney was still in Congress so I could understand how politics worked."

Now there was the nightmare scenario: Cassie learning the political system at the knee of John Mahoney. That would be like sending a kid to become an apprentice to Al Capone to learn how the liquor distribution system worked.

Cassie said, "Anyway, my dad had everything worked out. I'd go to Harvard, get an MBA so I'd learn how to manage my money. I'd work for him for a while to see how his companies operated. I'd go to work for the Gates Foundation or maybe Warren Buffett so I'd be ready to take over for him when he retired. But when he'd tell me these things,

I didn't really pay much attention. He was only forty-two years old and I always figured he'd be around for another thirty or forty years and I'd have plenty of time to decide what I wanted to do when I grew up. But now he's gone. What am I going to do?"

Jesus. "I'll tell you what you're going to do," DeMarco said. "You're going to be a kid. You're going to finish high school. You're going to be the shortstop on the varsity team. You're going to go to dances and have boyfriends and learn to drive and do what every other girl your age does. And when it comes time for you to decide what you want to do after college there will be a lot of good people to help you figure it out, people like Mary Pat Mahoney. So stop worrying about what you're going to do when you grow up. Just grow up."

"Easy for you to say."

Yeah, it was. He really needed Mary Pat. She'd know how to talk to Cassie. He certainly didn't.

***

Mrs. Aguilera was waiting on the porch when DeMarco and Cassie arrived. DeMarco had called her as they'd been driving back from New York, giving her an abbreviated version of what had happened.

Cassie got out of the car, dropping the blanket on the ground, and ran to her, and Mrs. Aguilera enveloped her in a hug. When DeMarco approached, she yelled, "You were supposed to protect her!"

Before DeMarco could respond, she said to Cassie, "Your godmother is here."

A wave of relief, one of tidal wave proportions, washed over DeMarco. He was saved.

Mary Pat was in the kitchen, preparing tea for Cassie. When she saw Cassie, she wrapped her arms around the girl and said, "Thank God, you're all right."

Mary Pat Mahoney, like her husband, had snow white hair and bright blue eyes—and that's where the similarities ended. She was trim; she glowed with good health. She rarely drank, she exercised daily, and she watched what she ate; Mahoney did none of those things. She was also Mahoney's polar opposite when it came to her personality: she was generous, caring, and compassionate, and DeMarco sincerely believed she wasn't capable of lying. If there had been an Olympic event for lying, Mahoney would have gotten a gold medal every four years.

But like Mrs. Aguilera, Mary Pat glared at DeMarco, shaming him with her eyes for almost allowing Cassie to be killed. DeMarco decided not to even try to explain why he'd thought Cassie would be safe at the cabin; he simply hung his head in shame.

Mary Pat said to Cassie, "Come on, honey, sit down, we'll have some tea and talk."

"I'm hungry. Can we order a pizza?"

Mary Pat spun toward DeMarco and said, "You didn't feed her? What's wrong with you?"

DeMarco was about to say that he had asked Cassie if she wanted to stop for food and she'd declined, but before DeMarco could offer up a feeble defense, Mary Pat said to Cassie, "You bet, sweetie, any kind of pizza you want. Now sit."

She turned back to DeMarco and said, "What are you still doing here? Don't you have something to do, like catching the guy who tried to kill her?"

As DeMarco, the leper of Beacon Hill, was slinking back to his car his phone rang. It was Lannigan.

"We got him," Lannigan said. "He was pulled over by the highway patrol a couple of hours ago. Right now, he's at the Suffolk County jail but we're going to ship his ass back to New York tomorrow. He's New York's problem, not ours."

"You're not shipping him anywhere," DeMarco said. "I want him prosecuted by the feds here in Boston."

As the attempted murder of Cassie Russell, Kathy Lee, and Jimmy Montgomery had occurred in Franklin County, New York, the Franklin County DA would most likely be responsible for prosecuting McGuire—and DeMarco didn't want this to happen. He wanted the feds involved.

"Why?" Lannigan asked.

"Because the feds can offer McGuire a deal if he rolls over on Mike or Erin Kelly. The feds can get Mike on a RICO thing if Paulie is willing to rat Mike out for all the crimes he's committed for him. And Erin Kelly, if I'm right about her, has been embezzling from the Russell trust and has committed federal crimes like tax evasion and wire fraud and God knows what else. Anyway, you want to get the feds involved in this, Lannigan. Not to mention, John Mahoney won't want his god-daughter having to go back and forth from Boston to New York for a trial. So go talk to the lawyers. The DA here in Boston, the DA in Franklin County, and the assistant federal attorney in Boston who handles mob-related shit."

Lannigan said, "Hey, it's not my job to talk to the lawyers and figure out who's going to prosecute the fuckin' guy. I'm just the detective handling Jerry Feldman's murder. "

"Which Erin Kelly paid for."

"You don't know that for sure," Lannigan said.

"But McGuire probably does, and he can solve your case for you too."

"Yeah, well, maybe, but I can't tell all the lawyers what to do."

"Well, I know a guy who can," DeMarco said.

DeMarco glanced at his watch. It was after eight and by now Mahoney would almost certainly be three sheets to the wind. And even if Mahoney was able to speak without slurring his words, it was probably too late for him to do anything; the people he needed to talk to would have already left their offices for the day. DeMarco would call Mahoney first thing in the morning.

He returned to his hotel, looking forward to seeing Shannon. She should be on duty tonight. Maybe the day would end much better than it had begun.

He walked into the bar but there was a guy behind the bar. He asked the bartender, "Isn't Shannon working tonight?"

"Nah, she took a couple of days off. Has the flu or something."

He called Shannon immediately. He said, "Hey, how are you feeling? The guy subbing for you said you were sick."

"I'm not sick. My agent said my novel really has potential but he wants me to make a few changes before he tries to sell it. I've been working on it nonstop for the last two days."

"Well, you want to take a break and maybe get a drink or—"

"I can't, Joe. I have to finish this. I'm sorry."

Well, poop. DeMarco had dinner alone and went to bed feeling sorry for himself.

35

DeMarco called Mahoney's office at seven the next morning, although he knew Mahoney most likely wouldn't be there. Mahoney didn't believe all that nonsense about early birds and worms. DeMarco told Mavis, who was usually in by six, "Get him to call me right away. Someone tried to kill Cassie Russell."

"Oh, my God!" Mavis said.

Half an hour later Mahoney called. He sounded hungover.

DeMarco told Mahoney what had happened to Cassie—at which point Mahoney started cursing—then told him how the guy who tried to kill her worked for Mike Kelly. He also explained why Mahoney needed to call the DOJ and get someone in Justice to take over the McGuire case.

"Yeah, all right," Mahoney said. "But, goddamn it, what do I have you for if I have to do all the work?"

All the work?

While waiting for Mahoney to do something useful, DeMarco called Tommy Hewlett to see what he'd learned about where Erin Kelly had been on the weekend the Russells were killed.

Tommy said, "I can't prove she went anywhere near Tupper Lake, New York. But I know she was up to something that weekend."

"What do you mean?"

"I mean, that weekend her cell phone never left her house. So that could mean that *she* never left her house or it could mean she left her house but didn't take her phone with her. Next, her car, which has an E-ZPass sticker on it, never passed through any toll booths. That could mean she didn't drive on any toll roads that weekend or it could mean she didn't drive her own car if she drove to New York. But here's the big thing. That weekend, she didn't have a single credit card charge. I went back a year looking at her credit card charges and there wasn't one day in which she didn't charge something. Not one. Almost every morning she gets coffee from the Starbucks near her house but, according to her credit card records, she skipped her morning coffee two days in a row. She eats out almost every day, but that weekend she didn't charge anything to a restaurant or a grocery. So either this woman spent an entire weekend inside her house living off leftovers or she kept her phone in her house and used another car to drive to New York and paid for everything in cash."

"If she rented a car, she'd have to use a credit card," DeMarco said.

"But she didn't charge a rental to her credit card," Tommy said. "So maybe she borrowed a friend's car or she has a credit card in a different name and she used it to rent a car. I don't know."

Tommy continued. "The geeks at Thurston Security did all the research on Erin's cell phone and credit cards. While they were doing that, I drove to Tupper Lake, went to all the motels and B and Bs in the area, but no one admitted to seeing her. Nor did they have any female guests who checked in using cash instead of a credit card. That doesn't mean a whole lot, though. She could have driven up there on

Saturday morning, sabotaged the plane that night, then driven back the same night."

"Well, shit," DeMarco said.

"I did see one weird credit card charge," Tommy said. "Two days before the Russells were killed she bought something from an Ace Hardware out near Waltham. Paid a hundred and thirty-eight dollars."

"Why's that weird?"

"Because Waltham is a long way from her place and there are half a dozen other hardware stores closer to her house. The other thing is that in the last year she's never used a credit card to buy *anything* from a hardware store. If she wants something fixed, she hires a plumber or a carpenter or whatever. This isn't a woman who's into home repairs or hobbies where she needs tools. I think it's possible that maybe she bought a battery-powered drill and some duct tape and whatever else she used to screw up the plane, but the guys at Ace didn't remember her. I showed them her picture."

"What about her finances?"

"She makes two hundred grand a year but back in 2008, 2009, during the recession, she took a major hit. At that time, she was making money off stock dividends and collecting rent on a town house she owned. Then the recession happens, she sells the town house at a loss, maxes out her credit cards, but she gradually gets things under control. Right now, it appears as if she spends every cent she makes but she's not carrying any debt other than the mortgage on her condo. But the thing is, if she's embezzling from the trust like you think, she could be paying for things out of the trust and that wouldn't show up in her personal accounts. Anyway, the bottom line is, her personal finances don't show she needs money but it's impossible to tell if that's because she's a thief or if she's just managing her money well."

When DeMarco didn't respond, Tommy said, "What do you want me to do next?"

DeMarco said, "I don't know. But there's something you need to know. This weekend Cassie Russell was almost killed by a guy I think Erin Kelly hired."

DeMarco filled Tommy in on the details of Cassie's weekend. When he finished, Tommy said, "Jesus, this woman's a fuckin' monster."

DeMarco met the assistant U.S. federal attorney assigned to take over Paul McGuire's prosecution at her office in the John Joseph Moakley U.S. Courthouse, which is on the waterfront in South Boston.

The attorney was a boney woman named Rita Harper. She was in her early forties and had the stringy, zero-body-fat build of someone who ran in marathons. She had dark hair, a narrow face, a sharp nose, and a sharp chin. There was something kind of witchy about her and DeMarco wondered if her ancestors had hailed from Salem.

Harper opened with: "I want you to know that I object to this entire situation."

"What situation?" DeMarco the Innocent said.

"I resent John Mahoney insisting that the U.S. attorney for Massachusetts take over an attempted murder case that occurred in New York just because Mahoney's goddaughter was one of the victims. And I resent being forced to meet with you."

"Let me explain something to you, Miss Harper. You should be thanking me instead of resenting me. This could be the biggest case of your career. It could *make* your career."

"What are you talking about?"

DeMarco explained that he believed Erin Kelly, the niece of the mobster Mike Kelly, had been embezzling from the Russell trust, and when an accountant named Jerry Feldman discovered this Erin sabotaged Connor Russell's plane, hoping to kill the entire Russell family.

She also went to her uncle Mike and asked for his help in killing Feldman and, later, Cassie Russell.

"Can you prove anything you've just said?" Harper asked.

Ignoring the question, DeMarco said, "If you can get Paul McGuire to flip on Mike Kelly you can make a RICO case against Kelly and convict him for all the shit he's pulled in the last thirty or forty years. The BPD suspects that McGuire has killed half a dozen people for Mike. You can probably also get Mike as a co-conspirator in the attempted murder of Cassie Russell, since McGuire wouldn't have tried to kill her unless Mike Kelly told him to. And then, once you have Mike Kelly, you can get Erin Kelly because, sure as shit, she's the one who paid him to unleash McGuire on Cassie Russell. Like I said, this case could make your career."

"Let me ask again. Can you prove any of these allegations you're making against Mike and Erin Kelly?"

"No. That's why you need McGuire to roll over on Mike and Mike to roll over on Erin. You need to get over to the jail and offer McGuire a deal to testify."

Telling Harper what she should do earned DeMarco a scowl. So he said, "Or at least that's what I'd do if I were you."

Rita Harper had to admit that DeMarco might be right: this case could be a career maker. The daughter of a big money Boston celebrity like Connor Russell. The future Speaker of the House, God help America. The biggest mobster in Boston since Whitey Bulger. These were front page characters who would dominate the media and she could see herself appearing on CNN in the not too distant future.

Paul McGuire was led into an interview room in the Suffolk County jail, his hands and ankles manacled. The guard who'd escorted him to the room asked if Harper wanted him to stay in case McGuire got violent. Harper said no. She didn't want a guard to hear the offer she was going to make to McGuire. It wasn't unheard of for the guards at the Suffolk jail to be on the payroll of men like Mike Kelly.

After the guard left, Harper said, "Do you want your attorney present for this interview, Mr. McGuire? You have a right to have him here."

McGuire didn't respond.

"Okay, that's your choice. But right now I'm a hundred percent certain that I'm going to convict you for the attempted murder of Cassie Russell, Kathy Lee, and Jimmy Montgomery. And if Montgomery dies you'll be convicted of murder. You're going to prison for the rest of your life. The only chance you have to get a reduced sentence is to testify against the person or persons who asked you to commit these crimes. If you can give us enough to send Mike Kelly to prison for the rest of *his* life, you may not do much time at all."

McGuire didn't say a word. In the fifteen minutes Harper spent with him, he didn't answer her questions, respond to her statements, or acknowledge her presence in any way. He didn't even nod or shake his head. He just stared at her, his eyes flat and dead.

An exasperated Harper concluded the interview saying, "Fine. Have it your way, knucklehead."

———◆———

What Harper didn't know about was what had transpired the day before, when Paulie met with his lawyer.

The first thing Paulie did when he was booked into jail was exercise his legal right to counsel. He called a lawyer named Louie Shapiro. Louie was Mike Kelly's lawyer and the lawyer Mike used whenever someone on his crew was arrested.

Paulie met Louie in the same interview room where he later met with Rita Harper, a room not monitored by a camera. Paulie was dressed in an orange jail jumpsuit, his own clothes having been taken by the cops so they could test for gunshot residue, blood spatter, and anything else that could tie Paulie to the crimes he was accused of committing. Louie Shapiro—possibly the homeliest creature God had ever created—was dressed in a dark blue suit with wide pinstripes, a bright yellow shirt, a purple and yellow tie, and yellow socks that matched his shirt. Paulie had always thought it was bad enough that Louie had a nose like an Irish potato and purple lips that made him think of earthworms mating; why the guy had to call attention to himself by dressing the way he did was a mystery. The good news when it came to Louie was that he was one of the best—if not *the* best—criminal attorneys in Boston. But Paulie knew, no matter how good Louie was, that he was screwed.

Paulie said, "I need you to deliver a message to Mike for me. They're going to nail me for three counts of attempted murder. They got two eyewitnesses who ID'd me—the girl I tried to kill and the girlfriend of the kid I shot—and they're probably going to get prints or DNA off the raft I used."

"The raft?"

"So I'm fucked. But I know the prosecutor is going to come to me and try to make a deal. He's going to offer to reduce my time if I'm willing to testify against Mike. They want Mike a whole lot more than they want me."

"I see," Louie said, now concerned because Mike Kelly was his real client, not Paulie McGuire.

"So this is the deal. I want Mike to set up a line of credit for seven hundred and fifty grand and it's to be used to provide for my mother until she dies. If Mike doesn't do this, then all bets are off. If he does what I want, and I know my mom is taken care of, then I'll do the time. Oh, also Mike pays you to defend me.

"And when Mike says he doesn't have the money, tell him I know that's bullshit. I know that greedy bastard has socked away millions. And if he doesn't want to pay it all himself, he can get his niece to chip in."

"His niece? Who's his niece?"

"Mike will know who I mean."

Paulie shook his head. "Tell Mike I'm sorry. I know I screwed up, but it's either him or my mom, and I'm not going to let my mom end up a zombie in some shitty state facility."

Two hours later Louie had a second meeting with Paulie.

"Mike will do what you want," Louie said.

Rita Harper called DeMarco to give him the news that McGuire wasn't willing, at least not yet, to give up Mike or Erin Kelly. Harper said, "Maybe when this guy is looking at thirty years behind bars, he'll change his mind, but right now he's a rock."

This was not good news and DeMarco decided to go for a long walk to think things over.

If McGuire wouldn't flip on Mike Kelly, DeMarco needed to come up with a plan B. And he really cared more about nailing Erin Kelly than he did about getting Mike Kelly or Paul McGuire. Erin was the head of the snake. He knew she'd killed the Russells; he knew she paid to have Jerry Feldman killed; and he knew she was the one behind McGuire trying to kill Cassie in New York. The problem so far was that he couldn't prove Erin had done anything. The slow-moving NTSB hadn't completed its investigation of the plane crash. Tommy hadn't been able to place her in Tupper Lake. Nor had Tommy been able to find any evidence that she had a motive for embezzling. But there had to be something he could do to prove that Erin was a criminal.

He walked through the Public Garden and the Boston Common, mulling the problem over, finally ending up at the Granary Burying Ground on Tremont Street. The cemetery had been established in 1660, had more than two thousand headstones, and was the final resting place of Paul Revere, Samuel Adams, and John Hancock. Some of the headstones were so sandblasted by wind and time that the names on them were barely legible. As he was standing there looking down at the grave marker of a woman named Mary Goose, wondering if Mary Goose was Mother Goose, DeMarco figured out how he was going to cook Erin Kelly's goose.

It wasn't easy for DeMarco to arrange a meeting with Tucker Whitely and Charles "Chip" Hanover. Tucker and Chip were two fabulously wealthy fellows who'd inherited buckets of money and spent little time working and a lot of time playing golf, sailing their yachts, and cavorting with their trophy wives. They were also the two men Connor Russell had appointed to the board that, along with John Mahoney, had the responsibility of overseeing Erin Kelly's management of the Russell trust.

It took half a dozen phone calls to track down Tucker and Chip and get them to agree on a mutually acceptable time and place for a meeting. The only reason they agreed to a meeting at all was because DeMarco had invoked Mahoney's name.

DeMarco was meeting them at the Country Club in Brookline where both men were members. The club was called simply *the* Country Club, as if it were the only country club in America. It was, in fact, the first country club in America. The Country Club had been the host to three U.S. Opens and a Ryder Cup. In addition to a twenty-seven-hole golf course it offered its members indoor and outdoor tennis courts, a curling rink, an Olympic-size swimming pool, a skeet range, cross-country skiing trails, and a skating pond. More important than the athletic amenities, it offered exclusivity. Membership was by invitation only and no Jews were invited to be members until the 1970s, no women were invited until 1989, and no blacks until 1994. Tom Brady, the Super Bowl–winning quarterback, and his famous model wife, Gisele Bündchen, were almost not invited to join the Country Club because current members were concerned the renowned couple might attract too many obnoxious paparazzi. As for the cost of a membership, no one knew for sure because the club wouldn't divulge such information to the pedestrian public. Informed guesses were that it was in the range of half a million.

DeMarco took a seat on one of the decks overlooking a fairway so lush and green it didn't seem real. DeMarco would have given a testicle to be allowed to play the golf course. Well, maybe not a testicle but a kidney. Tucker and Chip said they'd meet him after they finished playing nine holes, not certain exactly when that might be. He waited an hour for them to arrive, although the experience wasn't unpleasant as he sat there watching the golfers and drinking very expensive, very good martinis. (As a nonmember, he wasn't allowed to pay for the martinis; they would be added onto Chip's or Tucker's tab.)

Tucker and Chip were both the same age, the age Connor Russell had been when he died. They had gone to prep school with Connor and had belonged to the same clubs at Harvard. The only reason they were on the board overseeing Cassie's trust was that Connor trusted them completely, not only because they were lifelong friends but because he knew they were both so rich that it would never occur to them to steal from his daughter.

Chip had probably been a fine-looking specimen when he was younger: blond, blue-eyed, tall, and broad-shouldered. Now the blond hair was thinning, the muscle had turned to fat, and the broken veins in his cheeks indicated he might be overly fond of booze. Tucker, shorter than Chip, with dark hair (most likely dyed) and a patrician profile, had kept himself in shape and had aged better than his buddy.

DeMarco said, "As I told you on the phone, I'm here on behalf of John Mahoney, who is now Cassie Russell's guardian and sits with you on the board overseeing Cassie's trust. Well, I believe, and the Speaker agrees with me, that Erin Kelly may have embezzled from the trust. And she may have done things even worse than that."

DeMarco told the story of Jerry Feldman's audit, Feldman's death, his suspicions about Connor Russell's death, and how Paul McGuire, a man who worked for Erin Kelly's criminal uncle, had attempted to kill Cassie a second time. As he was speaking, Chip and Tucker responded with:

"My God, man, you can't be serious."

"Erin Kelly! I just can't believe it."

"Sabotaged the plane. That's, that's . . . preposterous."

"I need another drink for this."

DeMarco concluded with: "Mr. Mahoney wants to have the trust audited. Or I should say, he wants the audit that Jerry Feldman was conducting completed. As members of the board, you, along with Mr. Mahoney, have the authority to authorize another audit."

DeMarco pulled a document from an inside pocket and laid it on the table. The document had been prepared by a lawyer Maggie Dolan kept on retainer, like a pet mongoose chained to her desk. "That document, which you'll see has already been signed by Mr. Mahoney, authorizes the audit." (DeMarco had forged Mahoney's signature.) "After you both sign it, I'll arrange for Jerry Feldman's partner to conduct the audit."

Neither man picked up the document; they looked down at it as if a seagull had had the audacity to shit upon their table at the Country Club.

"Look, guys, what can it hurt?" DeMarco said. "If the audit proves that Erin Kelly is honest, then that's a good thing. And an audit will protect Cassie if she's not. Plus the audit was something that your friend Connor wanted done so you'll simply be honoring his wishes."

Chip said to Tucker, "Maybe we should consult with our lawyers before we sign anything."

"It's an audit, for Christ's sake," DeMarco said. "I'm not asking you to invest in anything or do anything else that poses any sort of legal liability."

Chip and Tucker eventually signed. When DeMarco left they were arguing over who should pay for DeMarco's drinks. Rich people were a trip.

———◆◆◆———

DeMarco's plan B was this: he was going to nail Erin Kelly for embezzlement. That wouldn't be as satisfying as putting her in jail for murder but it would mean she'd be convicted of a felony, spend a few years in prison, and her life, as she knew it, would be destroyed. Not the outcome he wanted but it was the best he could do. At least until he could think of something else.

36

DeMarco walked into Erin Kelly's office without knocking.

She said, "Uh, Mr. DeMarco. What are you—"

She stopped speaking when Clyde Jordan, Jerry Feldman's partner, and two other men followed DeMarco into her office. Jordan and the two men with him, a couple of super accountants Jordan had hired to speed up the audit, were all dressed in dark suits and somber ties. They looked like funeral directors.

Erin said, "What's going on?"

DeMarco walked over to her desk and dropped a two-page document in front of her. "That's signed by John Mahoney, Tucker Whitely, and Chip Hanover, the board overseeing Cassie Russell's trust. It authorizes these men"—he jerked a thumb toward Jordan—"to audit the trust. In other words, they're going to finish the audit that Jerry Feldman started. It stipulates that you are to leave your office immediately—an office paid for by the trust—and that you're not allowed to touch any of the computers in your office or take any files with you. It requires that you provide any passwords protecting the files and if you don't provide the passwords you'll be immediately terminated as the manager of the trust, and I'll bring in a hacker to crack the computers."

Erin Kelly stood up and shouted, "This is outrageous! You have no right to—"

"I don't have any rights," DeMarco said, "but the board does."

Erin stood there bristling. She was so angry her hands were shaking and her pale, freckled cheeks looked as if they were on fire. She said, "I want to know why the board—"

DeMarco cut her off. "I know what you did, Erin," he said, "and I'm going to nail you for it."

"What?" she screamed. "What did I do?"

"You killed Connor and Elaine Russell."

"That's—"

"And you hired someone to kill Jerry Feldman. You also tried to have Cassie Russell killed for a second time a couple of days ago up at her parents' cabin."

"What are you talking about?" she said. "Someone tried to kill Cassie?"

DeMarco got the impression the question was genuine and that Erin really didn't know about the murder attempt on Cassie. And maybe she didn't. The crime had happened in a small town in upstate New York and the media there had reported that a local teenager had been shot near Bear Lake but no names were released because all the kids involved had been minors. The names would certainly get out eventually, particularly when it became known that one of the victims was the wealthy daughter of the late Connor Russell, but so far, apparently, that news hadn't broken yet. As for the arrest of Paul McGuire, that had rated only a paragraph in the local section of the *Globe*. Whatever the case, Erin seemed genuinely surprised that someone had attempted to kill Cassie—but all that meant was her uncle hadn't informed her of what had happened.

DeMarco said, "You can play innocent all you want, but I know you're behind the attempt to kill Cassie."

"That's the most preposterous thing I've heard in my life. And if you repeat that story to a reporter, I'll sue you for defamation of character. I'm going to, I'm going to . . ."

Then she must have realized she had no idea what she was going to do next and she stopped speaking.

DeMarco said, "Give me the passwords for the files and the keys to this office. Then leave."

37

Erin had no idea what was going on. But based on what DeMarco had just said, her fucking uncle had bungled the attempt to kill Cassie. She called him.

She said, "What in the hell did you do?"

"Shut up," he said. "You're on a goddamn cell phone."

"Where are you?" She didn't want to have to drive all the way to Cape Cod to see him.

"At my place here in Boston."

"What's the address?"

Mike let her in, dressed in a purple bathrobe, his hair uncombed. Erin thought his white hairless legs and his splayed, pale feet were disgusting. Before he'd even closed the door Erin said, "What the hell happened?"

He turned and she followed him into the kitchen. He said, "You want some coffee?"

"No, I don't want any fucking coffee. I want to know what happened."

"Calm down. We don't have a problem. That is, we don't have one provided you can come up with six thousand bucks a month."

"What are you talking about? I already paid you three hundred thousand for a job you apparently bungled."

Mike explained what was going on, how Paulie had been caught by the cops after he tried to kill Cassie Russell.

"But you see, Paulie has this weird thing about his mom. She's got Alzheimer's and she's in this assisted living place."

"What does that have to do with—"

Mike told her that as long as Erin paid Paulie's mom's nursing home expenses, which could be as high as six grand a month for a number of years, Paulie would do the time and not say anything about who had hired him to kill Cassie.

"You trust him?" she said.

"Yeah. Paulie's a stand-up guy."

"Why don't you just have him killed? There must be a way to get to him in whatever jail he's in."

"Jesus, you're a murderous cunt. I'm not going to kill him, he's my friend. And I'm sure as hell not going to kill him when the problem can be solved with money, money which I know you got since you've been skimming from that trust."

"How do you know I've been skimming?"

"Why else would you have had the accountant killed?"

"Well, taking care of Paulie's mom is your problem not mine. He doesn't know who I am and there's nothing to connect me to him."

"Well, yeah, I lied about Paulie not knowing who you are. Paulie's the guy who let you into my house when you came to ask me to murder people for you."

"You son of a bitch."

"I'm telling you, you better watch your mouth with me, girlie. Giving you a good smack ain't out of the question."

"I'm still not going to pay. He's your guy and he may have seen me with you but that's not proof that I asked to have anyone killed. And remember that there's no money trail from me to you, much less from me to him. I made sure of that."

Mike pulled a small digital recorder out of the pocket of his robe. He punched PLAY and Erin heard:

"Who do you want taken care of?"

"Cassie Russell."

"Who's—"

"The daughter of Connor Russell, the one who survived the plane crash."

"A kid? You want to kill a kid?"

"Yeah. You have some kind of rule against that?"

Mike stopped the recording.

"You motherfucker," Erin said—and Mike backhanded her across the face, knocking her out of the chair she was in. "I told you to watch your mouth," he said.

She started to come up off the floor, her hands formed into claws, long red fingernails extended, ready to gouge out his eyes.

"Don't even think about it," Mike said, pointing a finger at her. "Now sit back down and show some goddamn respect."

Erin was so angry she could feel her cheeks burning. If she ever got a chance to kill him . . .

Mike said, "Now, look. This ain't a big deal unless you make it one. I know that trust you handle gives all kinds of money to charity. All you gotta do is set up an account that sends a lousy six grand a month to Paulie's mom's nursing home. And when the old lady dies, you can stop. That should be a piece of cake for you."

Erin couldn't tell him that with the audit being conducted she wouldn't be sending money to anyone and was liable to be indicted for embezzlement.

She nodded as if she knew she was beaten. "Okay. Tell Paulie I'll take care of his mother."

That was a lie.

She wasn't going to send a single red cent to Paulie's decrepit mother. When Paulie found that out, he might give up Mike, but he wouldn't be able to do damn thing to her. And neither would her treacherous uncle, in spite of the recording he had.

Erin Kelly had been preparing for this moment for a long time.

38

Erin returned to her condo. She looked in the mirror and saw her mouth was slightly puffy from Mike's blow, but nothing a little makeup wouldn't cover.

She turned on her computer. She could access all the trust's files remotely from her home or from wherever she happened to be. As soon as she was inside the files, she could see that the audit was still going on. Cursors were moving up and down the spreadsheets like ants going to and from their nest. She'd have to wait until later, until after all the damn accountants had gone home for the day.

She went to her bedroom and packed enough clothes for a couple of days. She'd replace her wardrobe when she reached her final destination. She walked over to a wall safe hidden behind a Monet print, opened the safe, and removed all her expensive jewelry, the ten thousand dollars in cash she kept for the day the ATMs didn't work, and the documents she would need. There was nothing else in the apartment that she would bring with her; she didn't see the point in lugging around photos of her parents or any other mementos from her past.

Next, she checked on flights for London, made a reservation for a first-class seat, then took a nap. The day had been exhausting and she had a long flight ahead of her.

At six p.m. she went back to the computer and accessed the trust's files. The accountants were no longer rummaging among them like squirrels digging for rotten acorns. The first thing she did was send a hundred and twenty million dollars to three different banks. She'd made sure a long time ago that at least a hundred million was always available in cash and not tied up in stocks or real estate or any other financial instrument that would take time to liquidate. She then spent the next two hours moving the money to various banks, the accounts in those banks not in her real name, until all the money ended up in two different banks in Switzerland. She'd made it as hard as she possibly could to trace the money but she knew that clever Treasury agents still might be able to follow the bread crumbs. But the one thing she knew for sure was that the two banks in Switzerland wouldn't cooperate with the U.S. government. These banks charged exorbitant fees for their silence—which was the reason why their major clients were corrupt dictators, weapons dealers, and drug lords.

The only thing she had to do before leaving for the airport was destroy her laptop. Not only did it contain a record of the banking transactions she'd just completed, but her browser history would provide a good investigator clues to her destination. She didn't have a hammer in the house, so she took the heaviest thing she could find—a brass candlestick holder—and went down to the garage where her Tesla was parked. (She was going to miss the car; she loved it.) She put on a pair of sunglasses to protect her eyes, opened her laptop, and then spent ten minutes smashing it to pieces. She was sweating by the time she was done; the fucking computer was harder to break than she'd expected. She left the garage, walked six blocks, then tossed the remains of her computer into four different dumpsters. She pitched her personal cell phone down a storm drain. Those tasks completed, she returned to her condo, took a shower, and Ubered her way to Logan Airport, calling on a clean burner phone.

It occurred to her as she headed for the airport that there was no one she'd miss in Boston. She had many friends—women at her gym, people she'd met in the course of her career, old school pals—but no *close* friends. And that was fine. She'd make new friends in the next phase of her life, people who would really appreciate her. She was actually looking forward to whatever came next.

39

DeMarco was in bed, sound asleep at eight a.m., when Clyde Jordan called him.

Jordan said, "She stole a hundred and twenty million dollars from the trust. She—"

"What? You've completed the audit already? I thought you said it would take at least a week."

"You didn't let me finish. She stole a hundred and twenty million from the trust *last night*. I don't know how much she stole before that because the audit's barely started. Anyway, when me and my guys got here this morning and turned on the computers we could see that someone had accessed the files. She had a way to do that remotely, which I knew was a possibility, so the first thing I did when I started the audit was make a backup copy of all the files. I made the backup in case of some fluke virus or a computer malfunction destroyed the originals, but I also made one in case she tried to alter the files remotely. But what never occurred to me was that she'd simply go in and steal cash from the accounts while the audit was going on. Anyway, last night she accessed the files and moved a hundred and twenty million to three offshore banks. Where it went from there I can't tell you."

"You gotta be—"

"So you don't need me to finish the audit, DeMarco, to prove she's a thief. What you need are FBI agents to arrest her before she flees the country and Treasury agents to try to figure out where the money is now and how to get it back."

———◆◆◆———

DeMarco called his personal U.S attorney, Rita Harper, and told Harper what he'd learned from Jordan.

"Can Jordan prove she stole the money?" Harper asked.

"Yes," DeMarco said. "And you can look at the proof any time you want, but what you need to do now is call the FBI and tell them to go arrest Erin Kelly."

Harper called DeMarco back a couple of hours later. "Erin Kelly has disappeared," she said. "We've got her name and photo out to every major cop shop in the country. The FBI is pinging her cell phone to locate her and they're watching for credit card charges. We've contacted the airlines to see if she's listed as a passenger on any overseas flight and we've passed out her photo to TSA in all the major airports within two hundred miles of Boston. And since it's possible that she might have a false passport, we're also using facial recognition software to see if she got on a plane, but it's going to be a while before we get back any results."

Five hours elapsed before Harper called him again.

"We got her on a camera at Logan. She caught a flight to London that left at ten p.m. last night, the same night she stole the money. She used a passport and a credit card with the name Bridget Pearson. The FBI confirmed Bridget Pearson arrived in London and then she disappeared. There's no record of a Bridget Pearson checking into any hotel in London or using her credit card to make any purchases there or to book another flight. It's possible, as smart as this woman is and with the money she has, she could have several false passports."

"What about the money?" DeMarco asked.

"Treasury is trying to find it. She moved it to three offshore banks as your accountant told you and Treasury is trying to get the banks to cooperate. But since the banks are located in Panama, Belize, and the Cayman Islands . . ."

"Well, shit," DeMarco said. "You gotta find this woman, Harper. I don't really care about the money but she's responsible for three murders and is an accomplice to three attempted murders."

Harper said, "I want her as much as you do, DeMarco, but she's not Osama bin Laden. The FBI is not going to assign a thousand agents to the case."

40

The funeral for Connor and Elaine Russell was held in the Cathedral of the Holy Cross as Erin Kelly had arranged. To DeMarco's surprise, Mahoney attended the funeral. Cassie, dressed in a black suit, sat between Mahoney and Mary Pat, Mary Pat's arm around the girl's shoulders for most of the ceremony. For once, Mahoney didn't make himself the center of attention. Nor was he one of the speakers who gave the eulogies. The people who did speak had been close to Connor and Elaine and they spoke of them eloquently, extolling their vitality, their contributions to the city of Boston, and their generous giving to many charities. After the service, a reception was held at Cassie's house on Beacon Hill. Mrs. Aguilera had organized the event, and with the help of a couple of local culinary students she put together a buffet with enough food to feed a village in Bangladesh. DeMarco was surprised that he'd been allowed to attend. He was the hired help, not a Boston blue blood.

At the reception, Mahoney appeared to have his own receiving line as wealthy Bostonians came over to congratulate him on soon becoming the Speaker again. At one point, however, Mahoney walked over to DeMarco, who'd been leaning against a wall, sipping a drink, admiring all the attractive women. Money was clearly an advantage when it came to preserving beauty.

Mahoney said, "You gotta find someone to manage Cassie's trust now that Erin Kelly's gone. And this time make sure it's not a fuckin' crook."

DeMarco knew it was futile to point out to Mahoney that it wasn't his job to find Erin's replacement. That responsibility lay with the board—the board consisting of Mahoney, Chip, and Tucker.

DeMarco waited until Mary Pat was by herself.

He asked her, "How's Cassie doing?"

"She seems to be doing okay. I was afraid that she would be so traumatized by almost getting killed that she'd be afraid to leave the house, but she seems all right." Mary Pat shook her head. "I still can't believe you left her alone that day."

"I told you that I feel terrible about what happened to her. I just never expected that Erin would try to kill her again."

"Anyway," Mary Pat said, "her arm's mending—fortunately it wasn't reinjured—and next week she'll start going to school again. She needs school. She needs to be around kids her age and doing something other than thinking about her parents."

"But what's going to happen to her in the long run? Who's she going to live with?"

"I don't know," Mary Pat said. "For now, I'm going to move in with her, and Rosa and I will take care of her. I'm actually looking forward to staying in Boston for a while."

Meaning: not being with her husband for a while.

"But long term I don't know," Mary Pat said. "I'll figure something out, whatever's best for her."

DeMarco had no doubt she would.

41

The day after the funeral, DeMarco called Chip and Tucker and told them that it was their job to find Erin's replacement and without complaint they agreed. DeMarco knew that Chip and Tucker wouldn't do a damn thing, but they had competent people working for them—the people who managed *their* money—and those people would form a committee to hire Erin's successor. DeMarco concluded his discussion with Chip and Tucker the same way Mahoney had when Mahoney spoke to him: *Try not to hire a fuckin' crook.*

Until Erin's replacement could be found, Clyde Jordan agreed to babysit the assets in the trust: pay any bills that came due, put dividends into a cash account; no investments or charitable contributions would be made until the new trust manager was onboard. The only good thing when it came to Erin Kelly stealing more than a hundred million dollars was that several billion still remained in the trust. Cassie was never going to want for money.

Mahoney returned to Washington after the funeral to continue his harassment of the president and to make sure the gears of government barely turned. Also on his agenda was a trip to Afghanistan, where he planned to spend Thanksgiving with the troops. For Mahoney this was not a sacrifice; he was genuinely looking forward to eating chow and joshing with the soldiers. Mahoney had many faults but there was one area where DeMarco had to admit that he did his job. Mahoney was a veteran. He'd enlisted in the Marines when he was seventeen, spent nine months in Vietnam, and still carried shrapnel in one knee from that experience. Since he'd been a member of Congress, he did everything he could to assist the military and help other veterans, and at least once a year he took a trip abroad, to wherever America's warriors were most at risk. Before leaving Boston, he told DeMarco to stick around for a while and make sure the FBI and federal prosecutor were doing their jobs when it came to Erin Kelly—as if DeMarco had the power to make the FBI do anything.

Cassie returned to school, which would soon be breaking for Thanksgiving. DeMarco had arranged with Nora Thurston to have bodyguards assigned to protect her, including an armed driver who would be taking her back and forth to school. Mary Pat said she was thinking about taking Cassie to New York for the holiday, where they'd see *Hamilton*, the musical version of the founding father's life by Lin-Manuel Miranda. Mary Pat had seen it but Cassie hadn't.

After calling Rita Harper to harass her and see what she was doing to find Erin Kelly, DeMarco called Shannon. She answered, saying, "God, I was hoping you'd call. I want to celebrate with somebody."

"Celebrate what?"

"I'll tell you when I see you."

"Well, if we're celebrating, we might as well do it right. I'll get reservations for dinner at some swanky place and pick you up at eight."

DeMarco lucked out and was able to get a reservation at No. 9 Park because a Saudi prince had apparently canceled. Dinner at No. 9 Park was going to cost him more than he normally paid each month for groceries. Or maybe two months. But what the hell. It was a celebration.

He picked up Shannon at her apartment, which actually was close to TD Garden, and she'd dressed for the occasion: a flimsy black cocktail dress short enough to show off her legs, cut low enough to reveal the tops of her breasts, and high heels with a complicated arrangement of straps that went around her ankles. All this was hidden by a trench coat because the dress had been intended for balmy spring evenings, not winter in Boston.

No. 9 Park was housed in a brick building with a small maroon awning over the door, the structure looking old enough to have been constructed when Paul Revere was a boy. Or maybe it had just been made to look that way. The lighting was romantically dim. The waiters wore unpretentious white shirts with the sleeves rolled up. All the pretentiousness was reserved for the food, served in small portions, each plate a work of art. The chef's six-course tasting meal cost two hundred bucks per person.

After they were seated and the champagne had been poured, DeMarco said, "So what are we celebrating?"

"Joe, you won't believe it. My agent's already sold the film rights to my novel to Reese Witherspoon's production company. Reese is going to play Claire."

"Claire?"

"The mother in my novel."

"Right. The mother living in the lighthouse with her pregnant teenage daughter."

"Yes. Can you believe it? Reese Witherspoon! And because of the film deal we have three different publishers bidding on the novel. David says—"

"David?"

"My literary agent. He says we're looking at a seven-figure book deal."

"Wow!" DeMarco said, thinking maybe she should buy dinner.

"I talked to Reese today—"

She was now on a first name basis with movie stars.

"—and she wants me to come out to California to talk with her and the screenwriter she's hired. So what have you been up to?"

"Well, nothing worth celebrating," he said.

DeMarco then told her what had transpired with Cassie at her parents' cabin, the arrest of Paul McGuire, and Erin Kelly splitting the country with a hundred million bucks before the FBI could catch her. When he finished, he concluded with, "The damn woman could be anywhere in the world right now and she might never be caught."

DeMarco was awakened by Shannon getting out of bed. The celebration had continued after dinner. He watched as she padded naked to the bathroom. There were those who liked waking to the sight of a glorious sunrise; DeMarco preferred waking to the sight of a beautiful, naked woman.

Shannon used the bathroom, then thinking DeMarco was still asleep she went into the kitchen to make coffee. Unfortunately, she'd put on a robe. After she'd started the coffee maker, she walked back toward the bed and noticed DeMarco staring at her.

"Oh, you're awake," she said.

"Wide awake," he said.

She shrugged off the robe—and it was twenty minutes later before they left the bed.

As they were drinking their morning coffee, Shannon said, "I was thinking about what you told me last night, that Erin Kelly could be anyplace in the world. That's probably not exactly true."

"What do you mean it's not true?" DeMarco said. "The cops have no idea where she might have gone."

"Well, think about it," Shannon said. "If I were Erin Kelly, I would want to go to someplace that doesn't have an extradition treaty with the United States. Now there are a lot of countries that don't have extradition treaties with us, but most of them aren't places where I would want to live."

"I'm still not with you," DeMarco said.

"Hang on," Shannon said and grabbed her iPad and tapped on it for a bit.

"Okay," she said. "There are about eighty countries that don't have extradition treaties with the United States. These include garden spots like North Korea, Somalia, Mongolia, Rwanda, Bangladesh, Afghanistan, and Yemen. In fact, just looking at this list on Wikipedia, I'd say that most of the places that don't have treaties with us are impoverished, dangerous, and corrupt. Now based on what you told me about her, Erin's a woman used to living in luxury and she has the money to afford luxury, so some jungle hut in Africa is not going to be all that appealing. Plus, she's white. A wealthy, white woman living alone would tend to stand out in places where people are predominately Asian, Arabic, black, or brown."

"Huh," DeMarco said. "So what are you saying? Someplace in Europe?"

"That would be my first choice if I were her." Shannon studied her iPad again. "In Europe, countries that don't have extradition treaties with the U.S. include Belarus, Macedonia, Moldavia, and Montenegro. Belarus and Moldavia are near Russia and Ukraine, which makes me think of Vladimir Putin, the Russian mafia, and tanks rolling across the border. So if I were a wealthy white woman looking for a country that didn't have an extradition treaty with the United States, I'd be thinking Montenegro might do. It's a beautiful place on the Adriatic Sea and the cost of living wouldn't be outrageous, particularly if you have a hundred million to spend.

"Anyhoo, just a thought," Shannon said. "You want to go out to breakfast?"

42

DeMarco returned to his hotel after breakfast, took out his laptop, and did some research on countries that didn't have extradition treaties with the United States—and concluded that Shannon might be right about Erin picking Montenegro as a nice spot to live.

Montenegro had once been part of Yugoslavia, along with Bosnia, Croatia, Macedonia, Serbia, and Slovenia. It was now part of NATO, though not yet a member of the European Union. It was a place with picturesque mountains and a coastline on the Adriatic Sea, and it was steadily gaining in popularity with tourists. And if one wanted to get away to someplace more sophisticated when it came to shopping and entertainment, Budapest and Vienna were only about twelve hours away by rail or car. Probably more important—from a criminal's point of view—was that law enforcement in Montenegro wasn't as robust as those in the richer European countries, such as Germany or France, and although Montenegro wasn't the most corrupt country on the earth, neither was it the least corrupt. The most interesting article DeMarco found was one that listed the five most popular places where criminals were likely to flee to avoid extradition. On the list were Brunei, Russia, China, the Arabian Gulf States, and, yes, Montenegro.

It occurred to DeMarco that the hunter would have some advantages if he were hunting for someone hiding in Montenegro. Fewer than seven hundred thousand people lived there—about the same number of people who lived in the District of Columbia. The country occupied only about five thousand square miles, which made it just a bit larger than Connecticut. Its largest city and its capital, Podgorica, had a population of about one hundred fifty thousand. Its second largest city, Nikšić—however the hell you pronounced it—had a population under sixty thousand. Some American football stadiums could hold all the people who lived in Nikšić. The size of these cities was important because DeMarco couldn't imagine a city girl like Erin Kelly living out in a shack in the woods, and in a relatively small city a rich foreigner was likely to stand out.

DeMarco then did a little research on retrieving criminals from foreign countries. He learned that this was not easy. In fact, sometimes it was really hard. There was one case where a guy wanted for murder fled to Thailand, and even though the United States has an extradition treaty with Thailand it took five years to get the guy home to face a jury. There were some countries that wouldn't extradite people to the United States if it was possible the person might be executed. He also learned that one of the main problems when it came to extraditing wealthy criminals from some countries was government corruption. There was a famous case involving a criminal financier named Robert Vesco who embezzled $220 million and fled to Costa Rica. Vesco wasn't extradited because he gave the guy who was president of Costa Rica at the time a two-million-dollar bribe to pass a law that prevented him from being extradited. It became known as the "Vesco Law." In fact, DeMarco learned that the worst thing the U.S. government could do was inform certain foreign governments that it wanted someone extradited because people in those governments would immediately go to the criminal and say, *How much will you pay us to let you stay?*

Now that he was about as informed on Montenegro and extradition as he was likely to get, DeMarco drove over to Rita Harper's office on the Boston waterfront. The weather had turned; the balmy autumn that the East Coast had been experiencing since DeMarco's arrival in Boston had disappeared overnight. The temperature was in the thirties and the wind coming off Boston Harbor stung DeMarco's ears, making him wish he was wearing a stocking cap, which upon reflection would have made him look like more of a thug than he already did. Harper initially refused to see him but eventually did so because DeMarco told her secretary that he was camping out in her waiting room until she relented.

Harper's friendly greeting was, "Why in the hell are you harassing me, DeMarco? If I had anything, I would have called you."

Her dark hair was tied back into a ponytail and she was wearing jeans and a faded Columbia University sweatshirt draped over her bony shoulders. DeMarco assumed she wasn't appearing in court today. Just looking at her office, he could tell she was overworked and he was only adding to her misery. There were cardboard shipping boxes stacked against the walls, the stacks about five feet high, and DeMarco figured the boxes contained files related to all the cases she was currently prosecuting.

Harper was still speaking. "The FBI hasn't been able to locate Erin Kelly. Paul McGuire won't talk to me. Mike Kelly won't talk to me. And the NTSB still hasn't completed its investigation into the Russells' plane crash."

DeMarco already knew about the NTSB's lack of progress because he'd called the agency again and learned that investigators had just gotten to the crash site to figure out how to get the plane out of there when Mother Nature decided to dump twenty inches of snow on the Adirondacks.

"I'm not here to harass you," DeMarco said. "I've got an idea."

He told Harper about the possibility of Erin Kelly being in Montenegro, explaining his reasoning.

"But that's just a wild-ass guess on your part," Harper countered.

"Not a wild-ass guess. It makes sense that she could be there."

"Yeah, maybe," Harper conceded. "I'll talk to the FBI, but I can guarantee you that they're not going to send a team there. If Kelly was a terrorist, they might, but an embezzler? I don't think so."

"She's not just an embezzler, she's a murderer."

"There's no proof she murdered anyone and she didn't steal money intended for orphans." Before DeMarco could object—or point out that Erin had indeed stolen an orphan's money—she said, "I'll call the Bureau. What I imagine they'll do is contact Interpol and law enforcement in Montenegro and ask for their help."

"Don't do that," DeMarco said. "I mean contacting Interpol might be okay but if you call the cops in Montenegro, they might locate Kelly and warn her that the FBI's hunting for her, then ask for a fat bribe to protect her. You need to send someone there to look for her and, if she's there, then just sit on her until you can figure out a way to get her back without alerting the local cops."

"That's not going to happen," Harper said. "The FBI is not the CIA. They're not going to snatch her and send her to some black op site. If she's there, the FBI will get the State Department involved and State will talk to the Montenegrins and try to negotiate her arrest and return to Boston. But, again, I doubt the FBI will send in a team to find her. They'll try to get someone else to do the footwork, especially since you don't have any evidence to prove she could be there."

"It's not my goddamn job to find the evidence!" DeMarco shouted. "That's what you and the FBI are supposed to do."

"Like I said, I'll talk to the FBI. Now you have to go. I'm due in court tomorrow and I'll probably be here all night preparing. Erin Kelly isn't my only case."

Upset by his conversation with Harper, DeMarco called Mahoney's office and told Mavis he needed to speak to the man.

Mavis said, "He's got no time for you, DeMarco. He's in a hearing the rest of the day and from there he's going to—"

"Aw, never mind," DeMarco said. It had occurred to him as Mavis was speaking that he didn't really need to talk to Mahoney. All he had to do was lie and *say* that he'd talked to Mahoney.

He called Chip Hanover and said, "I need to talk to you and Tucker about something, something that might help catch Erin Kelly."

An hour later Chip got back to him and said that he and Tucker could meet him at the Boston Yacht Club in Marblehead. They had to get together to do some planning for a regatta in December.

"You're going sailing in December?" DeMarco said. "Are you nuts?"

"Oh, it'll be great fun," the Chipper said.

The Boston Yacht Club bar was about what DeMarco had expected. Battered but expensive-looking furniture, photos of sailboats heeling in the wind, and what looked like an old brass compass that somebody might have stolen from the USS *Constitution*. Chip and Tucker were dressed almost identically in heavy cable-knit sweaters, which were appropriate as it was cold enough to freeze the balls off a brass Brahmin. DeMarco, not being sure of the yacht club's dress code, had opted for a dark suit when a parka would have made more sense.

"I think there's a possibility that Erin Kelly might be in Montenegro," DeMarco said, and for the second time that day he went through his reasoning. He concluded saying, "Now I realize it's a long shot, but I think it's worth taking a look."

"Okay," Chip said, "but what does that have to do with us?"

"It has to do with you in that I want to use some of Cassie Russell's several billion dollars to hire someone to search for Erin. I already talked to Mahoney and he agrees that spending a few bucks would be worth it. So Mahoney's already agreed, but I need your authorization as well. I could ask Cassie if she wanted to spend the money, and I'm sure she'd agree since I'm trying to catch the person who killed her parents, but I don't want to upset her."

"How much money are we talking about?" Tucker said.

"Hell, I don't know," DeMarco said. "But if it was a couple hundred grand, would it matter, considering the overall size of the trust?"

"I suppose not," Tucker said. "What do you think, Chip?"

"I think we should do it," Chip said. "I want that devious bitch behind bars."

DeMarco stopped at a coffee shop near Exchange Place, where Thurston Security was located. He had one thing left to do before he called it a day, but he decided to call Shannon to see if she might be available later for another celebration, one that wouldn't cost him quite so much and one that might end up with him back in her bed.

"How 'bout dinner tonight?" he said. "There's a guy I need to talk to but after that—"

"I'm sorry, Joe, but I can't. I'm flying to New York tomorrow to talk to my agent and I have to pack and get ready for the meeting."

"Well, maybe—"

At that moment Tommy Hewlett walked into the bar. "Sorry," he said to Shannon, "I gotta go. Maybe we can get together after you get back from New York."

"Sure," she said. "That would be good."

There was something about her tone that made him wonder if he'd ever see her again.

DeMarco said, "How's the job going?"

"Great," Tommy said. "It's like I never left. I can't tell you how grateful I am to you. Right now they got me and a couple other guys working on this case out in Winthrop. There's this scrap metal company there and the boss thinks a couple of his employees, who are both relatives, are ripping him off."

"Well, I want you to ask Nora Thurston to assign you to another job. I want you to go to Montenegro to see if Erin Kelly is there."

"Montenegro?"

DeMarco explained once more why it was possible that Erin might be there.

"But you don't know for sure," Tommy said.

"Nope. But I want you to look."

Tommy said, "Well, if that's what you want, I'm sure Nora will agree. But I should take someone with me to speed things up, and it probably should be a woman since I'll be hunting for a woman. And I hope you realize this isn't going to be cheap. You're going to have to pay our expenses. You know, flights, hotels, meals. And probably a few bribes."

"You're going to be paid out of Cassie Russell's trust. So money isn't a problem, but don't even think about flying first class. Now I'm guessing that if Erin's there, she'll almost certainly be using a false identity and not the one she used when she flew to London. I'm also guessing that she hasn't had time yet to buy a house, so you might start by looking at expensive hotels and rental properties. Whatever you do, you have to do it in such a way that any inquiries you make don't get back to her."

Tommy said, "I know what to do, DeMarco. I've hunted people before who didn't want to be found, I've just never hunted in Montenegro. But you gotta realize this is a long shot, so you need to decide how much time and money you want to spend on us looking for her there."

After Hewlett left, another idea occurred to DeMarco, which he knew was an even longer shot than Erin being in Montenegro. He didn't have anything better to do with his evening so he figured why not.

43

Mike Kelly sat alone at a table at the back of his bar in Charlestown, sipping a Sam Adams beer directly from the bottle.

The bar was a dive and probably the least popular place in gentrified Charlestown. It was dimly lit, making it hard to tell how dirty the beer mugs were. Moth-eaten red curtains covered the windows. The hardwood floor hadn't been washed or buffed in years. Wobbly bar stools covered with split red Naugahyde fronted the bar and the tables near the bar had mismatched chairs and no two tables were of the same design. The place didn't offer food other than pickled eggs and inedible microwave sandwiches. The paying clientele, which were few, were mostly alcoholic pensioners who went there because it was within walking distance of their hovels. And all of this suited Mike Kelly just fine. He owned the bar and it served as an office for him and he didn't want the place filled with annoying customers. And although it lost money as a bar, it was a moneymaking machine because Mike used it to launder money from his other endeavors and his accountant did clever things when it came to the bar and Mike's taxes.

Mike had just finished meeting with two of his main guys, guys who had brains in addition to meanness and muscle. They were the ones who handled the day-to-day operations of his business. And business was fine; he had no complaints when it came to his various criminal endeavors. Nonetheless, he was in a shitty mood.

For one thing, the fuckin' weather. A few days ago it had been one of the balmiest Novembers ever recorded in New England. Then overnight the weather changed and now Boston had become Canada. He should have been down in Florida, at his place in Naples, but with all the shit going on with Paulie and his psycho niece he hadn't been able to get away.

He was so pissed at Erin that if he could find her he'd kill her. That is, he'd kill her after she told him where her money was. His guy in the BPD had told him that she'd absconded with over a hundred million bucks, had taken a flight to London using a fake passport, and was now in the wind and no one had a clue where she was. And because Erin had split, he was now going to have to pay for Paulie's mom's nursing expenses.

It had occurred to him that he could send a guy over to the nursing home to smother the old bat with a pillow. That would be the end of paying to take care of her—it just killed him having to use his own money to do that—but murdering her posed a problem. If Paulie's mom died, what incentive would Paulie have for not ratting him out? And not just for the attempted murder of Cassie Russell but for a whole lot of other shit that Paulie knew about. Then there was the fact that Paulie hadn't been sentenced yet. His trial wouldn't be for another six months but, when it happened, Paulie was going to be found guilty and sentenced to at least twenty years in prison. Would Paulie change his mind about not testifying against him when he was looking at twenty years?

And what would happen as time passed? Say Paulie's mom lived for ten more years, as Mike continued to shell out money for her. But then what would Paulie do after his mom died and he was still looking at ten more years in the pen? Would Paulie, at that point, decide to give him up to get an early release? And what if the cops ever got their mitts on Erin? Would she give him up to get a reduced sentence? There was no doubt the bitch would. Shit, there were just too many different ways things could go and all of them were bad.

The best thing would be if everyone was dead: Paulie, Paulie's mom, and Erin. Paulie and his mom wouldn't be a problem but Erin . . . How could he find her before the FBI did?

A man walked into the bar, letting in a blast of cold air. Mike looked up, annoyed. The guy was wearing a brown bomber jacket and a black stocking cap. He was a hard-looking SOB—and there was something familiar about him. One of Mike's guys stopped him, the man said something to him, and Mike's guy patted him down for a weapon then got out of his way.

He walked over to Mike's table, started to say something, but Mike said, "Do I know you? You look familiar."

"My name's Joe DeMarco. I wanted to—"

"That's it! DeMarco! I knew a guy named Gino DeMarco when I was young. He worked for an old guinea in New York. You're the spittin' image of him."

"Gino was my dad," DeMarco said.

"No shit! He still workin' for the outfit in New York?"

"No, he's dead."

"Sorry to hear that. So what outfit do you work for?"

"An outfit called the United States Congress."

Mike laughed. "Now there's the biggest gang of fuckin' thieves to ever walk the earth."

DeMarco sat down. Mike said, "Did I say you could sit?"

DeMarco said, "I'm here to talk to you about your niece. Now you don't have to say anything. Just listen to me. There's a guy who works for you named McGuire in the Suffolk jail. He tried to kill Cassie Russell.

I also know that your niece paid you to sic McGuire on Cassie, then she split the country."

"You don't know shit," Mike said.

"Just listen," DeMarco said. "The FBI cares about getting you because you're a fuckin' gangster, but I don't care. What I care about is nailing your niece. Right now the FBI and Interpol are hunting for her. And I'm also hunting for her independently. When she's found, she's going to be arrested and extradited from wherever she is, then she's going to try to cut a deal with the U.S. attorney to reduce her time. But then it occurred to me that you might know where she is. Maybe you helped her get away. Maybe you got her stashed someplace. Well, Mike, I got the clout to make you a deal. You tell me where she is and I'll make sure you don't do any time no matter what she and Paul McGuire say."

"You got the clout to make that happen?"

"That's right."

"Well, sorry, but I don't know nuthin' about nuthin'. I don't know where she is and I don't know anything about what Paulie did. So pack your wop ass on out of here."

DeMarco rose. "Okay. But I'm going to find her eventually, and when I do you're going to jail with her if you don't help me. So think about it." DeMarco flipped a business card on the table that had only his name and a phone number on it. "You can reach me at that number if you change your mind."

DeMarco turned to leave and Mike said, "Hey, how'd your dad die?"

"Go fuck yourself."

───────◆◆◆───────

As soon as DeMarco walked out the door, Mike crooked a finger at a man sitting at the bar. The man was in his forties, had curly dark hair, and was short, only five-foot-six. In spite of his size he was one of the most lethal members of Mike's crew. His name was Epstein.

Mike Kelly was not an equal opportunity employer. He employed no blacks or Hispanics, and Epstein was the only Jew who worked for him. Had anyone asked him if he was a bigot, he would have replied, *Yeah. So what's your point?* The only reason he'd hired Epstein in the first place was that Epstein had married one of his guy's daughters, but he'd never regretted the decision. Epstein was smart.

Mike said, "That guy who just left. I want you to follow him and find out what he's up to."

Epstein didn't even think about asking why his boss wanted DeMarco followed. He turned and left the bar.

Mike didn't know what DeMarco had meant about independently looking for Erin. He wondered if DeMarco was some kind of private dick in spite of what he'd said about working for Congress. Whatever the case, maybe DeMarco could lead him to his niece. It was worth a shot and wouldn't cost him anything.

44

Thanksgiving Day arrived.

Mahoney was in Afghanistan eating with a bunch of young Marines, thoroughly enjoying himself.

Mary Pat spent the holiday with Cassie Russell in New York.

Tommy Hewlett flew to Montenegro to hunt for Erin Kelly. He enjoyed a hot turkey sandwich with cranberry sauce on the plane.

DeMarco also spent the holiday in New York, where he had Thanksgiving dinner with his mother. It turned out to be a rather gloomy affair because his mom was a rather gloomy woman. He would have preferred spending the holiday with Shannon but that wouldn't have felt right and, anyway, Shannon was having dinner with her family in Rhode Island. (Shannon was still waiting to hear back from her agent on the sale of her novel and was so nervous she was starting to act a bit squirrelly.)

Epstein, Mike Kelly's guy, spent Thanksgiving in his car, parked outside DeMarco's mother's house in Queens.

Mike Kelly had an uncomfortable dinner with his sister, the eccentric retired teacher, then spent the rest of the day watching football on television.

Erin Kelly had completely forgotten about the holiday. Nonetheless, she had a lovely lunch that day accompanied by a half liter of expensive red wine, followed by a relaxing massage.

DeMarco's phone rang. It was Tommy Hewlett calling.

"Got her," Tommy said.

"You're kidding," DeMarco said. He'd known that the odds of Erin being in Montenegro were better than the odds of her being in the Congo, but he still knew that finding her there would be like a hitting the lotto.

Tommy said, "We actually found her the second day we got here but I decided not to call you until we collected more information."

"How did you find her?"

"Cabdriver. Since we don't know the name she's using, we couldn't go to hotels and ask if she was staying there. And if we showed her picture at hotels or restaurants, the word might get back to her. So the first thing we did was spend a day at the airport showing her photo to every cabdriver we could find. One guy said he thought he recognized her and had taken her to the Hilton, which seems to be the best hotel in Podgorica and the one that rich tourists tend to use. We spent the next day hanging around the hotel and spotted her when she came out to go to lunch. She dyed her hair blond but didn't do anything else to change her appearance. After lunch she bought a pair of high heels that Dana said would cost nine hundred bucks in Boston."

"Who's Dana?"

"My partner. The next morning, she met with a real estate agent and they drove out to a house—I guess you'd call it a villa—that has a view of the Adriatic. It looks like she's shopping for a home."

"Hey, this is great news," DeMarco said.

"You haven't heard the bad news yet."

"What's the bad news?"

"Today she had lunch with a greasy-haired little guy who arrived in a Lincoln Town Car driven by an armed chauffeur. He reminded me of that old actor Peter Lorre. Anyway, Erin cheek-kissed him when he arrived, had a long lunch with him, which included two bottles of wine, and before the guy left she handed him an envelope. I had Dana follow the guy."

"Okay. So who is he?"

Tommy said, "All law enforcement in Montenego is under an outfit called the Police Administration, which is under their Ministry of Interior but operates independently. You know, sort of the way the Department of Justice is supposed to operate independently of the White House. The Police Administration is run by a police director, who is currently a guy named Milo Marković. Milo was the one Erin had lunch with. You see what this could mean?"

"Yeah," DeMarco said

But Tommy explained anyway. "If any foreign law enforcement agency, like the FBI or Interpol, is trying to locate Erin in Montenegro, Milo would know and would be able to warn her. Maybe more important, since Montenegro has no extradition treaty with the United States, Milo is also in a position to make sure Erin is never extradited as long as she keeps bribing him and whoever else she has to bribe."

"I realize that," DeMarco said.

"So what do you want me and Dana to do?"

"I don't know. But I'm coming to Montenegro. Just don't lose her before I get there."

———◆◆◆———

DeMarco called Mahoney's office, didn't bother to ask to talk to Mahoney, but told Mavis, "If Mahoney is looking for me, tell him I'll be in Europe."

"Europe? Are you taking a vacation?"

"No. I'm going there to catch the woman who tried to kill Cassie Russell. If he cares, tell him to call me."

⬥

Epstein called his boss.

"He's flying to Montenegro, wherever the hell that is," Epstein said. "His flight leaves in an hour."

Mike Kelly thought about the problem for five minutes. He Googled DeMarco, found an article that contained his picture, and pasted the link into a text message. He was surprised when he saw that the article containing the photo said DeMarco had been accused of murdering some congressman. What the hell was that all about? He'd read the article later but wondered if DeMarco was more than some politician's flunky, maybe a guy not a whole lot different than his old man.

Mike started to check his phone to see what time it was in Belfast, then realized he didn't give a shit what time it was. His call was answered by a man named Sean Murphy. Murphy was old-time IRA and had spent more than half his life in prison. Mike had supplied Murphy with a few automatic weapons back in the day when the IRA was running around tossing bombs and shooting people. Mike had provided the weapons, by the way, because Murphy paid him to do so and not because Mike gave a hoot about Ireland's never-ending pissing contest with the British. Now Sean, who was as old as Mike, was simply a thief and survived mostly on welfare, or whatever the Irish called welfare. But Sean knew some hard boys, boys who wouldn't have a problem doing what Mike wanted. He told Sean how much he'd pay, then texted him the article with DeMarco's photo.

"The main thing is, you don't have time to fuck around here," Mike said to Sean. "Your guys gotta beat him to Montenegro and be there when his plane lands."

45

It was an eighteen-hour flight from Boston to Podgorica, Montenegro, that stopped in Toronto and Vienna along the way. By the time DeMarco got there it was three p.m. local time but all he wanted to do was sleep.

He was met at the airport by a woman with short dark hair and smart brown eyes. She was short, maybe five-two, and muscular and DeMarco thought she had the build of a onetime gymnast. She was wearing skin-tight jeans and had enough muscles in her thighs to crack walnuts. She introduced herself as Dana Atkins, Tommy Hewlett's partner, and said that Tommy was currently following Erin Kelly. Dana drove DeMarco to a hotel called the CentreVille in downtown Podgorica. DeMarco was too travel whipped to care where he was going. Dana handed him a key card, DeMarco staggered to his room, and he collapsed on the bed without undressing.

The next morning DeMarco learned that the CentreVille was a modern hotel, as nice as you'd find in any European city. It was constructed mostly out of glass and the shape of the building reminded DeMarco of an old-fashioned steam locomotive. From his room he had a view of some mountain range; which one he didn't know. He met Tommy and

Dana in the hotel dining room for breakfast. After they'd all ordered coffee, Tommy said, "We got a plan here?"

"Yeah," DeMarco said. He'd figured out what he was going to do about Erin on the flight to Montenegro. Coming up with the plan had been simple. Executing it was going to be hard.

DeMarco said, "Let me ask you about Nora Thurston. How far is she willing to go for a client?"

"I don't know what you mean," Tommy said.

"Well, would she be willing to bend the law a bit?" Before Tommy or Dana could answer, DeMarco said, "Like when you got the information about Erin's cell phone location and her credit cards. That couldn't have been totally legal."

"It was absolutely legal," Tommy said. "Law enforcement would have needed a warrant to get that info but Thurston Security isn't law enforcement. All the information we obtained about Kelly is contained in databases and Thurston Security has contacts in the companies who maintain the databases. So Thurston didn't break any laws by asking for the information and I'm not even sure the companies who gave it to her broke any laws because they're allowed to collect the information in the first place."

"Huh," DeMarco said. That wasn't what he'd wanted to hear.

Tommy said, "Nora Thurston's a businesswoman and she wants to be successful, but she's got lines she won't cross. If you're a criminal she won't work for you. If you're a creep-stalker trying to find an old girlfriend she won't take you on. On the other hand, if she thinks the client's doing the right thing, like trying to catch a murderer, she's willing to do whatever it takes provided it doesn't put her company in any serious legal jeopardy. So I guess you could say she's willing to be flexible but there are limits."

"Well, let me tell you what I've got in mind for Erin Kelly and you tell me if you think it exceeds her limits."

When DeMarco finished explaining his plan, Tommy looked over at Dana and said, "I think I should call Nora."

"No shit," Dana said.

While waiting to hear what Nora Thurston had to say, Dana and DeMarco had breakfast.

DeMarco was surprised to learn that he'd been right about Dana: she had been a gymnast when she was young but hadn't had the talent to rise to the Olympic level. Or as Dana put it: "Fuckin' balance beam almost killed me. It's a good thing I've never wanted kids." After high school, she spent four years in the army, which included time in Afghanistan, then later hired on with the Boston Police Department. She decided after a couple of years that she didn't like being a cop. "The BPD is run by a bunch of sexist pigs and I figured I'd be riding around in a patrol car until I was fifty." Fortunately, she had the good luck to meet Nora Thurston. When army veteran Nora learned Dana was an ex-army MP, she offered her a job. Dana was now making almost twice as much as she'd made standing outside TD Garden, freezing her ass off, providing traffic control for Celtics games.

Tommy returned to the table; he'd been gone for half an hour.

Tommy said, "Nora said we could help you. If all Erin had done was steal the money, she probably wouldn't, but since she tried to have a kid killed we'll go along. But she also said to tell you that, if anything goes wrong, you're the guy who's going to take the fall, not me or Dana or Thurston Security."

"That's good enough for me," DeMarco said. "Now we got a bunch of logistics to work out"—then he explained what he meant.

Tommy said, "The home office can help us with some of that. I'll line things up here on the Montenegro end."

"And I need to get one other person over here to help," DeMarco said. "Until everything's in place you guys need to keep tabs on Erin. You don't need to follow her twenty-four seven. When it looks like she's in bed for the night you can knock off, but we need to make sure she doesn't split and we lose her."

"We won't lose her," Tommy said.

Dana glanced at her watch and said, "I better get going. If she sticks to her routine, she'll be eating breakfast at her hotel in about an hour. It's a good thing she's not an early riser. While I'm watching her, Tommy can talk to the guys in Boston about the, uh, logistics."

As Dana was leaving the hotel, she noticed a man sitting in the lobby, near the door to the dining room. He had receding dark hair and two days' worth of heavy beard. He was wearing a navy blue peacoat, faded blue jeans, and worn work boots. He seemed out of place in the upscale hotel but she'd learned a long time ago that rich people often didn't dress like they were rich, that they sometimes took a perverse pleasure in dressing down. The thing was, she thought she'd seen the guy before but couldn't remember where.

Oh, well. It would come to her eventually. It always did, provided she didn't try to force her brain to remember.

———◆———

Colin O'Brien was hoping he and Pat could finish the job as soon as possible. He'd never felt comfortable anywhere but Ireland. He'd been to mainland Europe several times—France three or four times, Germany twice, Amsterdam half a dozen times, also England, which was definitely a foreign country—and he'd always felt out of place. He didn't like being around people who weren't Irish. He didn't like the food and he didn't like the beer they served in their pubs. Then there was the job itself. He didn't know how the cops in a place like this would respond or what the penalties might be if he and Pat were caught. If he wasn't being paid so much he never would have agreed to do it. He just wished this fuckin' guy DeMarco would do what he was supposed to do quickly so he could get back home.

When Erin came down to breakfast, Dana was in the lobby of Erin's hotel, pretending to read a newspaper. Dana's back was to the elevator but she was able to see Erin using one of the mirrors in the lobby.

Erin took her time eating, looking at an iPad as she did, then went back up to her room, most likely to brush her teeth or touch up her makeup before heading out for the day. Dana wondered what would be on Erin's agenda today. More shopping? A spa? Certainly, lunch at someplace Dana wouldn't have been able to afford if the client wasn't picking up the bill.

Speaking of the client, she thought DeMarco was an interesting sort of guy. She'd been told he worked for John Mahoney but he certainly didn't come across as some slick, high-powered political operator. He was easygoing and more inclined to talk about sports than politics. On the other hand, when it came to getting Erin Kelly, it was apparent that he was willing to do whatever it took—which Dana liked. A woman who would attempt to kill a young girl deserved to be in a cage and she was going to help DeMarco in any way she could.

Ah, there she was. Dana had to admit the woman looked good: hair nicely styled, skin glowing, wearing trendy, pricey clothes. Today she had on a leather trench coat that Dana bet had cost a grand. Dana was twenty paces behind her as she left the hotel and jumped into a waiting cab.

Dana got into her rental car and followed Erin's cab to the real estate agent that Erin had visited before. Erin was inside the agent's office for

an hour, then the real estate agent—an overweight woman with earrings the size of Hula-Hoops—came out with Erin and they got into
the agent's car. Half an hour later they were at the seaside villa that
Erin had previously looked at. Dana figured she must be getting serious
about buying the place.

46

———◆———

Erin walked through the house, trying to imagine what it would look like once she'd decorated it with the appropriate furniture. She *loved* the exterior of the place. It was built from stone and had a red tile roof and red shutters on the windows. It looked at least a hundred years old because it was. But the previous owner had modernized it; the electrical system and the plumbing were only a decade old. The kitchen appliances would _do_ until she had time to replace them. The bathrooms were functional, although renovating the master bathroom would be a priority; the tiles in the shower were ghastly. What didn't need to be changed were the old hardwood floors, the exposed ceiling beams, the fireplaces—there were two of those—and a flagstone patio with an eye-popping view of the sea.

She'd been pleasantly surprised by Montenegro. No, *pleasant* wasn't the right word. She'd been *delighted*. She selected the country based solely on its extradition rules and the fact that it was European as opposed to African, Asian, or Arabic. She'd been afraid, however, that Montenegro would be some awful, third world backwater without the luxury or appeal of major European countries. She was thrilled to be proven wrong. Podgorica wasn't Paris, but it was certainly more cosmopolitan than about half the towns in the flyover country of the American Midwest.

The first week she'd spent primarily replacing her wardrobe and was again thrilled to discover Podgorica had several delightful little boutiques where she could purchase designer clothes and have them tailored. As for the country itself, she was impressed by its rugged mountains and lovely beaches, although so far she hadn't had time to go sightseeing. After she was settled into her new home she'd go exploring.

The most important thing she did the first week, however, wasn't shopping. It was safeguarding her status as a permanent resident. She did this in part by having dinner with a man named Teddy Parker, a doddering wreck of a man who'd been living in Montenegro for ten years. Teddy had come to Montenegro after fleeing Arizona with twenty million dollars he'd stolen from senior citizens who'd made the mistake of putting their faith in him. Erin's research had shown that the United States government had tried diligently for three or four years to have Teddy extradited but had not succeeded, and by now pretty much had given up on ever getting him unless he made the mistake of leaving the country. Erin wanted to know firsthand what Teddy had done to survive.

Teddy was now seventy-five but looked closer to a hundred and five. Among his many maladies, he had cirrhosis of the liver and his kidneys had failed and he was now getting dialysis treatments three times a week. Having dinner with him had been an excruciating experience as all the man did was whine about his health and how the Montenegrin government was bleeding him dry. But eventually Erin got from him the name of the man she needed to bribe and also learned it would be to her benefit to become a Montenegrin citizen. Money, of course, would expedite the citizenship process.

Her next dinner was with Milo Marković, director of the Police Administration, and she was frankly surprised at how easy it had been to come to an arrangement with him. He had done this sort of thing before with several other people; Teddy wasn't the only American criminal he'd helped. And Milo was as expensive as Teddy had said he would be, but fortunately her pockets were much deeper than Teddy's. If Milo got too greedy . . . Well, she'd cross that bridge when she came to it.

She stepped out onto the balcony of her new home, took in the view of the blue Adriatic, stopping a moment to think about what she'd accomplished. But she wasn't really surprised. When Erin Kelly set her mind to doing something she didn't fail. Like skiing. She didn't like to ski. She wasn't an outdoorsy sort of person, nor particularly athletic. She didn't like the cold, the windburn on her cheeks, and clumping around in ski boots. Nonetheless, she took lessons, quickly advanced to the intermediate level, and fearlessly plunged down mountain slopes. She did this because what she did enjoy were the form-fitting ski outfits that flattered her figure, soaking nude in a hot tub surrounded by snow, and, more than anything else, mingling with the Aspen jet set. It had just been a matter of deciding to become a skier and, once she'd decided, she did it well.

It was the same thing when she'd decided that Connor Russell had to go. She rented a plane identical to his but instead of flying it she spent two hours studying the engine while referring to a technical manual. She bought a drill, three bits of the appropriate size, a tube of plumber's putty, some red mechanic's rags, a vice she could clamp to her kitchen counter, a can of engine oil, and some tubing the exact size and composition as a particular oil line in Connor's plane. She then practiced in her kitchen until she was satisfied she could drill the hole precisely and without breaking the bit. When she'd arrived at the airstrip near Tupper Lake that night, she looked around to make sure she was alone, then acted quickly and decisively. She hadn't hesitated for an instant. She drilled the hole and applied a thin layer of black plumber's putty over it. The putty wouldn't harden completely as she hadn't mixed in the required amount of hardening agent, and it was barely noticeable on the oil line; it looked like a smudge of grease. She added oil to the engine to replace the amount that had drained out when she drilled the hole, then wiped down the engine to make sure no oil was visible.

And all this was done in the dark, using only a small flashlight that was magnetized so she could attach it to the engine while she worked. The job took less than thirty minutes.

Her planned escape to Montenegro had been executed with the same skill and precision. It also occurred to her that she was actually glad she'd been forced to steal the hundred million and flee to Montenegro. If her plan to kill Cassie Russell had succeeded, she would have continued to nibble pieces off the Russell trust and would have had a comfortable life, but she never would have been a person of significance in Boston. People would continue to see her as a competent professional, but still the hired help, and she never would have attained the status that came with enormous, inherited wealth. In Montenegro that would change. With money at her disposal, she would soon be on the local A list. People of stature—European royalty, Russian oligarchs, Greek shipping magnates—would invite her to their dinner parties and for cruises on their yachts. A yacht. She wondered what a small one would cost, say a sixty-footer with a competent crew. Certainly, she should be able get one for a couple of million.

Ah, life was good. She'd found a lovely home. After she'd finished decorating it, and when Podgorica began to bore her, and after her flight from the United States had ceased to be a priority for U.S. law enforcement, she'd travel around Europe provided she could find a way to do so safely and without the police in some other country arresting her. Also in the future might be a lover, some handsome Montenegrin a few years her junior, maybe one with the skills to pilot the yacht she might buy. An attractive woman with money would have no problem finding suitable companionship. And maybe she'd take up a hobby, like cooking. She'd never really cooked before but maybe it was time to learn; she'd hire a cute local chef to teach her. But first things first: she needed to go furniture shopping and find a contractor to redo the master bathroom in her new home.

47

DeMarco called Maggie Dolan. "I need a doctor," he said.

"So why are you calling me? If you're sick go to the emergency room."

"I don't need a doctor for me. I need one for this thing I'm doing in Europe."

"I still don't see why you're calling me," Maggie said.

"I'm calling you because you know everyone in Boston. Anyway, I need a doctor who isn't a stickler for the rules. A guy who's maybe hurting for money and would be willing to take some risks. And by the way, he doesn't have to have a current medical license, he just needs to be competent."

"So you're looking for a crooked, defrocked physician?"

"Well, I guess that's one way to put it."

"Give me a couple of hours," Maggie said.

Having nothing better to do as Tommy, Dana, and Maggie were doing all the work, DeMarco spent the next two hours walking around

Podgorica, playing tourist. The day was overcast, but the temperature was about sixty—thirty degrees warmer than it had been in Boston when he left. He strolled through Avanturistički Park and briefly along the Morača River. He was reading a sign in front of a church called the Church of Saint Great-Martyr George and Saint Neomartyrs of Momisici—curious as to who Great-Martyr George and Saint Neo-martyrs had been—when his phone rang. It was Maggie Dolan.

"Okay," Maggie said, "I got you a guy. His name is Adrian Eastwood. He lost his license three years ago for Medicaid fraud and he's in hock up to ears because of how much he had to pay his lawyers to keep from going to jail."

"Perfect," DeMarco said.

"You got a pen? I'll give you his phone number."

"No, I want you to talk to him."

"Me? I don't even know what you want him to do."

"You tell him that I'll pay him ten grand just to fly to Montenegro to talk to me. And tell him if he agrees to do the job I want him to do, I'll pay him fifty grand. But he'll get the ten even if he doesn't agree to do it."

"Why don't you talk to him?"

"Because I don't want to take the chance of him telling me no over the phone. I want to put him in a position of having to walk away from fifty thousand bucks, and if he's as broke as you say he is he'll have a hard time doing that. You can also tell him that what I'll be asking him to do isn't illegal, just a bit, uh, unorthodox."

That was probably a lie.

"I want him in Montenegro tomorrow," DeMarco said.

DeMarco never noticed the two men trailing along behind him, one of them wearing a navy blue peacoat.

At eight p.m. DeMarco was sitting in the hotel bar having a vodka martini, the martini just as good in Podgorica as the ones he'd been served in Boston. The bartender, however, was nowhere near as appealing as Shannon, making DeMarco wonder how things were going with her agent in New York selling her novel. Or maybe she was in California, chatting with her new pal Reese Witherspoon.

His phone rang. It was Dana.

DeMarco said, "Is Erin in for the night?"

"Yeah, she had dinner then headed up to her room. She spent the morning with a real estate agent looking at a place that I think she's about to buy. Or maybe she's already bought it. This afternoon, she spent her time looking at furniture and appliances. Anyway, forget about her. I think we could have a problem."

"What are you talking about?"

"I saw a guy this morning sitting in the lobby wearing a blue peacoat. Right now that same guy is outside the hotel, on a bench near the entrance, smoking a cigarette. I thought I'd seen him before but I couldn't remember where until I saw him again tonight smoking. He was outside baggage claim when I came to pick you up at the airport. He had the same coat on."

"Huh, what do you think—"

"I want you to go for a walk," Dana said. "A long walk. I want to see if this guy follows you. I wish I had a gun but I guess my baton will have to do."

"Your baton?"

"Combat baton," Dana said. "It looks sort of like a flashlight but with a flick of my wrist I'm holding two feet of lethal steel."

DeMarco went up to his room, grabbed a jacket, then headed out for a stroll. He meandered up and down the streets near the hotel, staying mostly in areas that were well lit and filled with people. An hour later he returned to the hotel, went to the bar, and ordered a nightcap. Dana called him ten minutes later.

"You're being followed," she said. "And there's two of them. The guy in the peacoat and another one wearing a jean jacket. You got any idea who they could be?"

"No."

"Tommy and I are going to hang around outside the hotel and see where they go. I'm guessing that after they think you've gone to bed they'll head back to wherever they're staying. I'll talk to you in the morning. In the meantime, go think about why someone would be following you."

48

DeMarco took a seat in the dining room, ordered coffee, and ten minutes later Dana joined him.

Dana said, "Their names are Colin O'Brien and Patrick Sullivan. They're staying at a cheap place three blocks from here, sharing a room."

"How'd you get their names?"

"By bribing the night manager. Anyway, based on their passports, they're Irish. This morning I got up early and called back to Boston to see if I could get any information on them. Thurston Security works with an outfit in the UK and I figured the UK company could get what we needed. It turns out that Pat and Colin have spent most of their lives in prison. Possession of illegal weapons, assault, extortion, theft, that sort of thing. And speaking of illegal weapons, Pat's carrying a gun. I saw it last night when his jacket rode up over the back of his pants. I'm guessing if Pat has one, Colin might too. So you got any idea why a couple of Irish gunsels with criminal records could be following you?"

DeMarco rubbed his chin for a moment, then said, "Maybe. When you said they were Irish, the first thought that popped into my head was Mike Kelly, Erin Kelly's mobster uncle. Mike knows that his niece got away with a hundred million bucks and my guess is that he wants a piece of that, or maybe all of it."

"So why is Mike having these guys follow you? And how would he know you're in Montenegro?"

DeMarco said, "I made the mistake of going to see Mike. I thought he might know where Erin was and I offered him a get-out-of-jail-free card if he'd tell me. I also told him that I was hunting for her. I don't know how he found out I flew to Montenegro, but he's a smart guy with a lot of connections. And if you saw Colin and Pat at the airport, that means they somehow managed to get to Montenegro before I did. So my guess is that Mike's got some sort of Irish connection and he hired these two guys hoping I'd lead them to Erin."

"Then what?" Dana said.

"I don't know. Maybe they'll lean on her in some way to get her money. Or maybe they'll snatch her and Mike leans on her himself. Or maybe Mike just blackmails her, threatening to tell the cops where she is unless she pays him. I don't know for sure, but I doubt Mike Kelly is having me followed to protect his niece. He just doesn't seem like that kind of guy."

"Well, one thing you said makes sense. If it was you they were after, they've had plenty of opportunities to get you, like last night when you went for a walk. So getting you isn't their objective. But the fact that they're packing heat is a bit nerve-wracking, especially since none of us are armed. I suppose I could look into getting a gun—I have no idea what the gun laws are here—or maybe there's some sort of black market where I could buy one."

"No, no guns," DeMarco said. "We're not going to shoot anyone, and especially not in a place where we don't have a clue how the legal system works. But we have to come up with a way to get rid of Pat and Colin before we make our run at Erin."

DeMarco was thinking that it was a good thing he hadn't attempted to see Erin since he'd been in Montenegro. He hadn't approached her because she knew what he looked like and he hadn't wanted to take the chance of her spotting him. He suspected, however, that if Pat and Colin were following him they'd probably noticed that Dana and Tommy were working with him.

"How do we get rid of them?" Dana said.

"I don't know yet. But I've got a doctor flying in from the United States today."

"A doctor?"

"Yeah. He'll be getting in about three, on the same flight I took. I don't want these guys to see me with him. So tell Tommy to stick with Erin and you meet the doctor at the airport. Make sure you're not followed. His name is Adrian Eastwood. He's from Boston. You can probably Google him to get a photo. Look under 'Medicaid fraud.'"

"Medicaid fraud? What kind of doctor—"

"Anyway, pick him up at the airport, check him into the hotel, and tell him I'll meet him later in his room. While you're doing that, I'm going to go for a walkabout to keep the Irish thugs away from the hotel."

"I hope they don't try to shoot you," Dana said.

"Me, too," DeMarco said.

DeMarco talked to the hotel concierge about a place to go sightseeing.

The concierge recommended the Ostrog Monastery, a seventeenth-century monastery that was built into the side of a cliff and contained ancient frescoes and altars inside of caves. According to the concierge, the monastery was the most popular tourist attraction in the Balkans and about an hour from Podgorica. DeMarco decided to take a tour bus there. He figured a bus filled with tourists would be safer than driving alone in a car where Pat and Colin might decide to run the car off the road.

He filed off the bus with the rest of the tourists and followed the tour guide—a woman who appeared to be fluent in at least six languages—and half listened as she discussed the history of the monastery. At one point he stepped outside and took in the view, a fertile valley running along the Zeta River. He looked around casually and noticed an unshaven man in a blue peacoat smoking a cigarette and looking everywhere but at DeMarco.

Fuckin' Mike Kelly. He had to come up with a way to ditch his Irishmen.

49

Mike Kelly was sitting in his Boston town house, watching TV, some show that was supposed to be a comedy, where the father's white, the mother's black, the son is gay, and the daughter has purple hair and what looked like a safety pin jammed through her nose. There was no doubt about it, the country was going to hell in a handbasket. One of his phones rang. The caller ID showed an overseas number. Only one guy it could be.

Mike said hello and the caller said, "This is one of Murphy's guys, one of the guys he sent to Montenegro. I called Murphy and he told me I should call you and tell you what's going on."

The guy's accent was thicker than Guinness beer and Mike could barely understand him.

"Why?" Mike asked. "If DeMarco has led you to Erin, I already told Murphy what you should do."

"He hasn't led us to her. I'm calling because I thought you should know that all this fuckin' guy has done since he got here is act like a tourist. He visits old churches and walks around the city."

"That doesn't make any sense," Mike said.

"Well, maybe it doesn't make sense, but that's what he's been doing. There's one other thing. DeMarco seems to be working with a couple here, an old guy and a young gal. The gal picked DeMarco up at the airport when he arrived, and the next day he had breakfast with them. But I don't know who they are and what their connection is to whatever DeMarco's doing. They don't hang around with him all day."

"Could they be cops?" Mike asked.

"I don't know. They're not dressed in uniforms. They just look like, I don't know, like ordinary people."

Mike wondered if the couple might be Interpol undercovers or local Montenegrin cops DeMarco had enlisted in the hunt for Erin. Or maybe they were Montenegrin PIs.

"Have you tried following this couple?"

"No. We were told to stick with DeMarco, but if you want we could snatch DeMarco and beat out of him whatever the fuck he's doing here. The other night he went for a walk by himself and we could have gotten him then. I mean, it's up to you but so far we're just wasting our time."

The idea of having the Irishmen beat the crap out of DeMarco was appealing. The problem was he didn't know if DeMarco had already located Erin or if he was still looking for her. But if he had located her, why would he be walking around visiting churches? And who was this couple and what were they doing with DeMarco? He bet they were locals that DeMarco had hired to find Erin, and DeMarco, the lazy fuck, was letting them do all the work.

He told Colin, "Stick with DeMarco for a couple more days. If he doesn't lead you to Erin soon, then maybe I'll let you have a little chat with him."

After he hung up on the Irishman, he tried to get back to watching the so-called comedy but his brain was still engaged with DeMarco—and the Irishmen he didn't know and didn't trust. He mulled the problem over for a bit and then picked up his phone again.

The Jew answered and Mike said, "Epstein, I want you to get your ass over to Montenegro."

Back at the CentreVille, after the monastery tour, DeMarco had dinner then went to meet his personal physician.

Adrian Eastwood turned out to be in his sixties, tall, thin, dyed dark hair, a face marked with old acne scars. DeMarco instantly disliked the guy. Maybe it was because he knew Eastwood was a thief, but there was just something greasy about him. On the other hand, if he had been an upstanding citizen he wouldn't have been the right man for the job.

DeMarco explained what Eastwood would have to do.

His reaction was: "Oh, I don't think I'd feel comfortable doing that. I mean, what if—"

"Doctor, did you think I was going to pay you fifty thousand dollars to take someone's blood pressure?"

"Well, no, but—"

"The main thing you have to do is get me what I need. I'll be the one taking the risk."

"I understand that but—"

"Fine," DeMarco said. "You can use part of the ten grand I already paid you to fly back to Boston and I'll find somebody else. I don't have the time to waste romancing you."

DeMarco started toward the door, knowing there was no way in hell Eastwood was going to turn him down. The man stank of desperation.

"No, I'll do it. As long as you promise no one will be hurt."

"I promise," DeMarco said. "Now how long will it take you to get what I need?"

"I'm not sure. I don't have any connections here. I need to call a few people and do some research."

"So get going. I want this done as fast as possible, and if you can't get what I want in the next couple of days I'll need to come up with a plan

B. And if plan B doesn't include you, you'll be flying home fifty grand poorer."

The next day DeMarco checked that everyone was doing what they were supposed to do: Eastwood getting the required supplies, Dana following Erin, and Tommy talking to the home office in Boston and people in Podgorica to make sure the logistical aspects of the operation were coming together. Satisfied that his small team was running like a finely tuned Montenegrin watch, DeMarco again decided to go sightseeing to keep Pat and Colin occupied. And while he was sightseeing he'd think some more about a way to pry them off his back.

He decided to take a tour recommended by the concierge to a town called Kotor, about an hour and half from Podgorica. On the tour bus, he spotted a man and his wife who'd also been on the Ostrog Monastery tour. He sat down next to them and learned they were from Nebraska. The man was in remission from cancer and was now scratching things off his bucket list, one of those being a long trip to Europe. He admitted that after four weeks on the road he'd rather be back in Omaha watching football in his den.

As for the city of Kotor, it had been around since about the fifth century. It was located on a secluded bay, surrounded by mountains and overhanging limestone cliffs. Fortified structures had been built there by the Romans, then the town was occupied over the years by the Turks, the Germans, the French, the Russians, and the British—apparently every country in Europe that had an army. DeMarco walked the city's narrow cobblestone streets, looking at old houses and even older churches, stopping periodically for a beer at different sidewalk cafés, all the time keeping an eye out for the Irishmen. Both guys were easy to spot, particularly the one in the blue peacoat. DeMarco hoped they were having a miserable time.

DeMarco met with his gang—he'd never had his own gang before—in his hotel room at ten p.m. Erin Kelly was back in her hotel room and appeared to be in for the night.

"So. Where do we stand?" DeMarco said.

The doctor said, "I can get what you need. I talked to a doctor I know in Germany and he referred me to an Albanian who lives here. The Albanian—"

"I don't need the details. When can you get it?"

"Tomorrow, but it will cost a thousand U.S. dollars."

"Not a problem," DeMarco said—the man dipping into Cassie Russell's trust. He also suspected that Eastwood was going to keep part of the thousand as a finder's fee.

"What about you, Tommy?" DeMarco asked.

"Everything's ready to go. All I need is twenty-four hours' notice."

"Good. And is Erin still sticking to her schedule when it comes to breakfast?" DeMarco asked Dana.

"Yep," Dana said. "Nine a.m. every morning in the hotel dining room, regular as a Rolex."

DeMarco nodded, then feeling like General Patton he said, "Guys, we're going after her the day after tomorrow. So, Doc, you get what you need first thing tomorrow but before that I have another little job for you. Tommy, you spend the day double-checking that everything's in place because we can't afford any kind of hitch once we start the . . . the operation. And while you're doing that, Dana and I are going to deal with the Irishmen."

"What am I supposed to do?" Dana said.

"Watch my back," DeMarco said.

50

Epstein was sitting in the lobby of DeMarco's hotel, having a cup of coffee, pretending to read a magazine. The Irishmen were waiting in their car outside the hotel.

Epstein had met with Colin and Pat the night before. Except for their accents, the two men weren't much different than the hoods Mike Kelly employed in Boston: average intelligence, if only barely, but hard boys who wouldn't have a problem stomping folks and killing them if it came to that.

Epstein had decided that he'd let the Irishmen continue to follow DeMarco—there was no point in *three* guys following him—and while they were doing that, he'd see if he could figure out who this man and woman were that were working with DeMarco.

At eight, DeMarco came down to breakfast. A few minutes later a stocky young gal and an older white guy joined DeMarco. The woman reminded Epstein of a cheerleader he'd known in high school, this bouncy way she walked. As for the man, he had the swagger you develop when you carry a badge and he was sure the old guy was a cop or had been at one time. Epstein had encountered a lot of cops and he knew one when he saw one.

DeMarco had a quick breakfast with Tommy and Dana. He could tell Dana was excited about his plan for dealing with the Irishmen and Tommy was disappointed that he wouldn't have an active role. While they were eating DeMarco reiterated to Tommy that he had the most important job: making sure that everything would come together without a hitch when they made their move on Erin.

Following breakfast, DeMarco had the hotel concierge set up a rental car for him, one with a navigation system. While waiting for the car to arrive he got a couple of maps from the front desk, then did some research online and made a few calls.

Epstein couldn't figure out what was going on. DeMarco was sitting in one of the lobby chairs looking at maps, pecking on a laptop, making a bunch of phone calls. At one point the concierge walked up to DeMarco and handed him a set of keys. The cheerleader was just sitting in the restaurant drinking coffee, reading a day-old copy of the *New York Times*, looking bored. The old cop was sitting in the lobby with DeMarco but in a chair several feet away, also making phone calls. What the hell were these people doing? If they were hunting for Mike's niece they were certainly taking their time about it.

Finally, DeMarco got up, signaled to the cheerleader, and they left the hotel together. Epstein followed them out of the hotel and watched as they got into two different cars and drove off, the woman following DeMarco. Epstein glanced across the street and saw the Irishmen start their car and join the caravan. Epstein walked back into the hotel. He'd stick with the old cop and see where he led him.

———◆◆◆———

Dana stayed behind DeMarco for about two blocks, checking her rear-view mirror to make sure the Irishmen were following. The next corner she came to, she made an abrupt right-hand turn, sped down a short block, and made another right. She checked the rearview mirror again. No Irishmen. They'd stuck with DeMarco as she'd expected.

Dana caught up with the Irishmen ten minutes later. She knew where DeMarco was headed so this was easy to do. She liked DeMarco's plan but figured it was going to take some luck—and maybe a bit of stupidity on the part of the Irishmen—to make it work.

———◆◆◆———

DeMarco's first stop was a café six blocks from the hotel, a café that had large picture windows facing the street. He parked his car but didn't look around to see if the Irishmen were with him. All he could do was hope they were.

He went inside the café, took a seat near a window, and ordered a cup of coffee. While drinking the coffee, he glanced several times at his watch, trying to give the impression of a man waiting impatiently. Fifteen minutes later Adrian Eastwood—whom the Irishmen had never seen—stepped inside the café, carrying a briefcase, wearing a trench coat, a trilby hat, and sunglasses. DeMarco thought the sunglasses were a little over the top, particularly as the day was overcast. Eastwood walked over to DeMarco's table, sat down, opened the briefcase, and handed DeMarco a buff-colored manila envelope. DeMarco pulled several sheets of blank paper from the envelope and pretended to study them. While doing that, using his peripheral vision, he spotted Blue Peacoat on the other side of the street, looking toward the café as he walked by.

He spent ten minutes in the café with Eastwood pretending to go over the documents Eastwood had given him. While doing so, he asked the doctor where he'd gone to medical school and learned he'd attended Stanford. That was good, DeMarco figured. The guy might be a thief but he probably wasn't a total quack.

DeMarco left the restaurant, taking the envelope with him, and drove to the American embassy in Podgorica. The embassy was on a street named John Jackson Street, making DeMarco wonder who John Jackson could be. The building was a white two-story structure with Doric columns and a red tile roof, which was fairly common in the region. Surrounding the embassy was an eight-foot spiked iron fence. To enter the embassy, DeMarco had to pass through a booth guarded by a couple of serious-looking young Marines. DeMarco knew that the embassy had been attacked by a Serbian suicide bomber in February 2018, and he assumed the rifles the soldiers carried weren't for ceremonial purposes.

Once inside the embassy, he joined a small queue in front of an information desk. Most of the people in the line were Montenegrin. DeMarco was in no rush. His plan was to spend half an hour in the embassy whether he needed to or not. Once he reached the head of the line, he explained that all he wanted to know was what he should do if he lost his passport and who he should call if he was arrested. He wasn't worried about losing his passport; being arrested, however, was a possibility.

His next stop was a police station located off Bulevar Mihaila Lalića. As he was driving he called Dana. "Are they behind me?"

"Yep," she said.

Inside the police station, DeMarco quickly found an officer who spoke English; he'd noticed that finding English speakers hadn't been a problem in Montenegro at all, English being the language of commerce and tourism. He asked the officer, a pretty woman with a mannish haircut, a few questions about what to do if he should happen to get into a traffic accident in Montenegro. Then he asked the one question he really cared about: the location of police stations near Montenegro's second largest city, Nikšić.

———————◆———————

The burner phone rang while Mike Kelly was talking to the Mexican or Cuban or whatever the hell he was who took care of his house in Naples, Florida. He was telling the guy that he'd be heading down there soon and to make sure the hot tub and the pool were up and running and that the air conditioner wasn't on the fritz like the last time. When the burner rang, however, and he saw it was an overseas call, he said to the caretaker, "Hey, I'll have to call you back."

He answered the burner, saying, "Yeah?"

"This is Murphy's guy," the caller said. "Something's finally happening."

"Say that again." The Mexican in Naples was easier to understand than the Irishman.

"I said, something's finally happenin'."

"What's that?"

"I don't know what he's doing but DeMarco met with a guy this morning and the guy gave him an envelope. After that, he went to the American embassy. Spent about half an hour there. Then he drove to a police station and spent half an hour there. Now he's driving somewhere—I don't know where—but we're behind him. Anyway, he's finally doing somethin'."

"Shut up a minute and let me think," Mike said.

It appeared as if DeMarco had been sitting around Podgorica waiting for information, maybe from the local cops, maybe from a local private investigator, maybe from this couple the Irishmen had seen talking to DeMarco. And most likely the information had to do with Erin. So maybe he goes to the American embassy to learn what it would take to arrest Erin and ship her narrow ass back to the States. Ditto his visit to the Montenegro cops. Mike would be totally screwed if the cops got their hands on Erin before he did. Not only would he not get her money, she might eventually rat him out to the feds.

"Where's Epstein?" Mike asked.

"He's watching one of the people working with DeMarco. He figured me and Pat could handle DeMarco and he'd see if he could find out what these people working for DeMarco are doing."

Huh. Mike would have preferred Epstein covering DeMarco, but there was nothing he could do about that now. "Okay, you stick with him," Mike told Murphy's guy. "Don't you dare fuckin' lose him. And keep me posted. I don't care what time it is, if something happens, call me."

———◆———

Epstein had no idea what the old cop was doing. After he made what had to have been a dozen phone calls from the hotel lobby he finally left, got into a car, and Epstein followed him to a hospital. But he didn't go *into* the hospital. Instead he walked around to the back where a couple of ambulances were parked and spent fifteen minutes bullshitting with one of the ambulance drivers.

Next, he drives back to the hotel and goes and sits in the restaurant, and a few minutes later a skinny guy in his sixties wearing a hat like a short-brimmed fedora joins him. The old cop and the hat guy talked for maybe ten minutes, and at one point the hat guy took a small case out of a pocket—like one for holding eyeglasses—and showed the cop whatever was inside the case. The hat guy finally stands up and walks to the hotel elevators, making Epstein think he could be a hotel guest.

Was the hat guy also part of DeMarco's crew? How many fuckin' people were helping him?

The old cop was on the move again. This time he drove about half an hour to a place where you could see the ocean, the sea, the bay, whatever they called it. He stopped for a minute in front of a house where a couple of guys were moving a mattress into the house, but he took off almost immediately, holding a cell phone to his ear. Epstein looked at the house as he drove past—fancy-looking old house—but didn't see anything but the mattress guys' truck in the driveway.

———◆◆◆———

When Tommy saw the guys moving the mattress into Erin's new house, an awful thought occurred to him: *Could she have checked out of the Hilton?* He called the Hilton and asked the front desk to ring her room. No one answered. He called back to the front desk and asked if Ms. Westover had checked out. Hannah Westover was the name Erin was using in Montenegro. He was told no, which was a huge relief. DeMarco's plan would have gone completely to hell if Erin had decided to move into her new home.

Tommy figured he was done for the day. He'd double-checked, then triple-checked that everything was ready. He might as well go back to his hotel and have lunch, then maybe after lunch just do a little sightseeing. He hadn't had a chance to do any sightseeing since he'd been in Montenegro and figured this might be the last chance he'd get.

He wondered how DeMarco and Dana were doing.

He wished his late wife were with him; she would have enjoyed seeing Podgorica.

———◆◆◆———

Epstein couldn't figure out what the hell was going on. The cop, or whatever he was, has a long lunch, then just goes for a stroll, walking along some river, through a park, and in and out of a bunch of shops that sold tourist shit. Bored, he called the Irishmen.

"What's DeMarco doing?" he asked.

"Beats the shit out of me," Colin said. "Right now he's driving around a town called Nikšić."

51

Nikšić is about forty miles north of Podgorica. DeMarco's first stop there was a real estate agent that he'd found online and had called to make an appointment before leaving Podgorica.

He spent forty-five minutes with the real estate agent, looking at maps and getting the information he needed. The agent was so desperate to make a sale that she followed him out to his car. He assured her he'd be back. He wouldn't.

To kill some time, he drove aimlessly through the city until he spotted a place with outdoor tables where he had a long, slow lunch. After lunch, he walked around and found a shop where he could buy bottled water and some snacks. Now fortified and prepared for a long afternoon, he left Nikšić, driving west on the M6 motorway, until he reached the exit for Slansko Lake. Slansko Lake is one of three man-made lakes built to support the Perućica hydroelectric plant. It's also popular with locals and tourists in the summer for swimming, fishing, and sunbathing. For DeMarco, its chief attraction was not its beauty but its proximity to a police station and how far it was from Podgorica.

He went halfway around the lake—catching sight several times of a maroon sedan behind him—then finally stopped at a spot on the road that looked down onto a small stone house perched on the shore of the lake. The house was almost surrounded by trees. He drove a short way to a place where his car couldn't be seen from the house, parked the car, then walked into some bushes and studied the house through binoculars he'd borrowed from Tommy. There was no sign of any activity in the house but he spent fifteen minutes staring at it, then returned to his car and called Dana.

"Where are they?"

"About a quarter mile from you. You can't see their car because there's a little bend in the road, but they're both standing in the woods watching you."

"Perfect," DeMarco said.

DeMarco sat in his car reading a novel on his Kindle, drinking water, and munching from the bag of popcorn he'd purchased in Nikšić. Every twenty minutes or so, he'd leave the car to stretch his legs while studying the house on the lake shore through his binoculars. One time, he pretended to talk on his phone for ten minutes while watching the house.

Finally, after three long, boring hours, the sun dropped below the horizon and the tree-shrouded house was barely visible in the darkness. Then lights came on in two rooms inside the house—and DeMarco smiled.

He started his car, made a U-turn, and drove back toward the highway that would take him to Nikšić. He drove right past the maroon sedan that had been following him but didn't look directly at it. He figured the Irishmen were either still in the woods or hunched down inside their car.

———— ◆◆◆ ————

Mike's burner phone rang. It was Murphy's guy again.

"He went to see a real estate agent in a town called Nikšić. I guess that's how you say it. Then he drove to this big lake and stopped by this house that's on the shore of the lake. He spent all afternoon watching the place, looking at it through binoculars."

"Was there anyone in the house?"

"I don't know. You can barely see the place. It's got trees all around it. Anyway, about five minutes ago, when it got dark, lights came on in the house and that's when DeMarco left. Right now, I'm guessing he's heading back to Nikšić or Podgorica, but I don't know for sure. I just thought you ought to know he's really interested in this house."

"Where are you right now?" Mike asked.

"We're behind him. Actually, trying to catch up to him."

"Hold on a minute," Mike said. "I need to think."

Could Erin be in the house? Why else would DeMarco have gone there? But why didn't he do something, like call the cops, if she was in there? Could be he wasn't sure she was there. Or maybe when the lights came on and he knew she was home, that's why he left, maybe to go get the cops. Shit, he didn't know what the hell DeMarco was up to. All he knew was that he couldn't let the cops get their hands on his psycho niece.

"Where's Epstein at?" Mike asked.

"Back in Podgorica, I guess. I told you, he was trying to get a handle on what the people working with DeMarco are doing."

"How far is Podgorica from where you are?"

"Over an hour," Colin said.

Shit, he wished Epstein was with the two micks but he couldn't wait for Epstein to drive from Podgorica to meet up with them.

"Okay," Mike said. "I want you to go back to the house and see if she's in there. If she is, take her then call me."

* * *

DeMarco saw the headlights behind him fade into the distance then disappear. He called Dana.

"What are they doing?"

"They were following you, but then they stopped and made a U-turn. I'm guessing they're heading back to the house."

"I know they are. Call the cops. Right now. I have no idea what the response time will be. Hell, I don't know if they'll respond at all."

Dana called 122, the 911 equivalent in Montenegro, then had to wait until a dispatcher who spoke English got on the line. Dana, whispering, trying to sound terrified, said, "There are two men outside my house. They have guns."

"Guns?" the dispatcher said.

"Yes."

"Who are they?"

"I don't know. Help me."

"Where are you now?" the dispatcher asked.

"Hiding in a closet."

"What's your address?"

Dana gave the dispatcher the address of the house.

"Stay where you are," the dispatcher said. "The police are on their way. But I want you to stay on the phone with me. Now, what's your name?"

"Oh, my God!" Dana shrieked—and hung up.

Colin and Pat parked as close to the house on the lake as they could get. They didn't drive right up to the house because they didn't want to alert anyone inside. They got out of their car and approached the house slowly and quietly. There were lights on in two rooms but they couldn't see anyone moving around inside.

"What do you want to do?" Pat asked.

"Let's just knock on the door. If she opens it, we take her."

"Okay, but what if she won't let us in? I mean, if you were a woman alone, would you let us in?"

Colin looked at his companion. "Probably not," he said. "Let's see what kind of door this place has."

They approached the front door, which was solid-looking and made out of wooden planks. Colin tried the doorknob. It didn't turn.

"Gonna be a bitch breaking through that," Pat said.

"Let's see what the back door looks like," Colin said. "Has to be a back door." They walked around the house, and when they reached the side facing the lake they saw a small porch and a back door. As they'd been walking, Colin noticed that the blinds were closed on all the windows.

The back door wasn't as hefty-looking as the front door. Colin again turned the doorknob to see if the door was locked and again it was. He stood for a minute, studying the door, then said, "Go back to the car and get the tire iron."

While waiting for Pat, Colin listened to see if he could hear anyone inside the house but didn't hear a thing. No television or radio playing. He was starting to get the feeling the place was empty and maybe that's why DeMarco had left. But he'd been told to see if she was inside and that's what he was going to do. The woman could be taking a shower or sleeping, but it seemed pretty early for her to be in bed.

Pat returned with the tire iron. Colin shoved the tip of it between the door and the door frame and yanked back hard. He ripped a good chunk of wood out of the frame and the sound of the wood ripping was like a banshee screaming.

"Shit! Gotta get her before she calls the cops," Colin said.

Pat went through the door first, his gun in his hand. The back door opened onto a small kitchen. They rushed through the kitchen and into what appeared to be a living room with a fireplace. In one corner of the room was a standing lamp near a window. There was no other furniture in the room.

"Aw, shit," Colin muttered. They quickly ran through the remainder of the house: two small bedrooms and a bathroom. There were no beds in the bedrooms but in one of them was another standing lamp and Colin noticed the lamp was plugged into a timer.

"Let's get the fuck out of here," Colin said. "I think we've been set up."

They fled out the back door, running now, reached their car, and jumped in. Colin turned the key in the ignition—and the car wouldn't start. "What the fuck!" he screamed. He turned the key again but all he got was a whirring sound, coming from what he guessed was the starter motor. Neither he nor Pat knew a damn thing about cars other than how to drive them fast.

"Are we out of gas?" Pat said.

"Fuck no, we're not out of gas."

"So what do we do?"

Before Colin could answer that question, an SUV came directly at them, blue roof lights blinking. Cops. Two cops got out of the SUV, holding machine guns—and they were pointing the guns at Colin's face and screaming something in a language he didn't understand.

He never should have left Ireland.

Dana called DeMarco. "They got 'em," she said.

"Thank God. I was afraid they'd get away before the cops got there."

"Well, I made sure they weren't able to do that. I sort of fucked up their car."

DeMarco said, "Dana, when this thing's over with, I'm gonna make sure you get a bonus."

DeMarco figured the Irishmen would spend the night in jail, particularly when the Montenegro cops saw they were packing weapons and learned they had records in the UK. At any rate, he was sure they wouldn't be back in Podgorica before nine a.m. tomorrow—and after nine it wouldn't matter.

52

"Did they ever show up?"

"No," Epstein said. "They never came back to their hotel and they're still not answering their phones."

"Well, shit," Mike said.

Last night, after the Irishmen had called him and said that Erin might be hiding in a house near Nikšić, they never called back. He waited a couple of hours, then called them but they didn't answer. He then called Epstein to see if he knew anything but Epstein said he hadn't heard from the Irishmen and now he was saying that they never came back to Podgorica.

"Do you think DeMarco could have wasted them?" Epstein asked.

"I don't know," Mike said. DeMarco had struck him as a hard guy but was he hard enough to kill? Maybe. Like they said, the apple doesn't fall far from the tree.

"What do you want me to do?" Epstein said.

"I don't know. Where are you at now?"

"I'm sittin' in the lobby of DeMarco's hotel. I couldn't figure out anything else to do. Hold on! DeMarco and his whole fuckin' crew just got off the elevator."

"His crew?"

"Yeah, the girl, the guy I followed yesterday, and this skinny old fart. I don't know who he is, but he's one of DeMarco's guys. They are all heading out. They got their game faces on."

"Well, follow them."

"I can't follow all of them."

"Then follow DeMarco. I think this is it, Epstein. I think he's going after Erin. And you can't let him get her. That bitch is worth a hundred million and I want her."

At eight forty-five, DeMarco was sitting in the lobby of the Hilton Podgorica Crna Gora, a copy of the *Wall Street Journal* hiding his face. At exactly nine a.m. Erin Kelly stepped out of an elevator and proceeded to the dining room.

The woman looked terrific, DeMarco thought. You'd never guess she was a criminal on the run from the law. She was wearing a white cashmere sweater, a necklace with a jade pendant, and small earrings inset with what might be emeralds. Her black slacks were form fitting; her shoes had two-inch heels, practical for walking. She was carrying a large leather purse, the strap over one shoulder.

The dining room hostess smiled at her and led her immediately to a table. A moment later, a waiter appeared and poured her a cup of coffee and placed a small glass of orange juice in front of her. The dining room staff clearly knew her preferences. Erin said something to the waiter and he laughed.

Erin pulled an iPad out of her purse and began to study the screen, sipping her coffee as she did. DeMarco waited until she was engrossed in whatever she was reading and approached her from behind. As he was walking toward her, he scanned the patrons in the dining room—there were about ten—and spotted Adrian Eastwood. The doctor was dressed in a suit, a white shirt, and a tie. He looked respectable and professional. His table was only about twenty feet from Erin's.

DeMarco walked up behind Erin and laid a hand on her right shoulder.

Erin said, "Ouch," and spun around to see who was behind her.

When she saw it was DeMarco, she said, "What in the hell are you doing here? And did you stick me with something?" As she said this, she put her left hand on her right shoulder, on the spot where DeMarco had touched her. She examined her fingers looking for blood; there was none.

"Of course not," DeMarco said.

"What are you doing here?" she said. She was angry but not apprehensive. His appearance annoyed her but didn't appear to worry her. The goddamn woman was a hundred percent confident she couldn't be extradited.

DeMarco said, "I'm here to take you back to the United States to be tried for murder, conspiracy to commit murder, and embezzlement. You're going to spend the next thirty years in prison."

"You're not taking me anywhere. You have absolutely no authority here and—"

Erin closed her eyes.

"Is something wrong?" DeMarco said.

Erin opened her eyes and continued. "And if you harass me, I'll call the—"

She closed her eyes again and muttered, "Don't feel right."

She started to stand and DeMarco said, "I wouldn't get up if I were you. You might hurt yourself."

Ignoring DeMarco, she placed her hands on the table to push herself up but then slumped back in her chair—then she fell out of the chair and onto the carpeted floor.

DeMarco quickly knelt beside her. A couple at a nearby table—two middle-aged women—stood up as well. While touching Erin's throat as if he were feeling for a pulse, DeMarco yelled in English, "Is there a doctor here? I need a doctor!"

Adrian Eastwood ran over to him and said, "I'm a doctor. Get out of the way." Adrian knelt down next to Erin, took her pulse, then opened her eyelids to look at her pupils. To DeMarco, he said, "Why are you standing there? Call for an ambulance. I believe she had a stroke."

To the couple who'd stood up, Adrian said, "Get my bag. It's over there." He pointed to the table where he'd been sitting. One of the women rushed over and grabbed Adrian's bag and brought it to him. He opened it and took out a blood pressure cuff and a stethoscope.

Had anyone thought about it, they would have been surprised by how fast the ambulance got there. Less than three minutes after Erin collapsed two medics dressed in white, carrying a stretcher, rushed into the dining room. One of the medics was Tommy Hewlett. They went over to Eastwood, he muttered something to them, and they placed Erin on the stretcher.

"I'll come with you," Eastwood said to the medics and grabbed the satchel containing his medical equipment. DeMarco grabbed Erin's purse, which had been on the chair next to her, and ran after Eastwood saying, "Hey, here's her purse. Her ID's probably in it."

Tommy and the medic carried the stretcher toward the hotel exit, Eastwood beside them, DeMarco following, carrying Erin's purse, a satisfied look in his eyes.

<hr>

Epstein had a front row seat to the whole . . . He didn't know what to call it. Operation?

DeMarco had obviously done something to Erin to make her pass out. Maybe he'd paid the waiter to put a drug in her coffee. Whatever the case, he'd set the whole thing up. The ambulance driver was the one he'd seen the old cop talking to yesterday and the skinny guy was pretending to be a doctor, fooling everyone while they . . . Hell, they *kidnapped* the damn woman in front of a dozen people.

He watched as the old cop and the ambulance driver slid the stretcher into an ambulance parked in front of the hotel. Then the old cop and the phony doctor got into the back with her and the driver got behind the wheel. While that was going on, DeMarco walked over to a car parked a short distance away from the ambulance. The cheerleader was driving the car.

It occurred to Epstein that he might be able to get Erin. He didn't know exactly what he'd do after he had her but he'd figure that out later. Right now, the important thing was to get the hundred-million-dollar bitch—and make sure that Mike Kelly gave him a big slice of the pie.

Without thinking more about the possible consequences of what he was planning to do, he looked around, whipped off his jacket, pulled his gun from the back of his pants, and placed his jacket over the gun so it was concealed. He then walked up to the ambulance. The back door was open. The old cop, dressed as a paramedic, was sitting on a little bench seat while the doctor was doing something to strap the stretcher down so it didn't move when the ambulance was in motion. The driver was looking back over his shoulder at the doctor.

Epstein raised the gun he was holding, the gun still covered by his jacket so that anyone looking at him from the side couldn't see it, but the men in the ambulance could see the barrel. He said, "I'm coming with you. You try to stop me, I'm going to kill you all right now and drive this thing away myself." He aimed the gun at the driver when he said this.

And that was his plan: get in the ambulance, make the driver take him someplace isolated, after which he'd most likely have to kill the old cop, the fake doctor, and the ambulance driver. And if DeMarco and the cheerleader followed, maybe he'd have to kill them too. Or maybe the ambulance driver—with a gun stuck in his ear—could shake

DeMarco and the cheerleader if they followed. He didn't know. There were just too many fuckin' details to work out—where would he take Erin once he had her?— but the main thing right now was to get into the ambulance and force the driver to take off.

Tommy raised his hands above his shoulders, which is what people usually do when someone is pointing a gun at them.

Epstein said, "Put your fuckin' hands down!"

———————————————

DeMarco saw the short, dark-haired guy holding a black leather jacket approach the ambulance, figuring he was a bystander who wanted to gawk inside and see what was happening. Then he saw Tommy put up his hands. DeMarco noticed then the way the short guy was standing, his right arm crooked at the elbow, the jacket covering his right hand, and he immediately thought, *Gun!*

"Give me your baton," DeMarco said to Dana.

"What?"

"Your baton, the combat baton. Hurry!"

Dana took the baton out of the right back pocket of her jeans and handed it to DeMarco. By the time she saw the man standing at the rear of the ambulance and figured out what was going on, DeMarco had already left the car, the combat baton now in the fully extended position, and he was running toward the ambulance.

———————————————

Epstein said to Tommy, "I told you to put your fuckin' hands down. If you don't—"

DeMarco said, "Hey."

Epstein turned—and DeMarco slashed downward hard with the steel baton and knocked the gun out of Epstein's hand. He broke Epstein's wrist in the process. Then DeMarco swung the baton in a backhand motion and slashed Epstein across the throat. Epstein fell to the ground, landing in a sitting position, and began to gag. The blow to the throat had made it almost impossible for him to breathe.

DeMarco said to Tommy, "Get moving," and slammed the ambulance door shut.

The ambulance, lights flashing, siren blaring, took off.

DeMarco said to Epstein, "Did Mike Kelly send you?"

Epstein croaked something that might have been "Fuck you."

DeMarco noticed that the two middle-aged women who'd been sitting near Erin were watching him and had most likely seen everything that happened. One of the women had both hands over her mouth. DeMarco pointed at Epstein's gun with the baton and yelled to the women, "Call the police. He had a gun." Then he put the tip of the baton in the gun's trigger guard—he didn't want to touch it and leave fingerprints on it—and swept it fifty feet away from Epstein.

DeMarco ran back to the car where Dana was waiting. "Go!" he said, and Dana took off, following the ambulance.

"Who was the guy?" Dana asked.

"I don't know. Probably one of Mike Kelly's guys."

She said, "You should have taken his gun."

"I told you, no guns. We're not going to shoot anyone."

"Well, you could have been shot," she said.

He said, "Where's her purse?"

"Back seat," Dana said.

DeMarco opened Erin's purse to make sure her passport was in there. It was, a British passport made out to Hannah Westover, the name she'd adopted in Montenegro. He didn't care what kind of passport she had as long as she had one.

Epstein knew he had to get away, even though he could barely breathe. And his wrist was killing him. That son of a bitch had broken it. He got to his feet, thought for a second about picking up the gun, then looked over at the two women—one of them was on the phone—and decided to forget the gun. If the cops got him the last thing he needed was to be packing a weapon. He ran to the parking lot, hopped in his car, then had to turn the ignition key with his left hand because of his broken right wrist. He was heading straight toward the airport and catching the first flight out of Montenegro, no matter where it was going. He'd call Mike on his way to the airport and tell him what had happened but no way was he sticking around to get arrested.

Tommy's job had been to take care of all the logistics—and he'd done his job well.

He'd arranged for the ambulance to be outside the Hilton at nine a.m. A large wad of American dollars had motivated the driver. With help from the home office in Boston, he had also arranged for the charter jet that was now waiting on the tarmac at the Podgorica airport. Someone working for Nora Thurston back in Boston had researched all the requirements for an unconscious patient, attended by her physician, to fly out of Montenegro and land at Boston's Logan Airport. All DeMarco could do at this point was hope that everything worked as he'd been told.

The plane was a Lear jet that would seat eight in comfort. The seats on one side had been removed for Erin's stretcher. As soon as they were onboard, and while Tommy was dealing with customs and the pilots were getting clearance for takeoff, Dr. Eastwood removed a vial from his medical bag and injected the contents of the vial into a vein in Erin's left arm. After he did this, he looked at DeMarco and said, "God help us if she's allergic to anything."

Frankly, DeMarco didn't care if the woman died—she was a heartless bitch—but he didn't want to have to deal with the complications of her death, one of which was likely to be him and Eastwood going to prison.

After Eastwood had medicated his "patient" he took her pulse and blood pressure, watching closely for any signs of an adverse reaction to the sedative he'd just given her. That was Eastwood's job from this point forward: to keep Erin Kelly sedated—and alive—until they reached Boston. As for the drug that DeMarco had used to knock Erin out while she was having breakfast, Eastwood had obtained an autoinjector containing a sedative from some Albanians. Why the Albanians would have such a device, DeMarco didn't even want to think about. An autoinjector is what medics use on the battlefield; it has a spring-loaded syringe and all the medic has to do is touch it to the patient to inject whatever drug the autoinjector contains, such as morphine. In this case, the autoinjector had contained a drug to immediately render Erin unconscious so they could get her out of the hotel and into the ambulance without her raising a fuss.

As the plane ascended into the sky over Podgorica, DeMarco couldn't help but recall a line from an old television show called *The A-Team*. The A-Team was a group of slick, ex-military operatives who pulled off complicated capers in the name of truth and justice. When they succeeded, which they always did, the star of the show, a handsome actor named George Peppard, would say: "I love it when a plan comes together."

53

Some days, God just decides to shit on you.

He looks down from His throne in heaven and says to His gang of archangels, "You see that guy, Kelly, sittin' there? Let's make the fucker miserable."

First, Mike gets the call from his IRA pal Sean Murphy in Ireland. Murphy says, "My boys were arrested in Montenegro. They said DeMarco set them up. They were caught after they broke into a house, and since they had guns on 'em and records goin' back to the time they were in diapers, the cops aren't letting them go. I talked to them and they said they were following your orders so, the way I figure it, you need to chip in when it comes to lawyers and whatever."

Mike said, "I'm not chippin' in shit. It's not my fault they're idiots and got caught."

He'd barely hung up from talking to Murphy when Epstein called. Epstein said, "DeMarco—"

"What's wrong with your voice?"

"DeMarco hit me in the throat with a fuckin' steel rod. And he broke my wrist."

"Jesus," Mike said. "Why'd he—"

"He kidnapped your niece. The son of a bitch drugged her in some way, stuck her in an ambulance, and drove off with her. I tried to stop him but—"

"So where's Erin now?"

"How the hell would I know? And I'm catching the next plane out of this fucking country before I get arrested." With that, Epstein hung up.

What the hell was DeMarco doing? And where would he take Erin? Maybe he was taking her to the American embassy or to the Montenegro cops, but he doubted that. The American ambassador to Montenegro wouldn't be part of some scheme where DeMarco drugs a woman, then takes her to the embassy to be shipped back to the United States. Nor did he think the Montenegro cops would be thrilled with the idea of DeMarco making what had to be an illegal arrest on their home turf. The only thing that made sense was that DeMarco was bringing her back to the United States so she could be arrested for stealing Cassie Russell's money. And where in the United States would DeMarco take her? Boston was the only place that made sense, and he'd most likely fly into Logan with her.

Mike sat scratching his paunch, thinking that maybe, just maybe, he'd be able to get one last shot at her. If a bunch of U.S. marshals or FBI agents were waiting at the airport when Erin arrived, then there wasn't anything he'd be able to do. But what if, when DeMarco landed, there weren't a bunch of cops waiting and DeMarco had to drive her to someplace, like maybe a police station or a courthouse? If he did that . . .

And that's when God decided to dump the third load of crap on his head.

His phone rang and the caller asked if he'd accept a collect call from the Suffolk County jail. It was Paulie calling.

"Be careful what you say," Mike said. "Those phones at the jail are monitored."

"Fuck be careful," Paulie said. "Did you have anything to do with my mother's death?"

54

Paulie had been in the jail dining room, playing cribbage with a guy he knew from high school.

It was funny. Paulie hadn't seen the guy in forty years—he'd never gone to any of the school reunions because he'd never graduated—and the next time he sees him is in a jail, awaiting trial for beating his wife half to death. It was weird how two men with nothing seemingly in common go their separate ways, then end up in exactly the same spot forty years later.

Anyway, he'd been playing cribbage when a guard walks up to him and says, "McGuire, you need to come with me."

"Why? I didn't do nothin."

Normally the guard would have said something like, *Get your dumb ass out of that chair*—but he didn't. In a soft voice, he said, "It's important, McGuire. Just come with me."

Paulie followed the guard to one of the rooms where the cons met with their lawyers. Inside the room, sitting at a table, was a priest.

The priest stood up when Paulie entered the room. The expression on the priest's face was somber.

Paulie looked at the guard and said, "What's going on?"

The priest said, "Paul, why don't you sit down. I have some sad news."

After the priest broke the news to him, the guard took Paulie back to his cell, Paulie not even remembering walking there. He sat on his bunk for a bit, thinking about the shitty life his mother had had. He was surprised he didn't start crying. He supposed the tears would eventually come but right now all he felt was empty inside. The last time he'd seen his mom she hadn't known who he was, but she'd seemed okay physically. She'd had a good appetite and she'd moved okay when he led her to the dayroom so they could sit and talk. Or so he could talk. All she did was stare out the window.

Then something occurred to him.

He asked for permission to call the assisted living place. Said he needed to find out about funeral arrangements and such. The guards were amazingly accommodating; even jailhouse screws could sympathize with a man losing his mother.

He ended up talking to a nurse with a Jamaican accent. He asked her, "How did she die?"

"We assume cardiac arrest, or possibly a stroke. An aide went into her room to take her to breakfast and found her lying on the floor next to her bed."

Paulie knew his mom had high blood pressure and took some kind of blood thinner to prevent strokes, but she'd never shown any symptoms that she was ill.

The Jamaican nurse said, "She was eighty-four years old, Mr. McGuire. I'm sorry she's gone but I think she was fortunate in passing quickly and not suffering."

"Yeah," Paulie said. "Did she have any visitors before she died."

"I don't know. Why are you asking?"

"Will you check, please?"

"Just a moment . . . No, you're the only one who ever visited her." Geez. Hearing that almost broke his heart.

"About the arrangements for her," Paulie said. "There's a priest, a

Father Delmonico. He'll be by to take care of things, so don't go ship-pin' her off in a cardboard box to the potter's field."

"We would never do that," the nurse said.

Paulie hung up on the nurse, still not buying that his mom had simply croaked in the middle of the night.

Mike Kelly was the cheapest son of a bitch who ever walked the earth. The man was so cheap he could squeeze the shit out of the buffalo they used to have on nickels. Since Erin Kelly had skipped the country, Mike had assured him that he'd take care of Paulie's mom's expenses but Paulie could just see the greedy bastard sending someone over to the nursing home to smother her with a pillow.

It was after he'd spoken to the nurse that he'd called Mike and asked him if he'd had anything to do with his mom's death. Mike, of course, denied doing anything.

Paulie started crying after talking to Mike. Not huge sobs, just tears streaming down his cheeks. He thought about the way his mom had always been there for him. How she'd protected him from the monster who'd been his father. The truth was that she'd been the best friend he'd ever had. And now he had no one. And just like no one had visited his mom when she was in the nursing home, he doubted anyone would be coming to visit him after he was sentenced to prison.

Prison. He'd been willing to do the time in return for Mike taking care of his mom but now . . .

No way would Mike Kelly do the time for him if the shoe was on the other foot.

55

Mike realized immediately that Paulie's mom's death was really bad news. Paulie would never have testified against him as long as he was paying for her care, but now that the old broad was dead . . .

Well, he'd worry about Paulie later. Right now he needed to get ready for Erin coming back to Boston. He called Casey, his underboss now that Paulie was locked up. He said, "I want you to get about twenty of the boys down to the bar in Charlestown. I'll be there in about an hour. Before I get there, you need to get online and find photos of a guy named Joe DeMarco and a woman named Erin Kelly then print out about thirty of the photos." Casey, of course, had no idea who DeMarco and Erin were, so Mike had to give him their backgrounds so Casey could Google them.

When Mike arrived at the bar, the few patrons who came to the place had been booted out and the bar was crowded with his men, about half of whom looked as if they were drunk. Great. Casey, a tall, dour-looking mick, passed out the photos of DeMarco and Erin, then Mike explained that everybody was to get their asses out to Logan and try to spot them as soon as they landed. Mike said he didn't know what time they were coming in or what gate they'd be using or anything else. All he knew was that they were coming from overseas, would most likely have to pass through customs, and would probably pick up their luggage from whatever baggage carousels were used for international flights. He told Casey, "You get everyone organized so they're not all standing in the same place looking stupid. And no guns inside the airport. Leave your guns in your cars." Then he added, "And hey! The one who spots them gets a grand."

After all the men filed out of the bar, Mike had another thought and called a guy named McDougall who worked for him at the airport. McDougall was one of the workers who took the luggage off the planes and Mike had used him several times when he had packages coming in that he didn't want going through customs. He explained to McDougall that a flight taking off from Montenegro was going to land at Logan in the next day or two and on the flight was going to be a guy named DeMarco and a woman named Erin Kelly. But that's all the information he had. He told McDougall to see if he could find out anything about passengers on flights originating from Montenegro or flights that stopped in Montenegro on the way to Boston.

"Well, shit, that's kind of a tall order," McDougall said. "I don't have direct access to passenger manifests."

"Just do the best you can, and if you get something useful you'll make five hundred bucks."

The charter flight from Podgorica was ten hours, including a refueling stop in Madrid. During the trip Adrian Eastwood made sure his patient stayed sedated and alive. Once, when DeMarco looked over at her, he thought she might have been dreaming. He could see her eyeballs moving rapidly beneath her eyelids. He wondered if she was having pleasant dreams or nightmares. The latter, he hoped.

When the plane landed at Logan, Tommy was dispatched to take care of customs, the pilots already having called ahead saying they had a sick patient and her doctor onboard and had an ambulance waiting to take the poor woman to a hospital for surgery.

Now all DeMarco had to do was deliver Erin into the warm embrace of the law.

Mike's phone rang as he was sitting on the toilet. It seemed these days that he was always constipated. Getting old was a bitch.

"Hey, this is McDougall," the caller said. "A charter flight that originated from Montenegro just landed. I don't know who's on board but there's an ambulance waiting for whoever it is."

"That's it!" Mike said. "You got a pen?"

"Yeah."

"Write this number down." Mike gave him Casey's number. "Call that number and tell the guy who answers where the plane is and where he should go to follow the ambulance when it leaves the airport. You understand?"

"Yeah. What about my five hundred bucks?"

"You'll get it. Now make the call."

Twenty minutes after landing at Logan—it was a good thing that Erin wasn't really having a medical emergency—DeMarco, Dana, and Dr. Eastwood left the airport with Erin asleep in the private ambulance arranged for by Thurston Security. Tommy would make his way home from Logan on his own; there wasn't room for him in the ambulance and he wasn't needed to execute the remainder of DeMarco's plan.

Fifteen minutes later they arrived at a Marriott hotel located a short distance from the airport.

Dana checked Erin into a room on the first floor using one of Erin's phony credit cards. DeMarco and the doctor then placed Erin in the wheelchair that came with the ambulance, DeMarco rolled her to her room, and he placed her on the bed. When he did she said something unintelligible.

"How long will she be out?" DeMarco asked.

"Maybe two hours, but maybe less," Eastwood said.

───── ❖ ─────

Casey said, "They just pulled into a Marriott near the airport."

"How many guys does DeMarco have with him?" Mike asked.

"I don't know. I haven't seen him or anyone else yet. I just followed the ambulance when it left the airport."

"Do you see any cops? Did a cop car escort the ambulance to the hotel?"

"No. Hold on. A broad just got out of the ambulance and went into the hotel."

"Is it Erin?"

"No. It's a short gal with short dark hair. Wait a minute! Now two guys are getting out of the back of the ambulance and pulling a stretcher out. One of them is DeMarco, I can see him clear as a bell. I don't know who the other guy is. There's someone on the stretcher but I can't see a face."

"It's Erin," Mike said. "How many guys you got with you?"

"Three."

"Then go get her. Stick a gun in DeMarco's face and take her. Dump her into the trunk of your car."

"There's too many people around," Casey said.

There weren't too many people around. There was only one guy standing near the hotel entrance smoking, but the reason Casey had spent only three years in prison—the average time for the guys on Mike's crew was ten years—was because he was a cautious man.

Before Mike could say anything else, Casey said, "They're putting her into a wheelchair. Now they're rolling her into the hotel." Casey turned to one of the guys in the back seat of the car and said, "Pete, get your ass into the hotel and follow that wheelchair. Find out what room they're taking her to."

To Mike, Casey said, "Once they got her in a room I'll scope the situation out and get her."

"Fuck! You should have taken her before she went to the room."

"I'll call you back," Casey said and hung up before Mike could give him another stupid order.

Five minutes later Pete, the guy Casey had sent to follow the wheelchair, came back to the car and said, "She's in Room 112. There's a door down at the end of the hall, a fire door, and we can go in that way so we don't all have to go through the lobby."

DeMarco told Dana and Eastwood, "You guys can take off and tell the ambulance driver he can go too. I'll catch up with you later this evening at my hotel." To Eastwood he said, "I'll write you a check for the money I owe you at that time. And thanks, you did a good job." *You Medicaid stealing scumbag.*

After Dana and Eastwood left, Eastwood pushing the wheelchair, DeMarco looked down at Erin. She stirred occasionally, muttering as she slept. He could tell the sedative was wearing off. He called Rita Harper, his pal the federal prosecutor.

Harper didn't answer, probably because she saw it was DeMarco calling, so he left a message. "This is DeMarco. Erin Kelly is here in Boston, at the Marriott near Logan, in room 112. She's using a British passport under the name of Hannah Westover. But in less than an hour she'll be gone, so I'd suggest you arrest her before she splits."

Five minutes later Harper responded to DeMarco's voice mail.

"How do you know she's at the Marriott?" Harper said.

"I just do."

"But why's she back in Boston?"

"I have no idea," DeMarco said.

"This makes no sense."

"Rita, whether it makes sense or not, the woman who stole a hundred million bucks from Cassie Russell, killed Cassie's parents, and attempted to kill Cassie twice is at the Marriott. I'd suggest you send a couple of FBI agents over there to put her in handcuffs. If you don't, and she gets away, I'm going to make sure folks know that you're the one responsible."

DeMarco hung up. He didn't want to be there when the cops arrived but decided to stick around for a short time, no more than fifteen minutes. It wouldn't be good if Erin woke up before the FBI got there and escaped for a second time.

Casey saw Dana and Eastwood come out of the Marriott's front entrance. Eastwood put the wheelchair in the back of the ambulance, the ambulance drove off, and a few minutes later a cab pulled up and Eastwood and Dana left in the cab. Casey figured that DeMarco must still be in the room with Erin.

He also figured he was probably going to have to kill DeMarco to take Erin.

He turned to the men in the back seat and said, "Denny, you go walk around the hotel and see if there's anybody who looks like a cop. Pete, you go back inside the hotel and check out the lobby, make sure there's no cops or security guards there. If there is, call me. If not, walk down to the fire door at the end of the hall on the first floor and wait."

While waiting to hear back from Pete and Denny, Casey sat, tapping his fingers on the steering wheel. The third man in the car, an idiot named Charlie, said, "What are we going to do if—"

"Shut up," Casey said.

Five minutes later Casey's phone rang. It was Denny. He said, "There's no one around that looks like cops to me. No Crown Vic with a couple of big guys sitting in it, no vans without windows, nothing like that."

"Okay, come back to the car."

Casey called Pete. "Where are you?"

"Standing by the fire door like you told me."

"Okay, open the door, make sure it doesn't lock behind you, and stand outside where I can see you. I'm going to drive around with the other guys and meet you there."

Denny got into the car, Casey started it, and he drove slowly toward the back of the building, scanning the parking lot for potential witnesses as he drove. He didn't see anybody.

"How are we going to get into the room?" Charlie said.

"You're going to bash in the door with your head. Your fuckin' head has gotta be good for something."

Casey turned a corner and saw Pete standing near an open door. He parked the car near the door and popped the lid for the trunk. He, Charlie, and Denny got out of the car and walked over to Pete. Casey said, "Where's Room 112?"

"About halfway down the hall," Pete said.

"Okay. We're walking down there and I'm going to knock on the door, say I'm hotel security, and when DeMarco opens the door we're busting into the room. I'm going to shoot DeMarco, whoever the fuck he is, and Denny and Pete are going to grab the woman and dump her in the trunk. We gotta move fast because my gun's going to make a lot of noise."

Charlie said, "What if he doesn't open the door?"

At that moment, a door halfway down the hallway opened and DeMarco stepped into the hallway.

DeMarco looked at his watch. He'd been sitting in the chair next to Erin's bed for fifteen minutes. He was sure the FBI was going to be there soon and he needed to get going. He absolutely did not want to be there when the FBI arrived. He took one last look at Erin, still sleeping restlessly, and said out loud, "Have a nice life, honeybunch."

He opened the door, stepped into the hall, pulled the door closed, and made sure it was locked. Then he heard a noise to his right and turned his head and saw four men at the end of the hall, near an open fire door. *Aw, shit.*

The men didn't look like FBI agents. Two of them had on stocking caps. They looked like the kind of thugs Mike Kelly would employ.

Before DeMarco could decide what to do, he heard the sound of men running toward him from the other end of the hallway. When he saw who it was, he smiled slightly and walked calmly in that direction, away from the men standing by the fire door.

When Casey saw DeMarco, he pointed to Charlie and said, "Get him! He's probably got a key to the room on him. Stick a gun in his fucking face and bring him back to the room."

Charlie started forward—and then stopped abruptly when he saw four FBI agents dressed in full body armor and helmets with face shields, armed with automatic rifles, shotguns, and pistols, come running down the hallway. You'd have thought they were coming to arrest a bomb-packing terrorist and not a five-foot-six female lawyer.

The lead agent saw DeMarco walking down the hallway toward him and screamed, "FBI! FBI! Stand aside! Stand aside!"

DeMarco pressed his back to the hallway wall as the FBI team thundered past him.

Casey said to his crew, "Let's get the hell out of here." Seconds later, Casey and his three guys were in Casey's car, the tires squealing as they departed the Marriott parking lot.

Charlie said, "Boy, Mike's really going to be pissed."

"Will you *please* just shut the fuck up," Casey said.

DeMarco watched as one of the FBI agents used a sledgehammer to bash in the door to Room 112. He wondered why they hadn't just asked the front desk for a key.

Two of the FBI agents rushed into the room, M4 rifles at the ready, screaming, "FBI! FBI! Raise your hands! Raise your hands!"

The agents were surprised to find Erin Kelly, apparently sleeping, lying on the bed, fully clothed, her purse on the bed next to her. Wakened by the commotion, but still half asleep, her mind turned to mush by drugs, she said, "Wha? Wha? What's going on?"

DeMarco, a small smile on his face, continued down the hallway to the lobby and asked the lady at the front desk to please call a taxi for him.

56

Erin was taken to the female wing of the Suffolk County jail, the same jail where Paulie McGuire was residing. The whole time she was being processed into the facility, she kept screaming that she'd been kidnapped from Montenegro by some guy named DeMarco but no one knew what she was talking about. A matron at the jail finally said, "Honey, just shut the fuck up. Nobody cares. You can tell your lawyer once we're through here." The matron snapped a latex glove on her big right hand—she could have easily palmed a basketball—and said, "Now take off your clothes."

Four hours after arriving at the jail, Erin held a meeting with her lawyer, a young guy, only in his thirties, but one with a stellar reputation for defending white collar criminals.

Erin said, "I'm telling you, I was kidnapped from Montenegro. My arrest has to be illegal."

"I don't know," the lawyer said.

"What do you mean, you don't know?"

"I mean, I'll argue that it was illegal and that your rights were violated, but I'm not sure that's going to make any difference. This is sort of like a case I read about, where a bounty hunter went into Mexico and hauled a drug lord across the border so the U.S. could prosecute him. The Mexican's now spending thirty years at the supermax in Florence, Colorado, and, as far as I know, nothing happened to the bounty hunter."

"I think I need a different lawyer," Erin said.

———◆———

Erin and her new lawyer met with Assistant U.S. Attorney Rita Harper an hour before Erin was scheduled to be arraigned.

Erin said, "You can't hold me. I was in Montenegro, which has no extradition treaty with the U.S., and I was kidnapped."

"Who kidnapped you?"

"An asshole named DeMarco who works for John Mahoney."

"Can you prove DeMarco kidnapped you?"

"Prove it? How else would I have gotten here? Do you think I came voluntarily? Anyway, proving he kidnapped me is your job."

"Not my job," Rita said. "I don't prosecute crimes that occur in Montenegro. My job is to prosecute you for embezzlement, which will be a slam dunk. In addition, I'm going to charge you for attempted murder if I can get the man you hired to kill Cassie Russell to cooperate."

"This isn't right," Erin shrieked. "You can't just kidnap me and drag me back to the U.S. for a trial. There are laws."

Rita said, "The U.S. government didn't kidnap you, Ms. Kelly. But what I'm not going to do is let you leave the country. I'm going to argue against bail at your arraignment, and because you stole over a hundred million dollars and we arrested you with a false passport in your possession, I'm pretty sure you won't be granted bail."

"Aren't you going to say anything?" Erin said to her lawyer.

"I've got one piece of good news for you," Harper said. "I've been led to believe that you conspired with your uncle Mike Kelly to have

Cassie Russell murdered. If you can provide evidence or testimony that will result in the arrest and conviction of Mike Kelly for any crimes he may have committed, that could reduce the time you spend in jail."

Erin was returned to the jail after her arraignment, where she'd been mortified to be seen in an orange jail jumpsuit, her hair uncombed, and without makeup.

She was not granted bail.

The judge didn't care that DeMarco had kidnapped her.

After the arraignment, a female guard led her to the cell where she'd remain until her trial, which might not happen for another nine months, thanks to a backlog of pending trials. Her heart almost stopped when she saw her cellmate. She'd been told that she was being placed in a section of the jail housing the nonviolent inmates and lesser psychos, but one look at her roommate and she wondered if she'd been lied to. The woman outweighed her by a hundred pounds. Her untamed Afro sprung out in all directions and her eyes bulged from her head, making Erin suspect that the woman had a thyroid condition. Either that or the bulging eyes were an indicator of an advanced state of lunacy. Erin had seen all the seasons of *Orange Is the New Black* and she knew what was likely to happen to a delicate woman like her. She was going to become this huge woman's sex slave and be forced to wash her underwear and make her bed and do God knows what else.

The woman stared at her for a moment when Erin entered the cell, then said, "Hi, honey, my name's Nettie. Now I hope you're not one of those nonstop talkers or someone who cries all night. I get cranky when I don't get a good night's sleep."

"I'm not," Erin said softly.

"That's good," Nettie said. "We'll get to know each other better after I've had my nap." Then Nettie stretched out on her bunk, turned her back to Erin, and almost immediately started snoring.

Relieved, Erin lay down on her own bunk and stared up at a tiled ceiling that appeared to be spotted with dried blood. How the hell had blood gotten on the ceiling?

She figured the case against her was rock solid when it came to the cash she'd stolen from the Russell trust. She also figured that if she returned the money, she'd be given only four or five years in prison. If she didn't give it back, she'd probably get twenty years, and when she got out of jail they'd make sure she didn't have the chance to spend any of the money she'd stolen. But that was the best deal she was going to get: less time in return for pleading guilty, saving the government the expense of a trial, and giving back the money she'd taken.

As for the offer that skinny bitch of a prosecutor had made—the one about her testifying against Mike for being an accomplice in the attempted murder of Cassie Russell—no way in hell was she going to touch that. For one thing, why should she admit to having anything to do with an attempted murder? Once she did that, who knows what kind of prison time a judge might give her, no matter what the prosecutor said. And there was another reason why she had no intention of accepting the prosecutor's offer. If her darling uncle Mike learned that she was going to testify against him, sure as shit, he'd try to get one of the bull dykes in the jail to cut her throat—then *her* blood would be on the ceiling. No, she was going to have to do the time, give back the money, and then . . . Then she had no idea what her life would be like in the future.

The guy who could upset everyone's applecart was McGuire. Right now he wasn't talking but if he decided to talk he'd implicate Mike and Mike might implicate her. And Mike, that evil prick, had a recording of her asking him to arrange for Cassie to be killed. So it wouldn't be just Mike's word against hers. She wondered what Mike was doing to make sure McGuire didn't talk. He'd said McGuire was a "stand-up guy"—whatever the hell that meant when it came to a cold-blooded killer—but if she were Mike she'd have McGuire killed, as she'd suggested once before. If she could find a way to get a message to Mike—she didn't dare call him—she'd make it clear that she wasn't going to testify against him and strongly recommend that he have McGuire permanently silenced.

She started crying, muffling the sound with a blanket so as not to disturb her bug-eyed cellmate. It was all so unfair, DeMarco, that son of a bitch, breaking the law and kidnapping her. That just wasn't right! And it was Connor Russell's fault for hiring the accountant to do the audit in the first place. The small amount she'd embezzled over the years—it was less than three million dollars—hadn't hurt Connor or his family at all. He hadn't even noticed that the money was gone. If Connor had given her a raise or a decent bonus every year, as she deserved for all her hard work, she wouldn't have been forced to steal. But instead of raising her salary, the entitled bastard had insulted her by ordering a damn audit, and when that little toad Feldman had been on the verge of exposing her she'd had no choice but to kill him and all the Russells. It wasn't as if she'd *wanted* to kill them. And then when DeMarco continued to harass her by ordering a second audit, the only option she'd had was to empty the cash account and flee the country. What else could she have done? There just had to be some way to make a jury understand how people had taken advantage of her and that she'd been compelled to do what she'd done.

57

Paulie McGuire stood between two federal marshals, his hands cuffed in front of him, tears streaming down his cheeks as his mother's casket was lowered into the ground on a bitterly cold December day. Mike Kelly stood behind Paulie, his face solemn, bright red from a winter wind that stung like a whip's lash. Accompanying Mike were about thirty of his guys. Mike had made them attend the service because he wanted to show Paulie how he and everyone else in his crew understood Paulie's grief.

It about killed Mike to watch the casket go into the ground. He'd spent ten grand on it, the casket being the finest one the funeral home had. He'd spent another eight grand on the marble headstone, a headstone suitable for Rose Kennedy. Just looking at it, you'd never guess that Ada McGuire had been a simple girl from Southie whose only claim to fame was giving birth to a man now charged with attempting to murder three teenagers.

Mike was doing everything he could to keep Paulie on his side. He'd bribed officers at the jail to make sure Paulie had a cell to himself and he wasn't being kept in a cage with some animal. He'd sent him books, candy, magazines, booze, and a contraband cell phone. His lawyer, Louie Shapiro, had met three times with Paulie to assure him he was doing everything he could to get Paulie the best possible deal. But the truth was that Paulie was screwed. He had three witnesses willing to testify against him: Cassie Russell and the boy and girl who saw him try to kill Cassie. Fortunately, the boy had survived the gunshot wound so at least Paulie wasn't being charged with murder.

In spite of everything that Mike had done, he knew in his heart that Paulie was going to flip on him. Now that his mom was dead, Paulie had no incentive for doing the time and he had to be thinking about cutting a deal with the federal prosecutor, saying he'd be willing to talk about the many things he'd done for Mike over the years. Mike had a couple of options. One was to kill all three witnesses willing to testify against Paulie, but that wasn't going to be easy and was liable to land Mike in even more hot water. And killing the witnesses, who'd already made videos of their testimony against Paulie, might not change the outcome of Paulie's trial. The best thing would be simply to kill Paulie, as much as he'd hate to do that. And if he was going to kill Paulie, he'd better do it soon and he'd better make sure the attempt on Paulie's life was successful. If he tried and failed to kill him there was no doubt that Paulie would sing like a fuckin' canary.

The casket, thank God, was finally at the bottom of the grave. Mike was afraid he was going to catch pneumonia if he stood outside much longer; at his age, pneumonia could kill him. Paulie was allowed to toss a bouquet of roses into the grave—roses that Mike had paid for—then the marshals were nice enough to let Paulie stand there for a couple of minutes muttering inaudibly to his dead mother. When the marshals started to lead Paulie away, Mike said, "Hey, Paulie, I'm so sorry. You just let me know if there's anything you need." Paulie said, "Thanks for taking care of the funeral. I appreciate that." But Mike noticed that Paulie didn't look him in the eye.

No doubt about it, the guy was going to flip.

58

Paulie sat at a table by himself in the cafeteria, drinking lukewarm coffee, the coffee laced with Jameson whiskey thanks to Mike. Pretty soon the guards would shoo everyone out of the room and make them return to their cells, but he figured he had a few more minutes to sit there and think.

The question he'd been asking himself since his mother's funeral was this: *Who am I? Am I one of those guys?*

He'd known a lot of rats in his time. These were men without honor, men with no sense of shame or loyalty, who testified against those they used to call their closest friends. He remembered seeing this movie, a documentary actually, about a guy named Sammy "the Bull" Gravano. Sammy, who'd killed nineteen people, had ratted out the entire Gambino crime family in New York and brought down John Gotti and about thirty other mobsters. In return for squealing, and in spite of all the people he'd killed, Sammy spent only a few years in prison. A book was even written about him, making Sammy maybe the most famous rat in history. Anyway, Paulie remembered seeing the documentary, Gravano bragging, trying to sound like a tough guy, when he was nothing more than a punk. Watching the guy had made Paulie want to puke, and he swore at the time that he'd never do what Sammy had done, that if he was ever caught he'd do his time like a man.

But now he was wondering if he was going to become the next Sammy Gravano.

The prosecutor had promised him that if he'd give her Mike and Erin Kelly, he'd get off having to do barely any time at all. And if it had just been Erin he would have given her up in a heartbeat. He didn't owe her shit. But Mike—that was a different story.

Paulie had come to accept that Mike hadn't killed his mom. She'd been old and her heart just gave out as the nurse at the assisted living place had told him. And although he was sure that Mike hadn't wanted to pay for his mom's nursing care, he would have done it, just as he'd promised. Mike kept his word. And look at the money he'd spent on his mom's funeral. Paulie had never expected Mike to go all out the way he had with a grand casket and a fancy grave marker and all the flowers. No, Mike had always done right by him, and in the end he did the right thing for his mom too.

Come to think of it, Mike had always acted more like a big brother than a boss. Mike took him on when he was only a kid, gave him the opportunities to prove himself, gave him more responsibility than the other guys in his crew, and trusted him enough to let him live with him. And what was he going to do in return? Rat the guy out? Is that who he was?

If he didn't rat him out, he could see his future and it was grim. They'd most likely give him fifteen or twenty years, and he might be eligible for parole in ten. Thank God that boy he'd shot didn't die. But by the time he got out he'd be seventy, the same age Mike was now. And by then, Mike would most likely be dead. So he'd spend ten years in prison, surrounded by lowlife scum, and when he got out he'd be old, completely broke, and with no place to live or any prospect of finding a job. What then? He lives in a flophouse, gets a few bucks a month from some kind of welfare, and dies alone?

Yeah, it was an awful future to think about but who did he have to blame but himself? It was his fault that he'd bungled the job on the girl, and no one else's. It certainly wasn't Mike's fault.

All right, he knew the right thing to do. He was a man, not a rat. He'd live with the mistake he'd made and all he'd ask of Mike was to make his time inside as pleasant as possible.

One of the cafeteria screws yelled, "Assholes, time to clear the room. Get back to your cells."

Paulie got up and headed for the door along with everyone else. As he walked he was thinking that he had to get the word to Mike that Mike didn't have to worry when it came to him. He knew Mike must be concerned. He'd set up a meeting with the Jew lawyer tomorrow.

He reached the door along with about twenty idiots all trying to cram through it at the same time, like they actually had someplace to go.

Behind him he heard a guy say, "I'm telling you, it's time to dump Brady. The fuckin' guy's probably the oldest quarterback to ever play the game."

Paulie turned his head to see who was talking. It was a long-haired white guy with tats all over his arms and neck, talking to another guy who looked just like him. Paulie was thinking about telling him that Tom Brady had gotten them to the playoffs once again and the Pats had just as good a chance as any other team to win another Super Bowl, all due to Brady—but then he decided, *Fuck it*. There was no point trying to reason with a fool.

He kept going, shuffling along with the herd going through the door, as the other white guy was saying, "Yeah, maybe, but I read that Brady's got these trainers who . . ."

That was the last thing Paulie heard as he felt a pain in his back, near his right kidney, a pain like someone had shoved a red hot poker into him. Then he felt the pain again and again and again as the shiv was jammed into him.

59

DeMarco was sitting at the bar of his hotel, feeling lonely, sorry for himself, and frustrated.

Shannon wasn't on duty because she was in New York and planned to be there several more days. And when she returned to Boston, she was going to quit her job as a bartender and move out to California for a couple of months to help with the screenplay being adapted from her novel. By then DeMarco would almost certainly be back in D.C.

Her agent, by the way, had sold her novel to Random House for seven figures and then sold the foreign rights to a dozen different publishers across the planet for another seven figures. She had also been given a contract to write a sequel to the first book, something she might collaborate on with Reese Witherspoon, to make sure the sequel would be appealing to Reese's production company. She was on cloud nine, suddenly rich, living her dream, and DeMarco felt really good for her—and he doubted that he'd ever see her again.

He had known it would have been hard to sustain a long-term relationship with her, her living in Boston and him in D.C., but he'd been willing to try. He liked her sense of humor and her intelligence. He liked that she was an optimist, which was good as he often wasn't. He liked that she was athletic and had been hoping he might be able to convince her to take up golf so they could play together. That wasn't going to happen now, not with her in California, completely committed to her writing career.

Thus, the self-pity and the loneliness.

The frustration he was feeling came from two things. One of those was a call he'd received from Mahoney's chief of staff and the other was his inability to put Erin Kelly in jail for murder or even attempted murder.

The NTSB still hadn't completed its forensic autopsy of Connor Russell's plane and probably wouldn't until spring when the snow in the Adirondacks melted. But even if the NTSB investigators concluded the plane had been sabotaged, and even if it could be established that Erin Kelly had the means and the motive to commit sabotage, there was still no evidence linking her to the crime. One bit of good news. The slug removed from the chest of the kid McGuire had shot in New York matched the slugs taken from Jerry Feldman's body. The only problem there was that the gun McGuire had used had not been found so an argument could be made that the gun had been used by someone else to shoot Feldman. But as long as Paulie McGuire remained silent, there wasn't anything tying Erin Kelly to Feldman's murder or the attempt on Cassie's life. So it appeared as if Erin was going to be sentenced to four or five years for embezzlement, contingent upon her returning the money she'd stolen, which she'd agreed to do. Being a nonviolent offender, she would serve her time in a medium-security prison and most likely be eligible for parole in three years and maybe sooner if the prison was overcrowded. If a black kid had robbed a liquor store and stolen fifty bucks, he probably would have been tossed into Attica for ten years. The whole thing with Erin Kelly made DeMarco furious but he couldn't think of anything to do about it.

As for the call he'd received from Perry Wallace, Mahoney's diabolical chief of staff, Perry had called to tell him that he needed to wrap things up in Boston and head for Minnesota.

"Minnesota?" DeMarco had said. Minnesota in the winter was like fucking Antarctica. It was even worse than Boston. "Why?" he'd asked.

"Do you know who Tim Duncan is?"

"No."

"He's the representative from Minnesota's first congressional district."

"Okay, but so what?"

"Duncan, the moron, made a claim that he was part Native American, and when people called bullshit on him he took one of those Ancestry dot-com DNA tests. Well, sure as shit, the test proved he was like four percent Native American."

"So what's the problem?"

"The problem is when he took the test, he checked the block that said his DNA information could be shared with others, and the test proved he has an illegitimate son from some woman he screwed more than twenty years ago."

"But what the hell does this have to do with me?" DeMarco asked.

"It has to do with you because your job is to go see the bastard."

"Which bastard?"

"The literal bastard, the kid, and make him shut up about Duncan being his father. Duncan barely won the last time he ran, and Mahoney doesn't want to lose him because he's easy to manipulate."

"Yeah, but why me?" DeMarco whined.

"Because this is your new job, DeMarco. You're going to have to start doing what your position description says and provide legal services to other members of Congress instead of playing golf all the time. Plus, Mahoney doesn't want you hanging around Washington until after he's formally elected Speaker."

"But Minnesota?"

"Quit bitching. You're lucky to have a job at all. Call Duncan today. He's expecting to hear from you."

So DeMarco sat, feeling gloomy, trying to work up the energy to go up to his room and pack. He was saved by a call from Rita Harper.

She said, "Did you hear what happened to McGuire?"

60

When Paulie opened his eyes, it took him the longest time to figure out where he was. He was pretty sure it wasn't heaven. Finally, he realized he was in a hospital room. There was one of those blood pressure things on his finger, something rubbery was jammed into his nostrils, and he could see a tube going from a needle stuck in the back of his right hand to a bottle hanging above his head. He heard a soft beeping sound off to his left and turned his head slowly. There was a screen that displayed his pulse rate and blood pressure. He didn't know if the numbers were good or bad, all he knew was that he was too weak to move.

A few minutes later, a black woman, a nurse, came into the room and looked down at him, studying him like he was some kind of bug. "How are you feeling?" she asked.

Talk about a stupid fuckin' question. He tried to tell her that he was thirsty but his throat was so dry he couldn't talk. Before he could say "water," she said, "Well, your vital signs look good. The doctor will be here in a few minutes to talk to you." Then the damn woman left before he could ask for water.

Ten minutes later a dark-skinned guy in a white lab coat came into the room, looked at some notes on a clipboard at the end of the bed, then told Paulie his name was Dr. Banerjee and that he was the surgeon who'd operated on him. Paulie figured Banerjee was some kind of Indian or Paki. His mother's doctor hadn't been white either; she'd been from Trinidad or Barbados, one of those fuckin' places. When he was a kid all the doctors he'd ever seen had been old white men but now none of them seemed to be.

Banerjee told him he'd been stabbed seven times and had lost a kidney, which, according to the doctor, wasn't that big a deal. Easy for him to say. The doctor said that as long as he ate right, didn't drink too much, and in general took care of his other kidney, he should have a normal life—as if being in prison was a normal life. According to the doctor, the only reason he hadn't died was because the guards at the jail had acted so quickly in transporting him to a trauma center. "You're a very lucky man, Mr. McGuire," Dr. Banerjee said.

Yeah, he felt real fuckin' lucky, all right.

But come to think of it, he was a lot luckier than Mike Kelly was going to be.

61

"So what happens now?" DeMarco said.

He'd been surprised that Rita Harper had agreed to meet him for a drink. Paul McGuire's near-death experience had significantly improved her attitude.

She said, "I'm going to nail Mike Kelly, probably put twenty of his guys in the can with him, and clear a dozen open homicides." Rita was positively glowing. It was as DeMarco had predicted: the Erin Kelly case had just made her a DOJ superstar. If she'd known DeMarco better she would have stood up and high-fived him.

"Did the guy who stabbed McGuire admit that Kelly paid him?"

"No, he wasn't ID'd even though there were ten eyewitnesses standing five feet away. But it doesn't matter. McGuire knows Kelly paid for the hit and he's willing to flip, which means I'm going to RICO Mike Kelly's fat Irish ass into a cell for the rest of his life."

RICO—the Racketeer Influenced and Corrupt Organizations Act—was invented to put mob bosses in jail. Basically, what RICO did was allow the leaders of a syndicate to be prosecuted for crimes they'd *ordered* others to commit, as opposed to crimes they'd committed personally. RICO had been used to bring down crime families in New York and Chicago. It had also been used against other criminal organizations such as the Hells Angels Motorcycle Club and the corruption-ridden Los Angeles Police Department. It had been used against individuals such as the inside trader Michael Milken. And what this all meant when it came to Paul McGuire and Mike Kelly was that McGuire would testify to all the crimes he'd committed on Mike's behalf, providing sufficient detail to be considered credible—such as identifying where bodies were buried—and Mike would go to jail for the rest of his life.

"What does McGuire get in return?" DeMarco asked.

"Five years, including time served, but he'll serve the remainder of his time in the nicest prison I can find. I'll let him pick. I can't let him off completely because he tried to kill Cassie Russell and two kids, but mainly Cassie. The richest, most influential people in Boston don't care if McGuire killed a bunch of gangsters, but they'll demand that he do some time for trying to kill one of their own."

"And what about Erin Kelly?"

"What do you mean, what about Erin Kelly? I've already got Erin."

"Bullshit, you got her," DeMarco said. "She's going to spend maybe three years in a Club Fed for embezzlement. You need to get her as an accomplice for Jerry Feldman's murder and for paying McGuire to kill Cassie."

"I can't get her for those crimes, DeMarco. McGuire met Erin when she came to see Mike, and Mike told McGuire that she was the one who paid to have the girl killed. But McGuire never spoke to Erin or received money from her directly and she's not in the circle of Mike's criminal enterprise. If I try to prosecute Erin as an accomplice to attempted murder I'll most likely lose, and I don't like losing."

Seeing the expression on DeMarco's face, she said, "Hey, quit acting like you lost your puppy. Getting Mike Kelly is a huge win for the Justice Department and it's not like Erin is getting off scot-free. A felony record will destroy her life."

62

DeMarco flashed his congressional badge at the cop sitting outside the door to McGuire's hospital room and lied to the cop about his reason for coming to see McGuire. The cop didn't care; he was too busy flirting with one of the pretty nurses.

McGuire's bed was tilted up so he could watch TV. He was watching *Judge Judy* when DeMarco entered the room. DeMarco thought the guy looked okay, considering how close he'd come to being killed. He also thought McGuire didn't look like a cold-blooded homicidal maniac, which he obviously was. He looked just like any other sixty-year-old man wearing a hospital gown, recovering from a serious injury: pale complexion, rumpled hair, a couple days' worth of gray stubble.

"What do you want?" McGuire said when he saw DeMarco. DeMarco figured that McGuire recognized him—he must have seen him when he was at the cabin with Cassie—but he doubted McGuire knew who he was or what authority he had. Or, to be accurate, he doubted McGuire knew that he didn't have any authority at all.

DeMarco had decided to go see McGuire himself. It was obvious that Rita Harper didn't care about Erin Kelly—as far as Rita was concerned she already had Erin's scalp on her belt—but DeMarco cared.

He was determined to make sure she spent more time in prison and not a minimum-security prison reserved for white collar criminals where the most she'd suffer would be boredom. DeMarco wanted her in an overcrowded federal prison filled with violent psychos, where every day would be a preview of hell.

"My name's DeMarco," DeMarco said. "I represent Congressman John Mahoney. Do you know who he is?"

"Of course, I know. I watch the news. And if I wasn't a convicted felon I would have voted for him." DeMarco would have to remember to pass on to Mahoney how he'd been endorsed by a gangster. "But what does Mahoney have to do with this?" McGuire asked.

"He's Cassie Russell's godfather."

"You're shittin' me," McGuire said. "So now he wants a piece of me too?"

"No. Mahoney wants Erin Kelly, not you. You're just the hired help. Now I know the federal prosecutor made you a deal to serve only five years, but I'm willing to make you a better deal if you can give me something that will nail Erin."

"What kind of deal?"

"I don't know. It all depends on if you have something. Like when you killed Jerry Feldman—"

"Don't know anyone named Feldman."

"Well, hypothetically, if you did, did Erin Kelly give you any information about him directly? Where he lived or where his office was, anything that ties her to the crime?"

"No," McGuire said. "I mean, hypothetically."

"And when you went after Cassie, did Erin assist you in any way? Like, how did you know where Connor Russell's cabin was in New York?"

"I didn't know. I just followed you when you took the kid up there."

Well, shit. "So you got nothing, nothing that can tie her to a murder or attempted murder?"

McGuire studied him for a moment, saying nothing. "If I can give you something, can you get me immunity?"

"Immunity?"

"Yeah, immunity. No prison time, Witness Protection, new name, a place to live, a job, the whole nine yards."

"Why would I do that if you don't know anything useful?"

"But can you do it *if* I know something."

"Yes," DeMarco said emphatically. Harper was going to kill him.

McGuire said, "Go get a cup of coffee or something. I need to think this over."

Paulie had one thing and only one thing going for him, and ever since he'd decided to flip on Mike he'd been trying to figure out a way to make it happen.

The way things stood right now, he'd spend five years in prison. And he'd have to spend all five years in solitary; he'd made solitary one of the conditions of his deal. He'd spend the time in a cell by himself because he knew—he was absolutely positive—that Mike would have him killed. And if Mike couldn't kill him while he was inside, he'd have someone whack him once he was released, and he'd probably tell whoever he hired to make sure that Paulie suffered the most gruesome death possible.

But if Paulie could pull one thing off *and* if he could survive, his future wouldn't be so bad. He'd not only have plenty of money but he'd have a way of making an income in the future without having to work because blackmail was the gift that kept on giving.

Yet he couldn't, for the life of him, figure out how to do it.

Mike had a small house he owned in Charlestown. The house was in his sister's name and two old spinsters lived there rent free. The reason

Mike owned the house was because down in the basement, hidden under a workbench, was one of the best safes ever made. Mike had always known that the cops might execute a search warrant on him at any time. They'd search his home in Boston, his place on Cape Cod, his bar in Charlestown, and his place in Florida. And the search would be conducted by pros using gizmos to find things buried underground or hidden in the walls. It was for this reason that Mike had bought the little house in Charlestown and put the safe there, figuring the cops would never know about it and, if they did, they'd have to come up with a reason for serving the search warrant on his sister.

Inside the safe was a treasure trove. There was probably a million bucks in cash in case Mike needed to run. There were false passports and driver's licenses and credit cards. Also, and maybe more important, there were documents and photographs that Mike had used to blackmail people. He had photos of city councilmen getting blow jobs from underage whores. He had proof of payments he'd made to bent politicians and judges to get them to cooperate. He had the names of dirty cops he'd used for years to give him the inside dope on BPD cases.

The problem Paulie had was that he could not figure out a way to get at the safe while he was in prison. If he hired a guy to break into the safe, the guy he'd have to hire would be a thief—and sure as shit, as soon as the thief saw what was inside the safe, he'd take everything and split. If Paulie waited until he got out of prison—assuming he lived that long—the contents of the safe would most likely be gone by then. Mike would use the money to pay his lawyers and he might use the information in the safe to cut some kind of deal.

Paulie never told the prosecutor about the safe because he'd been hoping he'd be able to figure out a way to get the goodies inside. But he couldn't. He just couldn't figure it out. Now it looked as if it was a good thing he'd kept that information to himself because, thanks to DeMarco, he could use what he knew to get himself a better deal.

63

———◆———

Rita Harper went ballistic.

"I ought to have you arrested for obstruction of justice!" she screamed. "How dare you offer him immunity!"

Before DeMarco could answer, she said, "I already told you I had to make sure McGuire did some time. He can't be allowed to get off scot-free for trying to kill Cassie Russell and two other kids."

"Well, it's a trade-off," DeMarco said. "Paulie gets a break but Erin Kelly spends ten years in prison for attempted murder in addition to the time she's already getting for embezzlement. I think—"

"I don't give a damn what you think. You had no authority to promise him immunity. You don't have the authority to promise anyone anything. You're nothing but Mahoney's goddamn bagman!"

"Calm down, Rita, and quit yelling at me. This could work out great for you if you don't screw it up. You'll take a little heat for McGuire not doing any time but you'll still get the credit for putting Erin in prison, for getting Cassie's money back, and for nailing Mike Kelly and maybe his whole fucking gang. But you also ought to consider your future. In two years there might be a Democrat in the White House, and maybe a Democratic-controlled House and

Senate, and when they start handing out lifetime appointments to federal judges it would be a good thing if you had a guy like John Mahoney on your side."

"Mahoney would do that for me? A seat on the federal bench?"

"If that's what you want. Or if you want to be the top guy in some district instead of an assistant federal attorney in Massachusetts Mahoney can probably make that happen."

At some point DeMarco would have to discuss with Mahoney all the promises he was now making—but he was pretty sure Mahoney wouldn't have a problem with what he'd done. Or, being Mahoney, he could always renege on the promises later if it became politically expedient to do so. But he wasn't going to tell Harper that.

Harper exhaled and said, "So what does McGuire have that makes immunity even a possibility?"

"There's a safe in a house in Charlestown and inside the safe is all the dirt that Mike Kelly has used to blackmail and extort cooperation from corrupt politicians, judges, and cops."

It occurred to DeMarco just then that he hoped there was nothing connected to Mahoney inside that safe.

"What does this have to do with Erin Kelly?" Harper asked

"Inside the safe is also a recording of Erin Kelly agreeing to pay Mike to have Cassie Russell killed."

"I'll be damned," Harper said. Then, being the ambitious creature she was, she added, "If I can put away a bunch of corrupt politicians in addition to Erin Kelly, that will make the immunity deal seem worthwhile."

"That's what I think too," DeMarco said. "But you need to get moving on this before Mike decides to clean out the safe."

So far Mike Kelly hadn't been indicted because Harper still needed a lot more details from McGuire to build the case against him, but Mike had to know that an arrest was imminent.

DeMarco said, "You need to give McGuire a promise of immunity in writing—I'd suggest you do it today—and he'll give you the address to the house where the safe is."

Harper studied him for a moment. "Okay, DeMarco. Now get out of here before I change my mind about having you arrested."

64

Paul McGuire would spend the next two years testifying against Mike Kelly and all the men in his gang, after which he'd enter the Witness Protection Program. He would be given a new name, dumped into some small town in middle America, set up with a minimum wage job, and most likely revert to a life of crime because all he'd ever been was a criminal.

Paulie McGuire was the lucky one. Erin and Mike Kelly both ended up in prisons in West Virginia.

During his trial, Mike resorted to the now common ploy of appearing each day in a wheelchair, sucking on an oxygen tank. He apparently thought this might garner him some sympathy when it came to his sentence. It didn't. He was given thirty to life and incarcerated at Hazelton, the same federal penitentiary where Whitey Bulger was incarcerated and then later beaten to death by his fellow inmates. During the year preceding his conviction, Mike ate almost nonstop, apparently his way of relieving the stress, and by the time he got to Hazelton he weighed over three hundred pounds. The first time he lined up for a meal a muscle-bound young inmate said, "Hey, fatso, back of the line. Wanna make sure there's enough food for the rest of us." Such disrespect was a harbinger of the days to come.

Erin was sentenced to fifteen years, would be eligible for parole in twelve, and became an inmate at the Alderson Federal Prison Camp, also in West Virginia. Alderson had been home to a number of celebrity female criminals including Lynette "Squeaky" Fromme, the Charles Manson devotee who attempted to assassinate President Gerald Ford, the singer Billie Holiday, and its most famous inmate in recent years, Martha Stewart. Ironically, Alderson was the basis for the fictional prison depicted in the Netflix series *Orange Is the New Black*—the show being the only insight into prison life that Erin had had before actually being sent to prison. Unfortunately, she found out that the show got a lot of things right when it came to how the prisoners abused each other. The second day she was there another inmate broke her nose when Erin accidently bumped into her in the cafeteria and spilled coffee on the inmate's jailhouse frock. An indifferent nurse in the prison clinic stopped the nosebleed by cauterizing a few veins but did nothing to straighten Erin's once perfect nose. Her bent nose would be a reminder of Alderson for the rest of her miserable life.

Before leaving Boston to travel to Minnesota and deal with the illegitimate offspring of the barely Native American congressman, DeMarco stopped to say goodbye to Cassie Russell and Mary Pat Mahoney.

It was a Saturday night and Mrs. Aguilera let him into Cassie's mansion. She said, "I thought you were leaving town."

"I am," DeMarco said. "I just came by to say goodbye to Cassie."

"She's with Mrs. Mahoney in the movie room on the third floor. I'll take you up." On the way, she said, "I want to thank you for getting that terrible woman. Mrs. Mahoney told me what you did."

"Yeah, well, that's my job."

"You got a funny job," she said.

"You're right about that. Has Mary Pat made any decisions when it comes to Cassie's future?"

"Yes, but you need to talk to her about that. Cassie's going to be just fine."

"How 'bout you and your husband?" DeMarco asked, wondering what was going to happen to Cassie's lifelong nanny if Mary Pat decided to relocate Cassie.

"Oh, we're going to be fine too," Mrs. Aguilera said, a small smile on her face. "Mrs. Mahoney is a wonderful person."

The movie room turned out to be a space with ten theater-style seats that had cup holders and could be tilted back like recliners. The television at the front of the room had a ninety-inch screen. In the room were Mary Pat, Cassie, and another girl Cassie's age named Sarah Levy, a small, dark-haired girl wearing big-framed glasses. All of them, including Mary Pat, were dressed in pajamas and eating popcorn. Mary Pat paused the movie when she saw DeMarco.

"What are you doing here?" Mary Pat said.

"I just came by to see how Cassie was doing and to say goodbye to her."

"She's doing fine," Mary Pat said. "We're having a pajama party and binge-watching *Game of Thrones*, although I'm not sure I should be letting them watch it. It's pretty racy."

"We told you, we've already seen it," Cassie said. To DeMarco she said, "She fast-forwards the show every time there's any nudity." She and Sarah giggled.

DeMarco had been hoping to talk to Mary Pat alone to see how Cassie was doing mentally, but it appeared as if he wasn't going to get that opportunity. Plus, just looking at her, he could tell she was okay and Mary Pat would make sure she stayed that way. He also imagined that Mary Pat was having a ball. It had been a long time since her own daughters had been teenagers and DeMarco could tell she was delighted to be there with the girls.

"Have you and Cassie made any decisions when it comes to Cassie's future?" DeMarco asked.

"Yes. We're selling this big place and Cassie's decided to use part of the money to pay for college for those two kids in Tupper Lake who saved her life. The rest of it we'll dump into Casssie's trust."

"So the boy's okay?" DeMarco said.

"He's going to recover completely."

"And where's Cassie going to live?" DeMarco asked.

"With me," Mary Pat said and clutched Cassie's hand. "Cassie and Rosa and Rafael are going to move into my house here in Boston. The place has plenty of room and I might as well get some use out of it. And this summer I'm going to teach Cassie and Sarah how to sail my boat. I'm also converting John's den in the Watergate condo into a bedroom for Cassie for when we go down to D.C. John doesn't use the den for anything other than drinking and watching sports on TV, and he can do that in the living room or his office."

DeMarco wondered how Mahoney felt about his wife residing in Boston most of the time, not to mention now having a live-in fifteen-year-old ward. He also imagined that Mahoney was going to miss Mary Pat more than she was going to miss him. However Mahoney felt, it didn't matter as Mary Pat had already made up her mind. DeMarco had always known that Mary Pat would do the right thing when it came to Cassie.

DeMarco called Shannon while waiting for the flight to Minnesota. He told her that he had a small job there, but afterward he could take some time off and maybe fly to California where she was temporarily living. He didn't bother to tell her the reason he could take the time off was because Mahoney didn't want him in D.C. until after the election for Speaker.

She said, "Oh, Joe, I'm sorry but my publisher's sending me on a twenty-city book tour as soon as my novel is released and after that, well, I just don't know what my schedule is going to be."

DeMarco didn't bother to ask if D.C. would be on the tour.

He could tell that Shannon had already moved on.

———————— ◆ ————————

The temperature in Minnesota was ten degrees above zero when DeMarco landed. He rented a car and drove to the apartment of the kid sired out of wedlock by Congressman Timothy Duncan. The kid's name was Brian Coleman. He was a mild-mannered, good-looking young guy in his twenties who had an IT job with 3M.

DeMarco introduced himself and said he was there on behalf of the congressman.

"I don't understand," Brian said. "What do you want?"

"Well, the congressman is a little concerned that you're going to be an embarrassment for him and might cause him to lose his seat in the House. He was wondering if he could come to some sort of an accommodation with you."

DeMarco was beginning to feel as if he were coated with slime.

"An accommodation?"

"As you probably know, the congressman has a wife and three kids, and if you've done the math he had the affair with your mother while he was still married."

"Yeah, I know that. My mother's dead. She died a couple of years ago of breast cancer. But she never told me who my father was and that's why I did the whole DNA search thing. I only wanted to know who my dad was. And I don't want anything from Duncan. I just wanted to meet him."

"Who knows that he's your father?"

"Just me and my girlfriend. So what's he worried about? That I'm going to talk to the press?" The kid was getting agitated and probably a little frightened, which made DeMarco feel worse than he already felt.

"Yeah, basically," DeMarco said.

"Well, I'm not. I just wanted to meet the guy. And what are you here for? To bribe me? To threaten me so I don't talk? Is that your job?"

"You know something, Brian? I don't know what my job is anymore. And, frankly, I don't care what you do. I'm going to catch the next plane out of this icebox down to Florida and play golf."